DEVONSHIRE
SCREAM

Tea Shop Mystery #17

LAURA CHILDS

BERKLEY PRIME CRIME
New York

BERKLEY PRIME CRIME
Published by Berkley
An imprint of Penguin Random House LLC
375 Hudson Street, New York, New York 10014

ISBN: 9780425281673

Berkley Prime Crime hardcover edition / March 2016
Berkley Prime Crime mass-market edition / March 2017

Printed in the United States of America
1 3 5 7 9 10 8 6 4 2

Cover illustration by Stephanie Henderson
Cover design by Leslie Worrell

This is a work of fiction. Names, characters, places, and incidents either are the product
of the author's imagination or are used fictitiously, and any resemblance to actual persons,
living or dead, business establishments, events, or locales is entirely coincidental.

PUBLISHER'S NOTE: The recipes contained in this book have been created for the
ingredients and techniques indicated. The Publisher is not responsible for your specific
health or allergy needs that may require supervision. Nor is the Publisher responsible for
any adverse reactions you may have to the recipes contained in the book, whether you follow
them as written or modify them to suit your personal dietary needs or tastes.

ACKNOWLEDGMENTS

A hearty thank-you to Sam, Tom, Amanda, Bob, Jennie, Danielle, and all the amazing people at Berkley Prime Crime and Penguin Random House who handle design, editing, publicity, copywriting, bookstore sales, and gift sales. Heartfelt thanks, too, to all the tea lovers, tea shop owners, bookshop folks, librarians, reviewers, magazine writers, websites, radio stations, and bloggers who have enjoyed the Tea Shop Mysteries and have helped to spread the word. You make it all possible!

And I am especially indebted to you, dear readers. You have embraced Theodosia, Drayton, Haley, Early Grey, and the rest of the tea shop gang as family. For that I am eternally grateful and pledge to bring you many more books.

1

❧

Crusted with emeralds, diamonds, rubies, and amethysts, the butterfly brooch glittered enticingly before Theodosia Browning's eyes. Perched in its own glass case, the butterfly looked as if it had just landed on some tasty, succulent flower. The butterfly's lithe wings were a virtual aurora borealis of precious gems.

The piece was whimsical yet spectacular, Theodosia decided. Like something the Duchess of Windsor might have pinned to the lapel of her chic Dior suit in an earlier, headier era. Or perhaps this bejeweled treat *had* belonged to the infamous duchess. After all, this Jewelry Extravaganza, which had just kicked off with a black-tie party, was intended to showcase antique and collectible gems and jewelry from the previous century.

Tiffany, Cartier, Bulgari, Van Cleef & Arpels. The names ticked through Theodosia's brain in a litany of jeweler's ateliers. They were the finest and most respected designers and purveyors of diamonds and gems in the entire world. And what a privilege to have been invited to this amazing event.

Of course, her invitation had come compliments of Brooke Carter Crockett, her good friend and proprietor of Heart's Desire Fine Jewelry here in Charleston, South Carolina. Brooke had negotiated with major jewelers and private collectors, dickered with two museums, and pretty much moved heaven and earth to bring this stunning show to fruition in her shop.

Though Theodosia adored feasting her eyes on fine jewelry (what woman didn't?), her immediate goals and dreams tended to be a bit more practical in nature. She knew she'd have to sell about a million scones and serve another million cups of Darjeeling tea to even begin to afford one of these pricey baubles. And with or without the adornment of fine jewelry, she was quite content to do what she'd set out to do in life. That is, create a romantic, relaxed environment at her Indigo Tea Shop, enjoy the company of Drayton and Haley as they served and soothed their customers, and still, knock on wood, manage a decent living.

But of course a girl could dream.

Theodosia's eyes bounced from the butterfly about to take flight to a tilted mirror that sat on the glass counter. As she caught her own reflection, her lips twitched in a fey smile and she immediately glanced away. Her grand inheritance was in her looks. High cheekbones and an almost porcelain complexion gifted from distant English ancestors, sharp blue eyes, full lips, a fine-boned oval face. An abundance of curly auburn hair that only she found problematic and that any reasonable woman would have killed for.

As champagne corks popped and bone china teacups clinked, Theodosia continued to take in the crowded shop. Well-dressed ladies on the arms of well-dressed titans of business drooled over Tahitian pearls and diamond rings, ruby earrings and emerald necklaces. Yes, the elite of Charleston had turned out en masse this crisp November evening for a little pre-Christmas shopping. And why not? Who didn't love to receive a blingy little trinket on Christmas morning? French perfume being so last year.

"Find something you like?" a cheery voice asked.

Theodosia turned to find Haley, her young baker and chef extraordinaire, smiling at her.

"Everything," Theodosia laughed. "It's all gorgeous."

Haley was accompanied by Kaitlin Crockett, Theodosia's friend Brooke's twenty-year-old niece. Brooke and Kaitlin both traced their ancestry back to the Crockett clan of Kentucky. *The* Crockett clan.

"How are the scones holding out?" Theodosia asked. She and Haley had baked eight dozen scones earlier today just for this occasion. In fact, Haley had come up with a special recipe for what she called *jeweled scones*—that is, cream scones studded with colorful bits of red, green, and gold candied fruit.

"We've still got plenty of scones in reserve," Haley said. "As well as Drayton's fabulous Devonshire cream to accompany them."

"Our customers are mostly drinking champagne right now." Kaitlin smiled. "But when that runs out and they're ready for a nosh . . ."

Theodosia touched a hand to Kaitlin's cheek and gently pushed back a strand of her dark hair. "What are you wearing there? Diamond earbobs?"

Kaitlin nodded eagerly. "Aunt Brooke said it was okay. They're almost identical to the ones Scarlett O'Hara wore. You know, in *Gone with the Wind*? The diamonds that belonged to Scarlett's mother?"

"Well, they look very glamorous on you," Theodosia told her.

Haley twisted a strand of her stick-straight blond hair and grinned. "I mean, duh. Who wouldn't look good in diamond earrings that probably cost fifty grand?"

"That's retail, not wholesale," Kaitlin said.

"Ah," Theodosia said. "I see you're learning the ropes."

Kaitlin lifted her chin. "I really want to work here with Aunt Brooke when I finish school. I think it would be inspiring to be surrounded by such beautiful things all day long."

"Are you interested in jewelry design, too?" Theodosia asked. Brooke was a terrific designer. Her forte was sterling silver free-form bracelets and earrings. And she sometimes crafted enormous knuckle-duster rings with gemstones wrapped in thin strands of gold wire, like enticing little packages.

"I'm taking a couple of design classes right now," Kaitlin said. Her eyes roved the shop, taking in the packed house, the busy buffet table, and her aunt Brooke, who was suddenly smiling and waggling her fingers in Kaitlin's direction. "Oops, gotta get back to work."

"Hey, Brooke," Theodosia said, raising a hand.

Brooke waved back. She was midfifties, yet athletically built, with a sleek mane of snow-white hair. Though she was juggling about a million details tonight, she still looked calm and in charge.

Kaitlin tried to push her way through the crowd, then hit an impasse as three women started jumping up and down and screaming over a canary yellow diamond bracelet. She changed course and headed toward the front of the shop, circling around the largest of the glass jewelry cases.

Theodosia's eyes followed Kaitlin as she cut across the shop, then Theodosia turned back to talk to Haley. Just as she was about to ask Haley if she should duck into the shop's small office and brew a couple more pots of tea, there was a sudden, earsplitting crack.

"What was that?" Haley's pale brows knit together. "Is there a storm coming?"

Startled, figuring some hapless soul had fallen headlong into one of the glass cases, Theodosia glanced quickly about the shop. Only to find herself stunned by what she saw.

The plate glass window at the front of the shop was suddenly bending inward, as if an F5 tornado were bearing down full force. A millisecond later, a spiderweb of cracks appeared. Then, like a knife slicing through butter, the shiny chrome grille of a black SUV shoved its way right through the showroom window.

Shards of glass flew everywhere, nicking and slashing the guests. Surprised cries turned into terrified screams as everyone lurched and fought to get out of the way. Even more frightening was the enormous black truck that relentlessly powered its way into the shop, all cylinders firing, its engine roaring like a runaway locomotive.

Reacting to the onslaught, Theodosia reached a hand out, fumbled for the top of Haley's head, and shoved her to the floor. More screams erupted as the SUV continued to accelerate and grind its way into the shop.

Like special effects in an action flick, two more panels of glass exploded inward like a hail of bullets. Everyone shrieked in terror again and Theodosia felt the sting of glass and plaster rain down upon the back of her neck.

Gripping Haley's hand now, Theodosia pulled her along as the two of them, on hands and knees, scrambled for refuge behind the counter at the rear of the store. Constructed of wood and metal, with only the front done in glass, Theodosia figured it might offer some protection versus the all-glass cases.

"What's . . . ?" Haley began. She was anxious to pop up and take a quick look.

"Stay down," Theodosia ordered. "Keep moving." Once they'd made their way to the back counter, where they were virtually hidden, she said, "Now roll into a ball and cover your head."

"But what about . . . ?"

"Please just do it," Theodosia said. She knew this was a bad situation. People were injured and screaming for help.

Loud, angry shouts added to the din, and glass was still exploding like mad. Slowly, carefully, fearful of what she might see, Theodosia peered around the end of the counter.

The jewelry shop was pure chaos, a war zone. The black SUV had rammed all the way into the shop, its throaty motor still rumbling. Slivers of glass lay everywhere while people crouched on their hands and knees, cut and bleeding. The truck's blast through the front windows had literally pulverized the jewelry cases in front and brought along a rush of cool air.

Theodosia's first thoughts were *Who's hurt?* and *How can I help?* Then her gaze shifted and she found herself staring directly into the blazing eyes of a red demon.

But no, the more rational part of her brain told her it was someone, a person, wearing a hideous demon mask. A terrorist? Here in little old Charleston?

Quick as a snapping turtle's bite, two more demons tumbled out of the black truck, all dressed head to toe in black clothing and looking like hellish clowns in some bizarre circus act.

"Down! Down! Everybody down!" one of the demons screamed.

Theodosia was pretty sure the screamer carried a snub-nosed pistol in his right hand.

Theodosia ducked down behind the case again, her wonked-out brain continuing to scream, *Terrorists!* But she knew it couldn't be. A split second later, a surge of adrenaline kicked in, and she realized she was probably smack-dab in the middle of a bold, highly orchestrated smash-and-grab robbery.

It was the kind of robbery she'd only *heard* about—the kind that took place in London or Paris or Monaco, where daring vandals slammed stolen vehicles directly through storefronts and made off with millions of dollars' worth of jewelry or Chanel and Dior purses.

She snuck another look just as one of the demon invaders pulled a silver canister from his jacket pocket.

"Go!" the demon shouted to his companions.

Now all three robbers pulled gas masks over their demon faces. The leader twisted the lid, there was a loud pop, and black smoke billowed from the canister. A smoke bomb!

Blind panic set in among the screaming, terrified guests. They stumbled and tripped over one another, fighting wildly to escape. Coughing and choking, some tried to lunge for the front door, some blindly tried to batter their way toward the back of the shop. Theodosia flipped Haley's apron over the girl's face and pulled her own scarf up over her own nose and mouth for protection.

The vandals, all wearing rubber gas masks that made them look like high-tech versions of the Elephant Man, went straight to work like practiced professionals. Brandishing crowbars and shiny hammers, they methodically smashed each and every showcase, snatching pearls, diamonds, and gold jewelry from their black velvet nests.

The robbers crunched their way toward the back counter where Theodosia and Haley remained hidden. The glass shattered in the front panel, and then Theodosia heard a hand scrabble around, grabbing jewelry and gold chains like crazy. The robber was so close to her she could hear his breathing, a kind of *ptew ptew ptew* through his mask.

White-hot anger surged through Theodosia. Slowly, carefully, she put a finger in the notch of the cabinet's sliding back door. If she could catch a glimpse of the robber, see anything that might identify him . . .

Theodosia waited, one eye tearing from billows of smoke, yet still pressed hard against the narrow crack. Her vigil was rewarded when a black-gloved hand reached over and grasped a spectacular blue-green alexandrite necklace. *Observe*, she told herself sternly. *Think. Try to take something away from this. Some kind of information or clue that will help the police.*

Just as she'd almost given up hope of seeing anything meaningful, the hand scuttled sideways and she caught sight of a small expanse of skin. Was that a woman's hand? Maybe. It was a smaller hand, that was for sure. And under the fingers of the stretchy black glove that the robber wore, could that be the bump of a ring?

Then the hand pulled away with the necklace, and Theodosia caught just a hint of light-blue lines etched against pale-white skin.

The smashing, screaming, and grabbing seemed to go on forever, although Theodosia later figured it was probably more like two minutes all told.

Just as suddenly as they'd begun, one of the robbers, the one who'd released the smoke bomb, yelled, "Time!" and they all jumped back into the black SUV.

They floored the vehicle and, like an Indy car in reverse, shot back out of the shop into the street. There were more loud revving sounds, almost like the scream of a motorcycle, and then a screech of tires on pavement.

Theodosia had been holding her breath, one hand clutching Haley. When she heard the SUV take off, she half stood and looked over the counter.

People were crying and coughing and moaning softly. Hunks of jagged glass lay everywhere, as if a giant kaleidoscope had exploded. A few larger pieces reflected the red-green of the stoplight down on the corner and the neon lights from the Red Peppercorn Grill across the street.

"Is it over?" Haley asked. Her voice was hoarse and shaky.

"Yes, but stay where you are." Theodosia could hear the faint wail of sirens several blocks away. An alarm had been triggered, or someone had dared to call 911 on their cell phone. Help was on the way, thank goodness.

Across the shop, Brooke scrambled to her feet, her eyes wild with fear, her body shaking uncontrollably. "Is anybody hurt?"

Loud moans and cries rang out in response.

"I'm cut."

"There are slivers in my hand."

"Please help me."

The sound of sirens was growing closer, Theodosia thought. Now they were just two or three blocks away.

"The police are coming," Theodosia called out over the screams, trying to sound braver than she actually felt. "There will be ambulances, EMTs to help all of you. Just stay where you are and try not to move." She figured the EMTs were the pros; they'd know how to triage the wounded. As far as everything else—the stolen jewels—that would just have to wait. The injured guests took precedence now.

"Kaitlin?" Brooke called out. She was hunting frantically for her niece. "Honey, where are you?"

"She's over here," a man cried out. "I think she's hurt pretty bad."

Brooke staggered her way across the front of the store, glass crunching underfoot as she tried not to step on the injured guests or fall headlong into the jagged, empty cases.

"Kaitlin?" Brooke called again as she finally reached her niece, who was lying prone on the floor. She bent down over Kaitlin's body. "Honey, I'm here." Her voice was ragged and tight with fear. Her hand reached out and gently touched Kaitlin's face. Then her voice rose in a strangled gargle. "Kaitlin?"

Theodosia, sensing disaster, began to pick her way toward Brooke and Kaitlin.

"Don't touch her," Theodosia warned. "The ambulances are here." Red and blue lights strobed out in the street. "Let them . . ."

Brooke was bent over Kaitlin now, clutching her and sobbing uncontrollably.

"Brooke." Theodosia's voice was a sharp bark, trying to get through to her friend. "Don't move her. Let the EMTs take care of her."

But Brooke would have none of it. Lifting Kaitlin's head, she gently pushed back her hair to reveal a daggerlike hunk of glass embedded in the girl's throat. Kaitlin's eyes had rolled back until only the whites were visible. She was no longer breathing. The poor girl was gone.

Brooke's scream rose in a pitch-perfect high C that melded with the blaring sirens of the police cruisers and ambulances that had finally arrived on the scene.

2

It was a catastrophe of epic proportions. Kaitlin dead, countless people injured, all the jewelry stolen, and Brooke's shop left in ruins.

How could this happen? Theodosia wondered as she watched a half-dozen EMTs and a dozen uniformed officers pour into the shop. One minute they'd all been sipping tea and gazing serenely at priceless jewels and gems, and now . . . everything lay in ruin.

"What are we going to do?" Haley asked, clutching at Theodosia's hand. She was trembling like a leaf. "People are bleeding . . . a lot of them are hurt really bad. And Kaitlin . . ."

They both turned to watch as an EMT knelt down over Kaitlin's body and did a quick life check. Despite Brooke's tears and loud protests, the EMT was shaking his head. No, Kaitlin was gone for sure. There was nothing that could be done.

"This is awful!" Haley cried. "What are we . . . ?"

Theodosia spun to face Haley and gripped her shoulders tightly. "Haley, we're going to pull it together, that's what we're going to do. We're going to take a deep breath and help wherever we can. We'll hold hands with the injured, carry stretchers if we have to, run and grab first aid supplies, and do whatever else the first responders might need. Okay?"

Haley wobbled her head. "I guess."

"Pull it together, Haley."

"Okay."

For the next five minutes they worked in what could only be classified as a disaster zone. That time stretched into another fifteen minutes of critical care. They comforted the wounded, helped some of them limp out to waiting ambulances and squad cars, and pretty much did whatever the uniformed officers and EMTs directed. It was hard work and the awful part was that Kaitlin's body remained in place, exactly where she'd fallen, with just black-and-yellow crime scene tape strung around it.

Finally, as the mess slowly began to get sorted out, the big guns arrived to investigate.

"Tidwell," Theodosia muttered when she saw the burly detective arrive on the scene. Burt Tidwell headed the Robbery-Homicide Division of the Charleston Police Department and he was a force to be reckoned with. Tight-lipped, tenacious, and pugnacious, Tidwell was a dogged investigator who drove his men with unbridled zeal. His detectives and officers feared him, trusted him, and depended heavily upon him. If push came to shove, they would probably walk across hot coals in their bare feet for him.

Tonight Tidwell wore a rumpled sport coat that barely stretched across his ever-expanding frame. His slightly bulging eyes never stopped moving as he took in the injured guests, the first responders still toiling away, and the smashed jewelry cases, where the only telltale signs of missing jewelry were faint impressions left on velvet.

Theodosia knew that Tidwell had noticed her, but he hadn't bothered to acknowledge her even though he was a frequent gobbler of scones and guzzler of tea at her shop. Instead, he stomped around the premises, taking everything in, seemingly unaware of glass shards crunching loudly beneath his heavy cop shoes.

"I . . . I think my hand got cut," a woman said in a small voice.

Theodosia whirled around to find Sabrina Andros standing there, looking slightly bereft. "Sabrina," she said. She vaguely recalled that Sabrina had visited the Indigo Tea Shop a few times in the past couple of months. "What's wrong? How can I help?"

Sabrina held out a trembling hand. "My hand got cut."

Theodosia peered at Sabrina's hand. There was just a faint abrasion on the back of her hand. "It doesn't look too bad," she said, trying to be helpful.

Sabrina's face crumpled and tears glistened in her eyes. "I knew I shouldn't have come here tonight. I just knew it."

Theodosia realized then that not all wounds were physical. Poor Sabrina's wounds were psychic and probably just as painful and upsetting as anyone else's cuts.

"Come here." Theodosia opened her arms and let Sabrina step into them. She hugged the woman gently. "You're going to be okay. The worst is over now and the police are here. There's nothing more to fear."

"But did you *see* what happened?" Sabrina snuffled. "Did you see those horrible men hacking away at the glass cases?" She exhaled deeply. "And then that poor girl got killed."

Theodosia gently rubbed small circles on Sabrina's back. "I saw the whole thing," she said. "And it *was* awful."

"Awful," Sabrina repeated. Then she pushed away and said, "I should go home. I should leave now." Her tears seemed to have dried up. Now she was talking in a more matter-of-fact tone of voice.

"I think the police want to interview everyone," Theodosia said. "I'm sure any information you can give them would be of value."

Sabrina shook her head. "No, I don't think I can do that." Now she just seemed nervous.

Theodosia grasped Sabrina's elbow. "Let's just go talk to one of these nice police officers, shall we?" She pulled Sabrina along. "Excuse me, Officer?"

A bookish-looking uniformed officer with blond, brush-cut hair and a pair of wire-rimmed glasses glanced her way.

"I have another witness for you to interview," Theodosia said.

"Very good," the officer said, turning his attention to Sabrina. "I just have a few questions . . ."

Theodosia backed away and studied the scene once again. Brooke was talking to Tidwell now. They were standing just inches from the crime scene tape that was draped around Kaitlin's body. From the droop of Brooke's shoulders and the despondent expression on her face, she was obviously relating her version of how the robbery had unfolded. Only her version wasn't that of an innocent, shocked bystander. It was from the perspective of someone whose shop had been rudely invaded by masked gunmen and her niece brutally killed in the process.

Theodosia shuddered. She knew Brooke must be completely devastated, though she seemed to be holding it together. *Amazing*, she thought. The inner strength of that woman.

Tidwell had handed Brooke off to another investigator and was now headed in Theodosia's direction. Theodosia squared her shoulders, preparing herself for a barrage of curt, no-nonsense questions.

"Well," Tidwell said. He beetled his bushy brows and peered at her, eyes bulging, chin tucked down. His feet were spread wide apart in an almost confrontational stance. "What can you tell me?"

"Probably not a lot more than you've already heard," Theodosia said.

Tidwell nodded abruptly. "Yes, yes, the black SUV, the devil masks, the wrecking of the glass jewelry cases, and of course . . ." His words halted abruptly and he jabbed his chin in the direction of two EMTs who hovered over Kaitlin's body.

"Kaitlin," Theodosia said. "Dead."

"Killed in a hail of shattered glass." Tidwell shook his head. "Obviously a terrible accident."

"If Kaitlin's dead," Theodosia said, "wouldn't that constitute murder?"

"A possible homicide, anyway," Tidwell said.

"But if it was intentional? Then wouldn't it be murder?"

"Why don't we leave the technicalities to the district attorney?" Tidwell muttered. "I'm not here to prosecute anyone, only to solve the crime."

"To apprehend the perpetrators," Theodosia said.

"I do understand what's involved, Miss Browning. I have done this before."

"Of course you have," Theodosia said.

"Now. What can you tell me?" Tidwell asked. He held up a hand. "And before you say anything, there's no need to rehash the story of the SUV crash. I've heard twenty versions already."

"Perhaps you'd like to hear some new information, then?" Theodosia said.

"Do you have something new?"

"I may have picked up a small clue."

Tidwell cocked his head at her. "Do tell."

"I think one of the robbers might have been a woman."

"And why do you think that?"

"This particular robber happened to have a much smaller hand. And I think was wearing a ring."

Tidwell rocked back on his heels. "Hmm." He didn't seem all that impressed with her observation.

"And I might have caught sight of something else, too."

"Please, Miss Browning, don't keep me in suspense."

"I think this same person . . ."

"The one with the small hand."

"Yes, I think that person might have also had a tattoo."

Tidwell frowned. "It was my understanding that they were all wearing gloves as well."

"I caught sight of something between this person's glove and shirtsleeve. It looked like . . . a small grouping of blue lines. Or maybe it was calligraphy. I'm not entirely sure; everything happened so fast."

"Interesting," Tidwell said. One of the uniformed officers suddenly shouted his name out and he jerked about abruptly. "Yes? What is it?" he asked.

"Crime scene techs are here," the officer called to him.

"Excellent," Tidwell said. Muttering to himself, his mouth working furiously, he stalked off without a word of thanks to Theodosia.

That was just fine with Theodosia. She hadn't expected much more and Brooke had hurriedly stepped in to take his place.

"Did I hear you right?" Brooke asked, a look of expectation on her face. "Did you just tell Detective Tidwell that you saw something on one of the robber's hands?"

"I told him I might have seen a tattoo," Theodosia said.

"That could be a clue," Brooke said, jumping on her words. "That could be important."

"And it might not be. Do you know how many people have tattoos these days?"

Brooke's eagerness turned to disappointment. "Oh. Well.

I suppose you're right." Tears welled in her eyes. "And whatever it was, it's not going to bring Kaitlin back."

Theodosia moved closer to Brooke and gave her a hug. "Oh, honey, I'm so sorry. I'm so sorry about Kaitlin." She saw that the crime scene techs were busily taking photos of Kaitlin's body now, their cameras strobing like mad.

All Brooke could do was bob her head.

"I know you feel absolutely devastated."

"You have no idea," Brooke said in a hoarse whisper. Then she stepped back from Theodosia and said, "Theodosia, you've got to help me."

"I will," Theodosia said. "I'll do anything I can to help."

Brooke glanced over at Tidwell and then back at Theodosia. "No. I mean with Kaitlin."

Theodosia frowned. She didn't know if Brooke wanted her to help plan a funeral or if . . .

"I want you to help find her killers," Brooke said urgently.

There it was. The "or if."

"Of all the people here tonight, you were the one who remained calm," Brooke said. "The only one who managed to come up with a clue."

Theodosia wanted to help, she really did. But she was reluctant to muscle her way into a major police investigation. "I wouldn't know where to start," she said, giving a helpless shrug.

"What if I gave you all the information that I have?"

"What do you mean, Brooke?" Theodosia flinched. The crime scene techs had just rolled Kaitlin's body into a black plastic bag.

"My list of jewels, the guest list . . . you know." A faint twitch played at the corner of Brooke's mouth. "Theodosia, you're the smartest person I know when it comes to unraveling this type of thing."

"Oh no, not really," Theodosia said. "Detective Tidwell has all the experience. He's the expert."

"But I know you've worked with him before on a couple of things." Brooke's tone had turned pleading, desperate.

Theodosia was silent for a few moments. And then she said, "Well, maybe I have. On a couple of things, anyway."

They both fell silent as two EMTs loaded the black plastic bag containing Kaitlin's dead body onto a gurney. They rolled it across cracked glass and strips of jagged metal, and then humped it through the doorway and out to a waiting ambulance.

Brooke dropped her head as tears streamed down her face.

Theodosia's heart went out to her. She wanted to help, really she did. But she wasn't a detective, private investigator, or even a *CSI* buff. She was a tea shop lady. An entrepreneur in her midthirties who served tea and scones with a smile, exchanged friendly banter with customers, did a bit of catering on the side, and had the same concerns about a shaky economy that every other small business owner did.

Of course, Theodosia was also smart as a whip, filled with curiosity, and possessed an almost poetic sense of justice. Maybe she'd inherited those qualities from her librarian mother and lawyer father, both gone now. Or maybe those traits had just incubated inside of her these many years until she'd finally witnessed enough injustice in the world.

Making up her mind, Theodosia grasped Brooke's hand and squeezed it hard. "All right," she said, her voice choked with emotion. "I'll do what I can. I'll try my absolute best."

3

❧

Monday morning should have been filled with excitement and promise for the coming week. Instead, it was a rehash of horrors from the night before.

Theodosia, Drayton, and Haley huddled together at a small wooden table in one corner of the Indigo Tea Shop. It was a cool day and they'd started a fire in the little flagstone fireplace. But no matter how merrily the flames crackled and danced, it couldn't lift the chill in their hearts.

Theodosia had slowly and sadly filled Drayton in on all the details of last night's debacle, Haley jumping in wherever she could. Her tea master had listened gravely, sitting ramrod stiff, allowing only his gray eyes to betray the concern he felt.

Finally, when Theodosia had exhausted herself with the details of the robbery, Drayton took a sip of his Assam tea, brewed extra strong today, and set his cup down in his saucer with a tiny *clink.* "So that's what this type of crime is typically called? A smash-and-grab?"

"That's what the police are calling it," Theodosia said. "As well as a homicide."

Drayton shook his head. "Tragic. Simply tragic. For someone to be killed during the course of a stupid robbery."

"Brooke is absolutely devastated," Theodosia said. "When I left her last night, she was just wandering through the ruins of her shop. And I guess making calls to funeral homes."

Drayton reached for a strawberry scone. They'd sat there for a while even though Haley had baked them less than an hour ago. Nobody was really hungry. "I can just imagine how terrible Brooke felt," he said.

Theodosia, Drayton, and Haley generally got together each morning to drink tea, enjoy the quiet, and exchange pleasantries before the Indigo Tea Shop opened its doors for business. This morning all they could do was commiserate. Everyone felt on edge, a little out of sync, and extremely upset that Brooke's event had ended so tragically.

"Not only that," Haley said. "I ran a search on the Internet first thing this morning. It turns out that smash-and-grab robberies have become a huge trend. I read about this Bentley dealership, I think it was down in Miami, that had a jewelry shop attached to it. I guess it was so fat cats could buy a Rolex and a Bentley. Anyway, *that place* got knocked off by a gang of robbers, a lot like the guys that hit Brooke last night."

"And they stole everything?" Drayton asked. He was mid-sixties, gray hair slicked back, and dressed in his trademark tweed jacket and bow tie. Though Drayton always appeared somewhat formal and brittle, a most proper Southern gentleman, he had a soft side to him, too. But only when you were allowed past his crusty, crunchy hard-shell exterior.

Haley was nodding solemnly. "Snatched all the Rolexes from that Miami dealership. Then they robbed the sales guys of their wallets and rolled away in a brand-new Bentley. Huh, some getaway car. It probably cost, like, three hundred grand and had six miles on the odometer."

"Haley's right about these bold robberies." Theodosia looked thoughtful as she spooned a dollop of Devonshire cream onto her scone. "I heard about a jeweler in New York, I think the shop was on Madison Avenue, that was robbed the exact same way. Vandals used a stolen truck to punch a hole right through the front window, then made off with the entire inventory."

Drayton's brows knit together. "All these tales have me worried. I was just thinking about the Heritage Society's Rare Antiquities Show that opens Saturday night. Maybe we should be proactive and enlist some extra security to guard our precious pieces. There's an outside chance those thieves—those murderers—might come back."

"Oh, I don't think . . ." Theodosia started to respond to him just as a sudden bang sounded at the front door.

"Customers?" Drayton frowned. "Already?"

Haley popped up from her chair, pushed back the chintz curtains, and peered out the leaded-glass window. "Oh no, it's Brooke."

Drayton was startled. "She's here? Now?"

"Better let her in," Theodosia said.

Haley scurried to the front door and pulled it open. Brooke, looking red-eyed and exhausted, tottered into the Indigo Tea Shop.

"How are you doing this morning?" Haley asked as she led her over to their table.

Brooke eased herself into the captain's chair directly across from Drayton. "Terrible."

Theodosia leaned over and hugged her, and then Drayton and Haley hugged her as well, expressing their heartfelt sympathies over and over.

"Thank you, thank you," Brooke said.

Theodosia thought Brooke seemed a little dazed and lost. Almost like the victim of a major, mind-shattering event, like an earthquake or hurricane. She was physically present but her mind was . . . someplace else.

Drayton poured Brooke a cup of tea and passed it over to her. "Here you go, dear lady."

Brooke accepted the tea. "Thank you."

Now Drayton was mock stern. "You know you probably shouldn't even be here."

Brooke took a quick sip of tea. "I know." She took another sip. "Good."

"It'll help fortify you," Haley said, putting a scone on a plate for her.

Theodosia figured it was probably up to her to jump-start the real conversation. The one she knew they probably had to have. "What's going on over at your shop?"

Brooke sighed. "The police were there pretty much all night long, digging through the rubble."

"For clues?" Drayton asked.

"I'm not sure there are any," Brooke said. "The only positive thing we have going for us right now is that the robbery was captured on CCTV."

"What on earth is that?" Drayton asked.

"Closed-circuit TV," Haley said. "Her security system."

"That *is* good news," Theodosia said. "Do you think there's a chance your video cameras captured some decent images of the robbers? That the police might be able to ID them?"

"I don't know." Brooke swallowed hard. "The whole thing's a complete nightmare. I can't quite believe that Kaitlin is gone. I mean . . . I even had to meet with the medical examiner first thing this morning and . . ." She stopped, her voice trembling, unable to go on.

"I know," Theodosia said. "It's very hard. No . . ." She corrected herself. "It's terrible."

"Kaitlin wanted to be a designer," Brooke said in a small voice. "She wanted to work with me."

"She told us about that," Haley said. "How she wanted to design jewelry just like you do."

"And now, besides talking to the ME and arranging to

have her poor body shipped back to her parents, the rest of my day will be spent dealing with frantic calls from multiple insurance companies, museums, private lenders, and major jewelers."

"It sounds pretty overwhelming," Theodosia said. "A lot to cope with."

Brooke nodded. "It is. Plus the crime scene people are still scouring my shop, along with a couple of investigators and some private security people I brought in."

"If there's anything I can do to help," Drayton said.

"Thank you." Brooke cocked her head and fixed Theodosia with a steady gaze. "But you're the one I'm here to presume upon. If you're still game, that is."

"Of course I am," Theodosia said. "I told you I'd try my best and I will."

Drayton's brow furrowed. "What's this . . . ?"

"I've completely imposed upon Theodosia," Brooke said. "Enlisted her good help. You know as well as I do how smart she is when it comes to puzzling out tricky situations."

"Really," Theodosia said, "I've just been very lucky."

"You're also tenacious and cagey," Haley said, jumping in. "You were the one who finally sorted out that crazy museum thing and figured out who killed that hotshot donor."

A ghost of a smile flickered on Brooke's face. "Yes, Theodosia was the one who finally solved the murder. I haven't forgotten that." She reached into her tote bag and dug out a stack of papers. "That's why I brought all my information along. Everything I could scrabble together, anyway. My guest list, the contracts and agreements for borrowing the gems and jewelry, pretty much everything I have that pertains to last night."

"You're going to take a look at all this?" Drayton was focused on Theodosia now.

"I said I'd try." Theodosia tapped the large stack of papers. "See if I can make sense out of anything."

"Well . . . good for you," Drayton said. He obviously approved.

Theodosia gave a faint smile. She'd been waiting for Drayton's endorsement. Needed it. Most people regarded him as a highly knowledgeable tea master and antiques collector, but he also served as her champion. Sometimes Drayton believed in her when she doubted herself.

Drayton inclined his head toward Brooke. "So what do the police have to say? What's the early report?"

"Not much of anything," Brooke said. "Mostly they're still asking questions. Oh, and they informed me that the FBI is being brought in."

"My goodness," Drayton said. "I wonder why?"

"Bringing the feds in won't make Detective Tidwell very happy," Haley said.

"Not a whole lot makes Detective Tidwell happy," Theodosia said. Then added, "Unless, of course, he gets a chance to shoot someone."

Once Brooke had taken off, loaded down with take-out cups filled with hot tea and a bag full of scones, they set about getting the Indigo Tea Shop ready for business. Haley scurried into the kitchen to tend to her baking and luncheon prep work; Theodosia and Drayton worked on arranging the tea room.

"I'm going to use the Spode china today," Drayton said. "Just because it's pretty and will give our spirits a nice boost."

"I think that's a lovely idea," Theodosia said. They had multiple sets of china and her collection of teacups and saucers just kept growing. Of course, if she could refrain from hitting every tag sale, auction, and antiques shop between Charleston and Savannah, then maybe they'd be able to fit all their pretty things into the limited cupboard space they had. But what fun was that?

"Do you really think you can make heads or tails out of all the papers Brooke gave you?"

"I don't know," Theodosia said. "But I'll give it a try."

"Bless you," Drayton said. He had just set glass tea warmers on the tables and was lighting the little votive candles he'd placed inside. The flickering flames leapt and danced, lending a cheery note. One that was sadly needed.

The tea room was half-full when Burt Tidwell ghosted in. Theodosia decided that he didn't so much enter a room like a normal person did, but rather stalked in. Head swiveling, eyes casting about, movement fairly contained, he always seemed to be cold-bloodedly hunting down his prey. She was constantly surprised that he was so light on his feet for such a large man. But she wasn't surprised when he stepped up to the front counter, rested his forearms on it, and then leaned in heavily so he could watch as she and Drayton prepped the tea.

Tidwell finally aimed an index finger at Theodosia and said, "You," in an omnipotent voice. "I need to talk to you."

"I figured as much," Theodosia said. She glanced at her watch. She had three pots of tea to brew for their existing customers and lunch was only forty minutes away. There'd soon be dozens of customers coming in for takeout as well as sit-down. "Only problem is," she told him, "I need to keep making forward progress here. I have to get things ready for our luncheon crowd. Could you please just ask your questions while I work?"

Tidwell lifted a bulky shoulder. "If you insist."

Drayton turned and fixed him with a gaze. "And I obviously need to be here, too."

Tidwell released a sigh. "Naturally."

Theodosia reached up and pulled a Chinese blue-and-white teapot off an overhead shelf. "Anything you have to say you can say in front of Drayton."

"Anything?" Tidwell raised a single bushy eyebrow.

"I meant within reason."

"Of course."

Theodosia set the teapot down and grabbed a tin of Dar-jeeling tea. "And I have a few questions myself."

"I'm not surprised," Tidwell said.

Theodosia measured out two scoops of Darjeeling and dumped them into her teapot. Then she added a pinch for the pot. "Are there any suspects?"

Tidwell shook his head. "Nothing concrete as of yet."

"Any clues?"

"Some. As well as the few bits of information you shared with me last night. Like you, I've been tossing around the idea that the smaller hand might have belonged to a woman."

"Are there women robbers?" Theodosia asked.

"It seems to be a growing trend."

"Interesting."

"Even more so when you factor in the notion that the blue lines on that smaller wrist might have been a tattoo," Tidwell said.

"Seems like everyone's getting tattoos these days."

"Not me," came Drayton's slightly scolding voice.

"Do you have anything else?" Theodosia felt frustrated at the lack of information Tidwell seemed willing to share. After all, the police had been at Heart's Desire all night long. They must have found something. "Surely somebody must have noticed something definitive about the three robbers?"

"It would appear not," Tidwell said, "though we questioned all the guests extensively. An awful lot of them claimed to be curled up in a fetal position, nursing cuts and bruises. Trying to avoid the noxious gas."

"It wasn't exactly poison," Theodosia scoffed. "I'm still here. All the other guests are still here."

Tidwell reached a chubby hand toward a tray of scones Haley had put there and helped himself to a strawberry scone. "The gas was your garden variety smoke bomb."

Theodosia slid a plate and butter knife across the counter to him. "Was it military grade?"

"Not even."

"Then what's it used for?"

"Goofy pranks, probably." Tidwell took a bite of scone and chewed thoughtfully. "We did recover the SUV, however."

Theodosia perked up. Here was something tangible. "Where did you find it?" She put a dab of Devonshire cream in a small bowl and gave it to him.

"Dumped in an alley near Hampton Park."

"So that tells you what?" Theodosia asked. "That the robbers live in the area?"

"Doubtful," Tidwell said.

"Then where did they disappear to? Outer space?"

"Huh. We're checking on that."

"Were there any fingerprints in the vehicle?"

"Wiped clean. These people were pros."

"You know . . ." Theodosia paused to recall the sights and sounds of last night. The robbery, as it unfolded, had blazed past like a bad experimental film. But there was one thing that had stuck in her brain. "I think there might have been a motorcycle, too. I'm pretty sure I heard the roar of a big motorcycle engine just as they were taking off."

Tidwell inclined his head toward her. "That's what another witness said, too."

"Well, did anyone *see* the bike? I mean, it wasn't ridden into Brooke's shop or anything, so it must have been waiting outside."

"So probably an outrider," Tidwell said. "A lookout."

"That's the feeling I got, too," Theodosia said. "So there were four people in this gang? But no motorcycle has been recovered? No bikes reported stolen or found stashed in a back alley somewhere?"

"Not yet."

Drayton, who'd been listening the entire time, turned

and placed a teacup in front of Tidwell and poured him a cup of tea. "We might have a small problem," he said.

Tidwell picked up his teacup and inhaled the aroma. "This is an oolong?"

Drayton nodded. "A fancy Formosan oolong."

"Ah yes. I'm picking up a slight oxidation now." Tidwell gazed over his teacup, his eyes slightly bulging. "And what exactly is your problem, Mr. Conneley?"

"The thing is," Drayton said, "the Heritage Society's Rare Antiquities Show kicks off this Saturday night."

"I see your concern and can easily put your mind at ease," Tidwell said. "I shall be happy to assign additional officers for added security."

"I'd appreciate that," Drayton said. "Since we have some particularly valuable items coming in for the show."

Tidwell didn't seem all that worried. "And those items would be . . . ?"

"Well," Drayton said, looking suddenly thoughtful as his brows pinched together. "There is the matter of the Fabergé egg."

4

❧

Theodosia had been reaching for a tin of Japanese green tea. She stopped, mid-reach, still balancing on her tiptoes and said, "What?" Had she heard Drayton correctly? The Heritage Society was going to put a priceless treasure on display? "You're putting a Fabergé egg on display?" she asked, her voice rising in alarm. She didn't know what the going price of jeweled eggs was these days, but she figured they weren't cheaper by the dozen and probably sold for a pretty penny. Especially since there weren't many reigning czars around anymore to wave their scepter and commission one.

"A *genuine* Fabergé egg?" Tidwell asked. Now he seemed startled by Drayton's announcement as well.

Drayton looked suddenly proud of the Heritage Society's big coup. "Oh yes. We managed to obtain an honest-to-goodness Peter the Great egg on loan from Virginia's Thuringer Museum."

"When is it supposed to arrive?" Theodosia asked.

"We're expecting it any day now," Drayton said.

"And what is the egg's value?" Tidwell asked.

Drayton fidgeted with his bow tie. "Oh, I don't know exactly."

"I'll bet you could make a good guesstimate," Theodosia said. "Come on, stun us with a ballpark figure."

Drayton looked around quickly, as if fearing he might be overheard. "By recent auction estimates, this particular Fabergé egg is worth somewhere in the neighborhood of twenty to thirty million dollars."

Theodosia's eyes went wide. "It's worth *millions*? Dear Lord. That must be some fancy egg."

"And some fancy neighborhood," Tidwell said.

"Well, yes," Drayton said. "The egg is practically price-less. So you can see why I might be worried."

Theodosia thought for a moment and decided they'd probably have ample security guards. "You know, you probably shouldn't sweat it."

Tidwell shook his head vigorously. "Oh no, he definitely should."

"What?" Theodosia said. "Seriously?" Now she put herself smack-dab in Tidwell's face. "But *you're* the one who's hard at work on this Heart's Desire mess, and the FBI has also been called in. I was assuming the robbery would be solved in a matter of days. That the jewels would all be returned to their rightful owners, and the robbers apprehended and cooling their heels in a nice dank jail cell."

"It doesn't work that way," Tidwell said.

Theodosia was sticking to her guns. "Well, it should."

"How does it work?" Drayton asked.

Tidwell grimaced. "Unfortunately, there are hundreds of major jewel heists that are never solved."

"Never?" Theodosia squeaked. This didn't sound good.

"Gems and jewelry," Tidwell said, "diamonds in particu-lar, are the most concentrated form of wealth. They're small, portable, and easy to convert into cash. They're the one form of currency that's pretty much accepted anywhere in the world. From Zaire to Zagreb. Moscow to Monaco."

"You're talking as if we're all playing parts in some grand caper movie," Drayton said. "*To Catch a Thief* with Cary Grant. Where jewels are stolen and everybody sits around on the Riviera drinking cappuccinos."

"I wish that were the case," Tidwell told him. "Unfortunately, in the U.S. alone, the jewelry industry loses more than one hundred million dollars a year to theft."

Theodosia poured a little more tea into Tidwell's cup. "Tell us about the FBI being called in for the Heart's Desire robbery. How will they help? What exactly are they expected to do?"

"Probably gum up the works," Tidwell said. He took a sip of tea, put his cup down, and then used a napkin to blot his lips. "They're not known for their skill or keen insight when it comes to actual field investigations."

"But you were an agent once," Theodosia said pointedly. "You were one of their best investigators." Tidwell had been an FBI agent, years ago, before he'd quit the agency and come to Charleston to head their Robbery-Homicide Division.

Tidwell reached for a second scone, sliced it in half, then twiddled his silver knife. "I worked many cases, yes. But I was always butting heads with useless bureaucrats. When I pushed to question witnesses and do field research that might lead to actual clues, they preferred to do wiretaps, amass information, and do a data dump." He snorted. "They wanted to write a *report*." He said the word *report* as if he was referring to camel dung. "A lot of good that does."

"So what now?" Drayton asked. He sounded a little frustrated. "Now what do we do?"

Tidwell gave a tight grimace. "I'd keep a close watch on that jeweled egg of yours."

*   *   *

"Did you hear any of what we were talking about out there?" Theodosia asked Haley. She was in the kitchen, leaning up against the butcher-block table, enjoying the aroma of fresh-baked scones and muffins, and watching Haley stir a big pot of corn chowder.

"I kind of did," Haley said. "Drayton said something about a Fabergé egg? What's *that* all about?"

"The Heritage Society borrowed it for their Rare Antiquities Show. A Peter the Great egg."

"Peter the Great from *Russia*?"

"That would be the place. And apparently this egg is the real deal."

Haley twiddled her wooden spoon and gave the counter a *tippety-tap*. "I'd say the timing on that fancy egg is seriously wrong. Can they hold off on displaying it?"

"Drayton tells me it's the key piece in their show. All their big-buck donors are coming Saturday night just to get a peek at it."

"What if somebody else shows up to take a peek at it?" Haley asked. "Like the same clowns who showed up at Brooke's shop last night?"

"Then we've got a huge problem."

"We? No, no." Haley looked startled. "Just leave me out of this, please. I've had enough robbery to last me a lifetime."

Theodosia realized that Haley was still deeply shaken by the robbery. And, of course, Kaitlin's death. "Yes, of course we will. Apologies if I upset you. Especially since I just came in to get today's luncheon menu."

"Whew." Haley looked relieved. "Hopefully we're back to our regular routine, then. Okay." She dug out a three-by-five-inch index card from her apron pocket and handed it to Theodosia. "Here you go."

Theodosia studied the card. "So lemon scones and your corn chowder as a starter."

"Yup. And a choice of three entrées today," Haley said. "Individual chicken potpies, zucchini quiche, and three kinds of tea sandwiches with either chicken salad filling, tomato slices with Cheddar cheese, or strawberry cream cheese. For dessert we've got toffee bars and chocolate brownie tortes."

"It all sounds perfect."

"With the cooler weather moving in, it's fun to come up with some heartier offerings." Haley smiled. "Heart-healthy ones, too."

"Atta girl."

Lunch was busier than Theodosia thought it would be. She greeted customers, poured tea, and took orders. And with the cooler temperatures moving in, customers *did* want heartier lunches. She brought out bowl after bowl of corn chowder and was beginning to fear that they'd run out of chicken potpies. But, somehow, through Haley's magic, they still managed to have a few left.

When one fifteen rolled around, Theodosia found herself with a slight break in the action. So she grabbed a carton of scone mixes from her office in back and carried it out to the tea room so she could restock her shelves.

Theodosia prided herself on her little retail area. There were two antique highboys chock-full of tea strainers, tea towels, DuBose Bees Honey, and shiny blue bags of Indigo Tea Shop tea. This time of year, Drayton's proprietary blends included Cranberry Razzle-Dazzle, Black Tea Orange, and Autumn Magic, which was a blend of white tea, apple bits, and black currants.

Her own line of T-Bath products lined the bottom two shelves. Her Chamomile Calming Lotion was by far the biggest seller, but they also sold lots of jars of White Tea Feet Treat as well as their T-Bath Bombs.

When everything looked perfect and organized, Theodosia glanced around the tea shop and smiled. The little shingled carriage house that she had freshened, decorated, and cozied up was her pride and joy. The tea-stained wooden floor lent rustic charm, while the candles, bone china, and fancy linens imbued it with a Victorian feel. Oh, and there were the decorated grape-vine wreaths and swags hanging on the walls, too. Wild vines she'd collected and dried at Cane Hill, her aunt Libby's planta-tion, then laced with velvet ribbons and hung with delicate floral teacups. So the whole shop projected a kind of rustic-Victorian-boho vibe, if there really was such a thing.

"Theodosia?" Drayton was calling to her, so she ambled over to the front counter, where he was chatting with a newly arrived guest. A man who was dressed almost on a par with Drayton. That is, a tweed jacket, pocket square, tailored slacks, and horn-rimmed glasses. But no bow tie, just a regular tie.

"Theo," Drayton said. "I'd like you to meet Lionel Rin-icker."

Theodosia shook hands with a smiling Rinicker and said, "But I kind of know who you are already. You're on the board of directors with Drayton. At the Heritage Society."

Rinicker, who was six feet tall and thin bordering on stork-like, beamed down at her. "That's right. And I have to say I'm loving it, even though I'm relatively new to Charleston."

"Lionel moved here six months ago," Drayton said.

"And you're already on the board," Theodosia said. "That's very impressive. Drayton and his merry band must think quite highly of you." She decided that Lionel Rinicker did look rather cultured and urbane.

"Lionel and I have very similar tastes in art," Drayton said. "In fact, he used to teach art history when he lived in Bous."

"And that city is where?" Theodosia asked. She gave him a rueful gaze. "Sorry, geography was never my strong suit."

"It's in Luxembourg," Rinicker said. "The southern part of the country. Though I'm afraid Luxembourg itself is only some nine hundred and ninety-eight square miles in total."

"And you were born there?" Theodosia asked. She'd never met a Luxembourger before. If that's what they were called.

"No, no," Rinicker said. "I'm not a native. I was born in Hollenburg, Austria, just outside of Vienna. I moved to Luxembourg some years ago so I could teach at the university just across the German border. The University of Trier."

"Wow," Theodosia said. "You're a regular citizen of the world."

"Hardly," Rinicker said as Drayton began to steer him toward an empty table.

"I'm sorry," Theodosia said. "I'm standing here gabbing away and you've come to eat lunch." She wiped her hands on her apron. "What can I bring you? Did Drayton show you our menu?"

"Why don't you bring him a cup of chowder, a scone, and a chicken potpie," Drayton said. "If there are any potpies left."

"Of course, there's one left," Theodosia told Rinicker. "And I'm pretty sure it's got your name on it."

He chuckled. "Lovely."

Theodosia cleared two tables, rang up tabs for departing guests, and handled a half-dozen take-out orders. Then, when everything seemed fairly copacetic, she plopped into the chair across from Lionel Rinicker. He was just finishing the last bits of his scone.

A smile lit his face. He seemed charmed to have her company.

"I'm curious," Theodosia said. "How did you pick Charleston?"

Rinicker rested his chin in his palm and looked thoughtful. "I think it was more a case of Charleston picking me. I came through here on a visit, not intending to stay. But there's something about this place that intrigued me." Now his eyes glowed with excitement. "It's very thrilling to live on a peninsula with the Atlantic Ocean pounding in at you and two rivers on either side. And then, of course, I was completely enchanted by the architecture."

"Some of it is very European," Theodosia said.

"It definitely is," Rinicker agreed. "But the larger homes carry such a distinct Southern flavor. I mean, who else but a Southern architect would take Italianate architecture and smatter on a few grand balconies and balustrades? It's absolutely charming! And then, of course, you add in Charleston's hidden walkways, churches, tumbledown graveyards, and the music, art, and theater scene, and it's all just very exciting and romantic." He clapped a hand to his chest. "As you might have guessed, I'm a romantic at heart."

Theodosia hated to break his mood, but she decided she had to bring up last night's robbery since it might impact the Heritage Society. "You know about the robbery that happened last night at Heart's Desire? And that the police have now officially ruled the young woman's death a homicide?"

Rinicker spoke in hushed tones. "Yes, I read about it in the newspaper this morning—it was the lead story. It must have been awful. And I'm to understand that the owner of Heart's Desire is a good friend of yours?"

"Yes, she is."

"Drayton told me you were there. That you witnessed the entire spectacle?"

"I feel like I saw bits and parts of it," Theodosia said. "The robbery was all very erratic and confusing." Actually, as she thought back over it, the SUV crash, the robbery, and the ensuing getaway had all felt like they'd happened in slow motion. What probably took sixty seconds seemed to have stretched into several minutes. Very disconcerting.

"Drayton mentioned that he's worried about extra security

for the Rare Antiquities Show," Rinicker said. "Particularly when it comes to the Fabergé egg."

"I think everyone at the Heritage Society should be worried," Theodosia said.

"Well, I haven't spoken to Timothy Neville yet, so I don't know what his plans are. Or if they've changed at all." Timothy Neville was the octogenarian executive director of the Heritage Society. He'd ruled the organization with an iron fist for decades and wasn't about to relinquish one iota of control now. If anything, his gnarled fingers would grip a little tighter.

"I spoke earlier with Detective Tidwell," Theodosia said. "He heads the Robbery-Homicide Division of the Charleston Police Department—and he's offered to send over some extra police officers."

"That's very generous of him," Rinicker said. "I think that would make us all rest a lot easier."

"I'm assuming the Heritage Society will hire extra security?"

"Like I said, I'm not sure what the plans are. But if Timothy agrees, we can for sure contact our security agency and double up on guards."

"I think that would be a smart idea," Theodosia said. "When is the Fabergé egg supposed to arrive?"

"We're expecting it any day now," Rinicker said. "It's supposedly being driven here in a Brink's truck. So it should be perfectly safe en route."

Theodosia smiled. The only thing that trickled through her brain was a memory of an old black-and-white movie that she'd watched a couple of weeks before—*The Great Brink's Robbery*. Millions stolen, the largest robbery in U.S. history at that time. Holy cats. She hoped there wouldn't be a sequel—*The Great Brink's Fabergé Egg Robbery*.

5

"Knock knock," Drayton said as he pushed open the door to Theodosia's office. "I come bearing a cup of rose hip tea. Any takers?"

"I'm dying for a cuppa," Theodosia said. She quickly cleared a space on her desk for the filled-to-the-brim teacup.

Drayton took in the clutter of papers. "You're looking through that rat's nest of papers that Brooke brought in this morning?"

"Yes, but it's not like I'm actually getting anywhere."

Drayton picked up a sheet of paper. "What's this?" he mumbled to himself. "Oh, I see, it's a list of jewelers and museums that contributed items to her show."

"This is so heartbreaking," Theodosia said. "Brooke did all this work, sweet-talking all these people and negotiating for rather rare pieces, and now it's all gone. Every bit of the . . . loot."

"That's probably how the robbers see it, too. Loot. Gems and jewels to be ripped apart and then disposed of. Fenced."

"Where would you fence pieces like that?" Theodosia wondered.

"You heard what Tidwell said. Pretty much anywhere, since gems and diamonds are so portable. You just stash them in your pocket and fly to Hong Kong or down to Rio."

"Because the good stuff, the shiny stuff, is always in demand." In Theodosia's mind's eye she could see fences picking over the jewels like a flock of wary crows.

"That's right," Drayton said. "I'd venture to guess that the buying and selling of stolen gems makes up a good part of the underground economy." He picked up another sheet of paper and shook his head. "How on earth would you even begin to find a clue here?"

Theodosia was a trifle more optimistic. "You never know." Then she took a deep breath and said, "I've been noodling this robbery over and over in my head. And the one thing that keeps popping to the surface is, what if it was an inside job?"

Drayton peered at her over his half-glasses. "Excuse me?"

"What if one of the guests at Brooke's party last night helped orchestrate the smash-and-grab?"

Drayton stood there rigidly, as if locked in place. "Why on earth would someone do that?"

"Oh, I don't know," Theodosia said. "Maybe to get filthy rich?"

He cleared his throat. "You know, I never would have considered that angle. You have a very devious mind, Theo."

"Thank you. I think." She waited a few moments. "So . . . what do you think, really? Am I completely off base or what?"

Drayton pursed his lips. "I think . . . I think perhaps we should take a closer look at that guest list."

But twenty minutes later they hadn't come up with much of anything.

"Look at the names on this list," Drayton said. "Two

Pinckneys, a Ravenel, and a Calhoun. All old-name solid citizens. Pillars of the Charleston community."

Theodosia had to agree. "Some of these families are so rich they don't need any more money."

"A bunch of jewels would be chump change to them."

Theodosia thought for a few moments. "Then let's look at the people who aren't so rich."

"Let me see." Drayton frowned as his eyes traveled down one of the pages. "Well . . . this is going to be rather difficult. I mean, how do you calculate the net worth of someone you don't really know that well?"

"I have no idea. But why don't you take a ballpark stab, for Brooke's sake. You actually know quite a few of these folks. Plus, you're on the board at the Heritage Society and you hang out with the opera crowd . . ."

Drayton held up an index finger. "Many of whom I shall be rubbing shoulders with this Wednesday evening, since *La Bohème* is opening our season."

"Excellent. So you see, you do hobnob with some of the wealthier folks around town, the socialites." She tapped the list. "Keep looking. See if any of these names arouse your suspicions."

"I suppose it wouldn't be very polite to ask them outright," Drayton said.

"I think not."

They checked and debated a few names for a good half hour.

Finally, Theodosia said, "I have another idea."

"Which is?" Drayton asked.

"What if our insider didn't take part in last night's robbery at all? But what if they put together a group?"

"You mean like in the movies?" Drayton said. "A gang of hired thugs?"

"Sure. Kind of like the Bling Ring that knocked off Paris Hilton's home. Stole jewelry, designer handbags, you name it."

"Sounds far-fetched," Drayton said.

"Okay, what about those crazy Eastern European gangs that have been in the news lately? The ones who've been hitting the Paris and London boutiques?"

Drayton considered this. "Yes, they are quite daring. And you really think one of those gangs could have landed here?"

"They could have," Theodosia said. "And if this is a well-organized smash-and-grab gang, and they decide to hang around Charleston for a spell, you can bet there'll be another disaster just like last night."

Drayton pursed his lips. "You're talking about our big show at the Heritage Society. You're trying to scare me."

"Yes, I'm trying to scare you," Theodosia said. "If it happened once and the thieves got away with it, it could happen again. You should have seen those guys. They were smart, perfectly coordinated, and fearless. I mean, they were *good*."

"Hmm, maybe we'd better take another look at that list."

They went over the list again and ended up putting red question marks by six names. They weren't exactly suspects; they were just people they didn't know all that well.

"This lady, Sabrina Andros," Theodosia said. "I spoke to her last night after the robbery. She cried a few crocodile tears, but in the end she didn't seem all that shaken up. She was more, um, *interested* in what was going on in the aftermath, though she really didn't want to speak to the police." Theodosia blew out a glut of air. "But I don't know a single thing about Sabrina and I'm pretty sure my suspicious mind is getting way ahead of me."

Drayton closed his eyes in thoughtful contemplation. "Andros. Andros. Something about that name sounds familiar."

"Well, I know Sabrina's come into the tea shop a couple of times."

Drayton snapped his fingers. "Wait a minute. Isn't her husband the yacht guy?"

"I don't know. Is he the yacht guy?" Theodosia didn't go sailing as often as she liked anymore. So she hadn't been hanging around the Charleston Yacht Club, sipping Sea Breeze cocktails and picking up the latest boat gossip.

"Andros. I think that's the name," Drayton said.

"Easy enough to find out." Theodosia picked up the phone and dialed the number for Heart's Desire. "I'll just ask Brooke."

"I'm going to grab us a fresh pot of tea," Drayton said as he disappeared out the door.

Then Brooke was on the line. "You found something already?" she asked.

"I'm afraid not," Theodosia said. "I'm just calling to ask you a quick question."

"You and two hundred other people. Angry people."

"But I'm not angry," Theodosia soothed. "Just a little curious about two of your guests."

"Which ones?"

"Sabrina and Luke Andros," Theodosia told her. "Their names are on your list and I'm not very familiar with them. Is Luke Andros the yacht guy? That's what Drayton thought, anyway."

"That's right," Brooke said. "Luke Andros owns Gold Coast Yachts. Apparently they specialize in custom and high-end yachts."

"And you invited him and his wife to your jewelry event?"

"Actually, they were kind of a last-minute addition. Luke Andros came into my shop last week looking for a tasty bauble to buy for his wife. When he found out about my upcoming show, he asked if they could attend."

"So what else do you know about Andros?"

"Just that he and his wife are relatively new in town," Brooke said. "They opened Gold Coast Yachts something like eight months ago."

"What else?"

"Well, I've been told the two of them wasted no time in doing a fair amount of social climbing."

"Trying to buy their way in," Theodosia said. It wasn't unheard of.

"More like trying to impress their way in," Brooke said. "Because they didn't buy a single thing from me."

"And they were both there last night? I remember talking to Sabrina but not to her husband."

"No, he couldn't make it."

"Interesting," Theodosia said. She put a second check mark next to Luke and Sabrina Andros's name just as Drayton came back with a fresh pot of tea.

"Is something going on?" Brooke asked. She sounded a little breathless. Anxious. "Did you find something?"

"No, I'm just trying to familiarize myself with your guest list," Theodosia told her. "In case I want to do a couple of low-key interviews."

"There's something I should tell you about," Brooke said. "Something we kind of stumbled upon this morning."

Theodosia perked up. "What's that?"

"We had a party crasher last night."

"Do you know who it was?"

"No. But when the police had me look at the surveillance tapes an hour ago, there he was."

"And you're sure he wasn't on your guest list?"

"Positive," Brooke said. "But the police have promised to track him down. I guess they're going to take a screenshot and run it against driver's licenses or something."

"Let me know what happens, okay?" Theodosia said.

"Absolutely," Brooke said.

"What?" Drayton asked once Theodosia had hung up.

"There was a party crasher last night."

"Does Brooke know who he was?"

"No, but the police are looking into it." She hesitated. "And we should probably do a quick check on Sabrina and Luke Andros. Just to kind of clear them."

"Why is that?"

"A couple of reasons. Brooke says they're fairly new in town and serious social climbers."

Drayton frowned. "What else?"

"Because Sabrina showed up last night, but Luke didn't."

"Okay," Drayton said. "That's mildly interesting."

"And because their high-end yacht business puts them squarely in contact with high-end people."

"I hear what you're saying. But how exactly are we supposed to compile a dossier on those two?" His eyebrows twitched. "Go purchase a yacht?"

Theodosia thought for a minute. "Maybe we could call Delaine?" Delaine Dish was a society mainstay, gadabout, and prolific fund-raiser. She owned Cotton Duck, an exclusive boutique, and professed to be one of Theodosia's very best friends. "I mean, Delaine knows everybody."

"It's funny you should say that, because Delaine just came in a few minutes ago for afternoon tea," Drayton said.

"Seriously?"

"Yes. Go see for yourself."

Theodosia did. She rushed out past the kitchen and peeked around the corner into the tea room. Delaine was sitting at the small table next to the stone fireplace. She was dressed in a stylish eggplant-colored suit, and her dark hair was swept up into a messy but very cute topknot that set off her heart-shaped face to perfection. She fidgeted nervously as she talked into her cell phone and shared her thoughts and observations with anyone in the nearby vicinity who would listen.

"What did Delaine order?" Theodosia asked.

"A chicken salad sandwich. Oh, and I brought her a pot of Mokalbari East Assam."

"That Assam is fairly high in caffeine," Theodosia said. She needed Delaine to be grounded when she talked to her.

Drayton shrugged. "A finer cut always means more caffeine extraction."

"So what isn't a caffeine bomb that'll send Delaine into orbit? I know, let's trade her out for a pot of Lapsang souchong."

"Fine with me," Drayton said.

"The-o-do-sia," Delaine purred when she caught sight of her friend. She leaned across the table and gripped Theodosia's hand. Her carefully made-up face looked sweet, but her dark eyes glittered with intensity. "I read all about that horrible robbery in the paper this morning. Awful. Just awful for poor dear Brooke to lose her niece like that. And you were really there?"

"I'm afraid so."

"Then you must tell me *everything* about it. Don't leave out a single, thrilling detail."

Theodosia ran through her version of the robbery. How the SUV had smashed its way in, how the people had screamed as glass shards exploded, how the masked robbers had dashed about, smashing open all the cases. And finally, how poor Kaitlin had been found dead in the detritus, a dagger of glass embedded in her neck.

Delaine hung on every word, her eyes getting bigger and bigger, her mouth pulling into a rounded O. "That sounds like a hideous way to die. Extremely painful. And you say the robbers stole every single piece of jewelry?"

"Everything that wasn't locked in the safe in Brooke's back room."

"Goodness." Delaine sat back in her chair. "What a chilling story."

"It was a pretty bad scene," Theodosia agreed.

"I'm glad I didn't attend." Delaine sighed and picked an invisible piece of lint from her expensive suit. As proprietor of one of the ritziest boutiques in Charleston, Delaine owned a wardrobe that wouldn't quit. And to Theodosia's sometime consternation (because she herself veered perilously between a size eight and a size ten), Delaine was also able to squeeze her skinny, carb-obsessed body into all the tiny sample sizes.

"The event started out beautifully," Theodosia said. She was going to ease her way into questioning Delaine. "Many of Charleston's most prominent families were guests."

Delaine took a tiny nibble of her sandwich, managing to avoid the bread. "I should imagine."

"There were even a few new people there." Theodosia squinted as if trying to remember. "I ran into a lovely woman. Sabrina Andros? Have you met her yet?"

"Yes, I have," Delaine said. "I met Sabrina at an opera fund-raiser last month. She and her husband Luke own Gold Coast Yachts."

"Mmn, sounds fancy."

"They sell some of the finest yachts available," Delaine smiled. "Marquis, Princess, Vantage. You know, Vantage is the kind of yacht that Calvin Klein owns."

"Wow," Theodosia said. "Then it sounds as if the Androses are rolling in dough."

Delaine waved a hand. "I'd probably classify them more as nouveau riche. Anyway, they've been throwing a lot of money around, supporting various charities, even though they seem to have come out of nowhere. I mean, they don't exactly have a proper Charleston pedigree."

"That's okay," Theodosia said. "Neither do the dogs at the Four Paws Animal Rescue."

Delaine practically spasmed in her chair. "You're so *right*. And look what adorable creatures they are. Did I tell you about the puppy I saw when I was dropping off a check from our recent fund-raiser? An adorable, sweet little pug. If I thought my darling Siamese kitties would tolerate him, I would have snatched the creature up and carried him home!"

Theodosia half listened to Delaine, then subtly threw in a few questions about some of the other people she'd marked on her list. When Delaine had rambled on about the third person, she suddenly turned suspicious.

"You're certainly quizzing me a lot," Delaine said, practically pulling her mouth into a pout.

"I'm sorry," Theodosia said. "I thought we were just having a conversation."

"You've been probing. Carefully and gently, but you're up to something, aren't you?" Delaine narrowed her eyes, catlike. "Theodosia, I know you. You're definitely *up* to something."

6

❧

So much for wringing information out of Delaine, Theodosia decided. Some of it had been proffered freely, most of it had been like pulling teeth.

It was late afternoon and she was back at her desk, jotting a few notes to herself.

"Did you find out what you needed from Delaine?" Drayton asked. He was lounging in the doorway, looking elegant and half-posed, like a retired ballet master.

"Yes and no."

Drayton gave a thin smile. "Why am I not surprised? Delaine's like a Chinese puzzle. Layers and riddles and infinite dead ends."

"She thought I was pumping her for information."

"That's because you were," Drayton said. "She's not stupid, she's just snooty."

"Hey," Haley said, pushing her way past Drayton. "Am I the only one around here who's working her little fingers to the bone?"

"You're the only one, Haley," Drayton said. "Theodosia and I have been lazing about, stuffing our faces with chocolate bonbons and watching soap operas."

Haley eyed him warily. "What do you know about soap operas? You only watch the Smithsonian Channel and the History channel. And public television."

Drayton gave a cryptic smile. "Which broadcasts *Downton Abbey*?"

"That's not a soap opera," Haley said.

"Come on," Drayton said. "You've watched it. The show's a bit of a potboiler. Or it was, anyway. Admit it."

"Theo?" Haley asked. "What do you think?"

Theodosia twiddled a pen. "Mmn . . . I'd probably have to say . . . potboiler. But a very entertaining and cultured one."

"Sheesh," Haley said. Then, "You know, we've got a super busy week ahead of us."

"So we've noticed," Drayton said. "Our Duchess of Devonshire Tea is scheduled for the day after tomorrow and then our Romanov Tea happens on Thursday."

Haley grinned. "The Romanov Tea that . . . hooray . . . Theodosia is going to promote to high heaven when she appears on Channel Eight."

"When is your interview scheduled?" Drayton asked.

Theodosia cast a quick glance at her calendar. "Um . . . day after tomorrow. Wednesday afternoon. So right after the Devonshire Tea, but just in the nick of time to publicize our other teas. And it's not really an interview per se. The station asked me to do a quick tea demo."

"That sounds like fun," Haley said.

"Anyway," Theodosia continued, "after the tea segment they've promised me about twenty seconds to promote the two event teas we have on this week's schedule."

"Please don't forget to mention our Full Monty Tea," Drayton said. This particular themed tea was his own idea and he was constantly fretting over it.

"Twenty seconds doesn't seem like very much time," Haley sniffed.

"If we were paying for that media off a rate card," Theodosia said, "it would cost us a thousand dollars."

Drayton dusted his hands together. "There you go. Case closed."

Theodosia thought about Brooke, who was so eager and trusting, placing all her hope in Theodosia to figure out who'd killed her beloved Kaitlin. Was that case closed? No, not by a long shot. In fact, she'd only just gotten started.

"Okay, I'm taking off now," Haley yelled as she hustled out of the kitchen and raced through Theodosia's office. She'd pulled on a beaten-up brown leather jacket and had her belongings stashed in a small backpack. Her long blond hair was clipped into a youthful ponytail.

She was almost at the back door when Drayton said, "What on earth is that horrific racket?" He was sitting across from Theodosia's desk on the overstuffed chair they'd dubbed the tuffet, drinking a cup of tea. Theodosia was basically ignoring him, working on orders and shuffling through invoices that needed to be paid.

Haley grinned at Drayton over her shoulder. "Oh, don't mind that. It's just a friend picking me up."

"He drives a Sherman tank?"

Haley rolled her eyes. "No, Drayton, he has a motorcycle. A Harley-Davidson, if you really must know. And it seems as if you must."

"Is this another one of your bad-boy boyfriends?" he asked.

"Bad boy . . . ?" Haley stuck a hand on her hip. "Look, he's a friend, okay?"

"Does this friend have a name?" he asked.

"What are you, my parole officer?"

Drayton had to smile at that one.

"Okay, his name's Billy Grainger," Haley said. "And he really is a nice guy. Not a maniac or a crazy person, so I'm perfectly safe. Now. Are you satisfied?"

"Yes," Drayton said. "Just please take care when you're clinging to the back of that thing, getting bugs stuck in your teeth."

"You got it," Haley said as she dashed out and pulled the door closed behind her.

Drayton stood up and peered out over a white lace curtain. "My, that certainly is a large motorcycle. Must be quite powerful."

Theodosia glanced up from her desk. She'd been paging through a half-dozen different tea magazine and catalogs, studying the contents. It was time once again to place orders for tins of tea, jams, jellies, and tea knickknacks. "Hmm?" she said. She'd heard Drayton's good-natured exchange with Haley and something had stirred within her brain. But what was it? She tried to pull it up, but it didn't want to come. Stayed stuck. Oh well.

Drayton turned and smiled. "I said I hope Haley is wearing a helmet."

Theodosia lived in an English-style cottage that went by the name of Hazelhurst. It had once been part of the larger estate next door to her. Now it was its own little principality ruled over by Theodosia and her dog, Earl Grey.

Thump, thump, thump.

Earl Grey's tail beat out a syncopated rhythm on the parquet floor as Theodosia opened the front door. She crouched down as he leapt up and squirted toward her, a bundle of fur driving forward to bury his sleek head in her hands.

"Hey, buddy," she said, giving his ears a gentle tug. "How was school today?" Theodosia employed a dog walker, a retired schoolteacher by the name of Mrs. Berry, who came by most afternoons. They all called it school (K through 9? K9?) even though it was mostly Earl Grey, a Scottie dog named Mr. Misty, two schnauzers, and a toy poodle named Tootsie that the dog walker led through the tony neighborhoods on most afternoons. The dogs had the time of their lives, sniffing and romping to their heart's content, dragging their human handler down narrow, seldom-traveled cobblestone pathways such as Stoll's Alley and Longitude Lane.

Theodosia hung up her jacket and bag and walked through her dining room into the kitchen. Ignoring the ugly cupboards that she still wanted to change out, she pulled open the refrigerator door and scanned the contents inside. Some lobster bisque that she could heat up, a slice of leftover quiche, lots of fruit and cheese.

Was she hungry? She decided no. Not at this very moment, anyway. So maybe a jog was in order to blow out the carbon and help her relax? She thought that might just do the trick.

Ten minutes later, dressed in workout pants, a hooded anorak, and Nike trainers, Theodosia and Earl Grey were out the door and bouncing down the back alley. It was full-on dark now, and as she raced through the historic district, some of the lighted windows offered glimpses of life in Charleston's grandest homes.

A dining room table was being set with gleaming silver and china. Drinks were being imbibed in a wood-paneled library. A man in a wine-colored jacket (was that really a smoking jacket?) poked at logs in a crackling fireplace. Lights were snapped on and, finally, heavy curtains drawn across elegant, arched windows.

Theodosia chugged along at a fairly brisk pace, idly wondering if the robbers from last night had ever cased homes such as these. Down here, along East Bay Street and Murray Boulevard, the enormous Georgian, Federal, and Victorian-style homes were the cream of the crop. They sold for multimillions in today's hot real estate market and housed many of Charleston's bankers, lawyers, and doctors. Their contents—antiques, artwork, silver, Oriental rugs, Chippendale furniture, what have you—were probably worth a small fortune. She hoped it all remained safe.

Earl Grey matched Theodosia stride for stride, his legs chugging along, his ears laid flat against his fine-boned head. Her heart filled with love for this wonderful dog that had become her dear companion. She'd found him, several years ago, as a shivering, frightened, homeless pup cowering in the alley behind the Indigo Tea Shop. She'd picked him up, wrapped him in a warm blanket, whispered to him, and never let him go. Now he'd grown into a magnificent dog—smart, friendly, good with people.

In fact, Earl Grey was now a registered therapy dog with the Big Paw organization. Several times a month, he'd don his bright-blue nylon service-dog cape and they'd visit hospitals and nursing homes. Sometimes just laying his head in the lap of a patient made their face light up. And sometimes the patients' sad smiles, as they no doubt remembered their own dogs from long ago, made Theodosia brush away tears of her own.

They ran down Tradd Street, hit Church Street, and hung a left, running past the darkened Indigo Tea Shop. Two more blocks and then they swung right again, running toward Heart's Desire.

Theodosia pulled back on Earl Grey's leash as they approached. When she heard voices and saw black-and-yellow tape flapping in the wind, she crossed to the other side of the street. It looked as though there were still some police officers present, along with two men in white overalls who were unloading large sheets of plywood from the back of a pickup truck that had the name JUNI'S HARDWARE painted on the doors.

Going to board up the store. Too bad that's the only thing that's being done right now.

Theodosia headed over to Concord and ran along the high embankment of the Cooper River. Lights from several small boats shimmered in the fog that was slowly beginning to drift in. Farther down, she could just make out the large docks where commercial vessels pulled in to unload cargo.

She slowed her pace and they veered off the path. Jogged along dry grass and over to a rocky patch. They stopped, both of them breathing hard from a good, long workout.

Off in the distance, a boat horn tooted mournfully, then a small tugboat came puttering into sight. Theodosia looked down at the river as the boat churned by. The water looked gray and cold and turgid. She shivered and thought of poor Kaitlin, lying in some mortuary on a cold slab.

Who would answer for her?

Who had put her there?

Who could have masterminded that robbery?

Theodosia clenched her jaw as she shivered in the November cold. She intended to pull out all the stops and find out who was responsible.

Make sure they were punished for their crime.

7

Just as Theodosia and Drayton were primping and priming the Indigo Tea Shop for Tuesday morning tea service, wouldn't you know it? The FBI showed up.

Theodosia took one look at their conservative dark-blue suits, white shirts, and narrow ties and thought *FBI.* They looked like they'd come directly from central casting. Or had stepped right out of an episode of *Criminal Minds.*

Drayton wasn't quite as observant. Or maybe he thought they looked more like front men for a retro doo-wop group.

"I'm afraid we're not open yet," Drayton told them. "If you'd care to wait outside?"

The lead agent's jaw tightened as he flipped open his leather ID case. He was tall with chiseled features, probing dark eyes, and just a hint of salt and pepper in his dark, curly hair.

"I'm sorry," Drayton said, not bothering to glance at the man's credentials. "There's no soliciting in here. The Indigo Tea Shop maintains a very strict policy."

Theodosia started to giggle. Sometimes, Drayton could be a complete stitch. She put a hand on his shoulder and brushed past him.

"Please come in," Theodosia said. "Of course, we really weren't expecting you."

"We really weren't expecting who?" Drayton asked, puzzled.

"I'm Boyd Zimmer," the taller of the two men said. "Federal Bureau of Investigation. I'm the AIC, agent in charge, and this is my assistant, Agent David Hurley."

"You're FBI?" Drayton stammered out. "Oh my."

"Nice to meet you," Theodosia said. Smiling and shaking hands, she introduced herself and Drayton to both agents. She was pleased that her courtesy had caught them off guard. "We've got a few minutes before we open the tea shop, so why don't we all sit down at a table?" She pointed to the one nearest the window and said, "Right this way, gentlemen."

The agents shuffled toward the table, looking stodgy and staid. They realized they were somehow being *handled* by this small Southern woman, but weren't sure what to do about it.

Once the agents were seated, Theodosia said, "If you'd like, we could all enjoy some tea and scones."

"Scones, ma'am?" Agent Zimmer said. He said it with a certain degree of mistrust. As if she'd just mentioned insider trading or the smuggling of illegal weapons.

"That's right," Theodosia chirped. "We have coconut cherry scones and maple nut scones today. Our baker has really outdone herself."

"They both sound good," Hurley grunted. He had thinning blond hair; an open, pleasant face; and intensely blue eyes. He seemed more relaxed than his partner, as if he was actually looking forward to some tea and scones.

"Then I'll bring you one of each." Theodosia figured if she could impart a bit of grace and civility to these men, there might be faint hope for the FBI yet.

Theodosia bustled back to the kitchen and stacked scones on a silver tray while Drayton fixed a pot of Panyang Congou tea.

When they were all seated, Theodosia passing around the scones and Drayton pouring tea, Hurley said, "I don't believe I've ever had brewed tea before. Except maybe in a Chinese restaurant."

"Those were probably tea bags," Drayton said, switching into tea master mode. "Bits of stalk and stems and tea dust. No, you really must drink freshly brewed leaves in order to enjoy the full, rich taste of a great tea."

"And this is a great tea?" Hurley asked, taking a sip.

"You tell me," Drayton said.

"Mmn, it's very good," Hurley said.

"I thought you'd like it." Drayton smiled with pride. "A nice Chinese black tea, easygoing and round."

Zimmer and Hurley watched as Theodosia sliced her scone lengthwise, and then followed her lead.

"And this whipped cream goes on top?" Zimmer asked.

"It's Devonshire cream," Theodosia said. She nodded at Drayton. "Made from Drayton's own proprietary recipe."

The agents slathered on Devonshire cream, bit into their scones, and nodded appreciatively. They actually seemed to be relishing their tea and treats.

Good, Theodosia thought.

"I was wondering," Theodosia said, addressing both agents, "why the FBI is involved with this jewel theft? When Detective Burt Tidwell and his team are really quite brilliant at what they do. I mean, we do have every confidence in our own Charleston Police Department."

"Mmn," Zimmer said, chewing. "I'm sure you do, ma'am. And we do, too. It's just that, from our experience, a jewel theft of this magnitude usually involves a gang of criminals that has moved in from another part of the country."

"So it's interstate." Theodosia could see the logic in this, even though Tidwell still resented their butting in.

"That's exactly right," Hurley said. He was busying himself with his scone. Slicing off small pieces then smearing them with a judicious amount of Devonshire cream.

"The other reason we're giving this our full attention," Zimmer said, "is because diamonds and gems are what the bureau calls an *influential means* by which to acquire drugs and weapons."

Theodosia sat back in her chair. "Oh. That doesn't sound good at all."

"It's not, ma'am," Zimmer said. "But we're seeing more and more of these robberies that indirectly threaten homeland security."

"What we'd really like," Hurley said, glancing at Theodosia, "is to ask you a few questions."

"That's fine," Theodosia said.

"We read the police report," Hurley said, "in which you were referenced several times."

"Because I was a witness."

"Actually, a pretty good witness," Hurley said. "Fact is, you were the one who got a good look at one of the thieves' hands. And conjectured that it might have even been a woman."

"A woman with a tattoo," Zimmer said.

"Not really their hand," Theodosia said, trying to recall exactly what she'd seen. "More like their wrist. I caught sight of a little slice of skin where the glove ended and the sleeve had ridden up."

Zimmer looked interested. "And you saw a tattoo."

Theodosia shook her head. "No, that's not what I told the officer who interviewed me. I said I saw faint blue lines *like* a tattoo. Seems to me a tattoo is generally a recognizable object or character or letters. These were more like, well . . . crosshatches. Do you know what those are?"

Zimmer pulled out a notebook and a pen and quickly scribbled a loose grid of crosshatches. "Like this?"

"Close," Theodosia told him. "Does that symbolism mean anything to you?"

"Not right now," Zimmer said. "But it's certainly an identifying mark."

"Does the FBI keep a database of tattoos and marks?" Drayton asked.

Zimmer nodded. "We do." He smiled. "But we prefer you not mention it to anyone."

"I won't." Drayton was all for giving his full cooperation.

Theodosia drummed her fingers against the table. She'd once again been replaying the robbery scenario in her head. The car crash, the smashing of glass cases, the almost precision-like work of the robbers.

"What, ma'am?" Zimmer asked. "Is there something else you can tell us?"

"Talking with the two of you about the robbery has sort of jogged my memory," Theodosia said.

"How so?" Hurley asked her.

"I think I just remembered something else."

Both agents leaned forward expectantly.

Theodosia raised her right hand in a pantomime. "One of the thieves was using a small hammer. To, you know, smash open the cases. But it was a different kind of hammer. An unusual-looking hammer."

Hurley was interested. "You mean like a tack hammer or an upholstery hammer?"

"Not exactly," Theodosia said. "I know what those hammers look like and this one was different. More like a silver hammer with a jagged clawlike thing on one end." She wrinkled her nose. "I wish I could describe it better, but I just caught a quick flash."

"Interesting," Hurley said as Zimmer made more notes.

"Do you think it could be an important clue?" Drayton asked.

Zimmer snapped his notebook shut. "We prefer to call it a lead."

"But only if it leads somewhere, right?" Theodosia asked.

Both men remained silent.

"I'm curious," Theodosia said. "Have you found out any more about the SUV that was used in the robbery? The one that was stolen and then dumped?"

"We've since located the owner," Zimmer said.

"Someone local?" Theodosia asked.

Zimmer shook his head. "No, the owner lives in Savannah. He believes it was probably stolen out of his garage on Saturday night."

"So the thieves are from Savannah?"

"Not necessarily," Zimmer said. "And we still don't have a bead on the motorcycle. Though we have located a couple of witnesses who saw it tear down Market Street. Leading the way for the SUV."

When Zimmer said *motorcycle*, Theodosia twitched. That's what had been tickling at the back of her brain. Tidwell had mentioned something about a motorcycle yesterday morning, and then Haley had rushed out last night and jumped on the back of one. An interesting coincidence.

"Has the motorcycle been recovered?" Theodosia asked.

"No," Zimmer said. "It's still out there somewhere."

And the surprises just kept on coming.

"Miss Browning," Zimmer said, "we'd like you to take a look at some photographs."

Theodosia smiled politely. "But they all wore masks; I never did see anyone's face. I don't think anybody did."

"Just work with us on this, okay?"

"Sure."

Hurley fingered a large brown envelope.

Drayton jumped to his feet. "Here, let me clear off this table."

"Are the photos you're going to show me of suspected jewel thieves?" Theodosia asked.

"*Known* jewel thieves," Hurley said. "Men and women who have stolen millions, perhaps even a billion dollars' worth of diamonds, Rolex watches, necklaces, rings, and bracelets. Some were full sets by Bulgari, Cartier, and Tiffany, others were loose, precious jewels."

"I'll look at your photos, but I don't think it's going to help," Theodosia said. She made a slightly helpless gesture. "The masks, you know."

They waited until the table had been cleared and Drayton had left. Then Hurley opened the envelope. Carefully, one at a time, he laid out a dozen different photographs. "These are all photos we acquired from Interpol, the International Criminal Police Organization," he explained.

Theodosia gave a cursory glance at the photos. There were ten men and two women, a dozen photos in all. Some were in color, some in black-and-white. She studied the one closest to her. The man was midthirties with dark hair, a hawk nose, and high cheekbones. Dangerous-looking, but a little intriguing, too.

As she made a concentrated effort to study each of the photos, Theodosia noted that all the faces had a somewhat cultured European vibe to them. They may have been thieves—or even dangerous killers—but they all looked like they'd lived a pampered lifestyle.

She worked her way through the photos, shaking her head as she went. When she got to the last row, she figured this whole thing had been an exercise in futility. The FBI wasn't getting anything out of this and she certainly didn't recognize . . .

When Theodosia glanced at the last photo, her eyes

widened and she let out a small gasp. The FBI agents were quick to notice.

"Do you recognize this person?" Zimmer asked.

Theodosia tapped the photo with a manicured finger. "Who is this man?"

"His name is Klaus Hermann," Zimmer said. "He's a German national, a jewel thief who has been working in Paris and Rome for the past couple of years. He also goes by a number of aliases that include Count Henri von Strasser, Lord Conroy, and Rupert Gainsborough."

"Where is he now?" Theodosia asked.

"We don't know," Hurley said. "He disappeared last year right after a particularly daring raid on a jewelry store in Cannes. We figured he might be cooling his heels in South America. Drinking rum and guava juice and relaxing on the beach at the Four Seasons in Buenos Aires." He paused. "Why? Do you recognize him?"

Theodosia stared at the picture of Klaus Hermann, aka Count von Strasser, Lord Conroy, and Rupert Gainsborough. And thought that, at the right angle, with the right lighting, he bore a slight resemblance to Drayton's friend Lionel Rinicker.

"I don't think I know him," Theodosia said finally. "But he mildly resembles someone I recently met."

"What?" The agents were ready to pounce on her information. Maybe even draw their weapons and make an arrest.

"I don't know if I should . . ."

"It's your duty," Hurley said.

"This isn't just federal, this is international," Zimmer put in. He was using his hard-edged FBI voice now. "We're working with our legal attaché offices overseas."

Theodosia twisted the moonstone ring she wore on her left hand. Should she or shouldn't she? And did she really have a choice? She'd promised Brooke that she'd help as much as she could. And these two guys standing over her *were* genuine FBI.

"This man looks a little bit like Lionel Rinicker," she said.

"Who is that?" Zimmer asked. "What do you know about him?"

"He's a fairly new Charleston resident and he serves on the board of directors at the Heritage Society."

Zimmer began scribbling notes like crazy.

Then, like a cat sneaking up on its unsuspecting prey, Drayton appeared at their table. He'd been eavesdropping on the entire conversation.

"Theodosia!" Drayton cried. "What are you telling these men?" He looked like he was about to have an explosive coronary.

Theodosia put a finger on the photo and spun it around. "Look at this guy," she said. "Who do *you* think he looks like?"

Drayton stared at the photo. Then he put the palm of his hand against his cheek and shook his head vigorously, as if trying to deny it.

"Drayton?" Theodosia said, pressing him for an answer. "Come on. Just say it."

Drayton finally met her eyes. "All right, it looks like Lionel. Just as you say, the man in this photograph looks a little bit like Lionel Rinicker."

8

❧

"Oh boy," Hurley said. His eyes danced with excitement, his fingertips twitched.

"But it's probably *not* him," Drayton said in an icy voice. He was upset and didn't care who knew it. "It must be a case of mistaken identity."

But Zimmer and Hurley were insistent, pressing Drayton for all the information he had on Lionel Rinicker. After two minutes of pressure Drayton folded like a cheap card table. He told the agents all about Rinicker moving to Charleston, his claim about living in Luxembourg and teaching art history at the University of Trier, and his being asked to join the Heritage Society's board of directors.

"Thank you," Zimmer said. "You've been very forthcoming."

"Not that I wanted to be," Drayton grumped.

"Now we need to share some information with the two of you," Zimmer said.

"Tell you a little story," Hurley said. "A true crime story."

"Have you ever heard of the Pink Panther gang?" Zimmer asked.

Theodosia and Drayton exchanged glances.

"Like in the movies?" Theodosia asked.

"This Pink Panther gang isn't quite as funny or light-hearted as it sounds," Zimmer said. "Interpol gave them the name early on and I'm afraid that it's stuck. Best we know, they're a group of Serbs who are responsible for over five hundred million dollars' worth of daring robberies in Dubai, Switzerland, France, Japan, Luxembourg, Spain, and Monaco. The members in the gang are all fluent in several languages and possess multiple passports."

Drayton scratched his head. "That all sounds rather amazing."

"There's more," Zimmer said. "The gang members that have been arrested have all managed to escape. One person actually escaped from a Monte Carlo prison while police officers fired machine guns at him. Poof—he was gone in a heartbeat. Another gang member masterminded a break from a prison in Lausanne, Switzerland, and took four other prisoners with him. And two others escaped from a Swiss prison in Orbe with the help of outside accomplices." He lifted his shoulders in a resigned shrug. "Did I mention they were daring?"

"And they enjoy their life of crime," Hurley said. "It's made them rich. Rich beyond belief."

"Your story is . . . fantastical," Theodosia said. "And you were wrong, it *does* sound like a movie."

"Except these Pink Panthers play for very high stakes," Drayton said. He'd been seriously impressed with the derring-do of the gang. And maybe a little frightened, too.

"What we're wondering now," Zimmer said, "is if your Lionel Rinicker could be one of them. If he's the leader of the gang that struck here on Sunday night."

"That would make Rinicker one of the escapees?" Drayton

asked. "Let me see, perhaps he hopped a tramp steamer in Marseille, landed in Charleston, and started up a new gang of jewel thieves?"

"Now, that does sound like a bad movie plot," Theodosia said.

"We don't know that any of this is related," Zimmer said to Drayton. "The thieves at Heart's Desire may very well have been a South American gang that we've also been trying to track. They're a particularly nasty gang that's been quietly terrorizing Miami. But we do need to have a sit-down meeting with your Mr. Rinicker."

"Couldn't you just check his fingerprints or something?" Drayton asked. "I mean, you must have fingerprints on those guys who escaped."

Zimmer and Hurley exchanged glances. "We did," Hurley said. "But not anymore."

"Nice work there," Theodosia said. "So what exactly are you telling us? What's the takeaway here? That you're hoping to nail Rinicker to the wall? A man who could easily be one hundred percent innocent? Or are you just going to wait around until this same murderous gang strikes somewhere else?" This time she threw a meaningful glance at Drayton.

The two FBI agents fell silent. Drayton fidgeted nervously.

"Okay," Theodosia said. She knew it was time to grab the bull by the horns. "Now *we* have a story to tell you." She glanced at Drayton. "Drayton? Please enlighten these two gentlemen about your Rare Antiquities Show."

So Drayton gave the agents a quick rundown on the Heritage Society show that was scheduled to open this coming Saturday. He told them about the big-buck donors that would be in attendance, who was doing the catering, the Etruscan coins that would be on display, and then, as their eyes began to glaze over, he told them about the Fabergé egg.

That little nugget of information woke them up and rattled their cages in a huge and meaningful way.

"A genuine Fabergé egg?" Zimmer asked in disbelief. "You mean one that . . . one that . . . ?" He was sputtering now.

"A Fabergé egg that belonged to a *Russian czar*," Drayton said. "Yes, that's exactly what we're talking about."

"Creepers," Hurley exclaimed. "We're gonna need to bring in more agents."

Once Zimmer and Hurley had left, Drayton remained preoccupied for the rest of the morning. He greeted customers amiably enough, brewed tea, and even managed to charm the usually crusty Mrs. Merriweather, who'd dropped by for morning tea and scones. But Theodosia could tell he was still awfully upset.

"I'm sick at heart," Drayton confided to Theodosia when she stopped at the front counter to grab a pot of black currant tea. "I never in a million years thought something like this could happen. Lionel has been a good friend and now I've betrayed him. I may have even ruined his life—caused catastrophic consequences for him that can *never* be put right."

"You did no such thing," Theodosia told him.

"But I did. Now those two FBI agents are going to be sniffing all around poor Lionel. Digging into his bank accounts, talking to his friends, probably interviewing him in some frightening room with bright lights and a two-way mirror. And it's all because of me." Drayton dumped three scoops of tea into a Chinese teapot, seemed to lose count, and then haphazardly added another scoop.

"Actually, it's because of me," Theodosia said. "I looked at that photo and his name pretty much flew out of my mouth. I mean, the guy in the photo really did look like Rinicker." She gazed at Drayton. "Come on, he did. You thought so, too."

"I know there was a slight resemblance, but I'm seriously regretting that I ever seconded your opinion."

"Drayton . . ." Theodosia's voice was cajoling.

"Do you think I should call Lionel?"

"No. Absolutely not," Theodosia said. "If Rinicker really is an international criminal and you tip him off, that makes you an accessory to a crime."

"Oh dear. Now I don't know what to do."

"Don't do anything," Theodosia said. "Play dumb. Pretend this never happened. If Rinicker mentions that the FBI came calling and wanted to chat with him, just act surprised. Or commiserate with him if you want. Look down your nose and act haughty and outraged."

Drayton nodded. "I can do haughty and outraged. I've got that down solid."

Theodosia patted him on the arm. "See. There you go. It's all gonna work out fine."

"You think?"

"Sure. Unless Rinicker really is this guy . . ."

Theodosia poured tea, served plates of scones, and ferried a small bowl of strawberry jam to Leigh Carroll, the woman who owned the Cabbage Patch Gift Shop next door. She was an African American woman in her midthirties, fairly close in age to Theodosia. She was tall with beautifully burnished skin, sepia-colored hair, and almond eyes. When men first caught sight of her, they often fell madly in love.

"I heard you were at Heart's Desire when that big jewel robbery took place," Leigh said. She dropped her voice. "And that Brooke's niece was killed by a piece of flying glass?"

Theodosia sighed. "It was awful. The robbery was bad enough. But Kaitlin . . ."

Leigh looked concerned. "How is Brooke taking all this?"

"She's heartsick, as can be expected."

Leigh let loose a little shiver. "Makes you wonder. How

safe are we, anyway? Church Street has always felt like this sweet little slice of charm and gentility. And then something like this happens. It just shatters your faith in people and your own neighborhood."

"I know," Theodosia said. "It does make you wonder."

And Theodosia was wondering about something else, too. As if the FBI's suspicion about Lionel Rinicker wasn't bad enough, she needed to ask Haley about her motorcycle-driving boyfriend.

In their postage stamp–sized kitchen, Haley was doing her chef's spin-and-twirl ballet. With a white chef's hat the size of an overblown mushroom atop her head, Haley sliced and diced, then leapt over to her oven to pull out fresh-baked loaves of date-and-walnut bread.

Theodosia hovered in the doorway, a little unsure of how to launch the conversation. "Can we talk?" she finally asked.

Haley smiled and gestured for her to come in. "Entrée, please. Come into my domain, my little fiefdom, if you dare."

"You're in a good mood this morning," Theodosia said.

"I'm always in a good mood," Haley said. "How are my maple nut scones faring out there? Everybody liking them?"

"They're loving them."

"Thought so." Haley picked up a knife and began slicing an English cucumber. "What's up, Theo?"

"You heard some of what was going on out there this morning?"

Haley gave a crooked grin. "You mean with those hunky FBI guys?"

"Yes, but I never realized they were hunky." Theodosia was a little flustered. "Did you think they were? Really?"

"The tall one was. What was his name? Zimmer?"

"Special Agent Zimmer," Theodosia said.

"I like that 'special agent' stuff. It reminds me of secret agents. You know, like Tom Cruise in *Mission: Impossible* with his self-destructing tape player and rubber human head masks."

"Mmn." Theodosia picked up a wooden honey stick and played with it. "But do you know what they were asking about?"

"Sure. About the robbery and stuff at Brooke's shop. And about Kaitlin getting killed. And then you picked out that photo that looked like Drayton's friend."

"Except it's probably *not* Drayton's friend," Theodosia was quick to assure her. "We're pretty sure that Lionel Rinicker is a different guy entirely."

"And, then again, he could be an international jewel thief."

Theodosia decided to tackle the subject she really wanted to know about.

"Haley, I'd like to know a little more about your motorcycle-driving friend."

Haley continued to slice away at her cucumber. "There's not much to know."

"Then how about his name, for starters?"

"His name is Billy Grainger. You know, Drayton already quizzed me about this."

"Please bear with me," Theodosia said. "And I know this next question is really going to sound strange . . . but do you know where Billy was on Sunday night?"

Haley glanced up and gave a blank stare. "Sure, I do. But . . ." Then she stiffened and her eyes did a slow reptilian blink. "Wait a minute. Why are you asking about him?"

"The police and FBI think there was a guy on a motorcycle who served as a kind of lookout for the jewel thieves."

Haley's good mood suddenly evaporated. "And you think it was Billy?" She sounded shocked.

"Not really. But it just feels like an awfully weird coincidence. There's a guy on a big bike who leads the getaway car through town and suddenly you have a friend who rides a big bike."

Haley shook her head so defiantly her blond hair almost escaped from her kerchief. "He wouldn't. I mean he would *never.*"

"I didn't think so, either, Haley. But I'm just . . . well, I'm kind of looking out for you."

"And for Brooke."

"Yes, of course, for Brooke."

"And you want to find justice for Kaitlin."

"That's a huge factor, too," Theodosia said.

"Which is why you want to know where Billy was Sunday night."

Theodosia peered across the butcher-block counter at Haley. "Do you know where he was?"

Haley stabbed murderously at a cucumber slice. "He told me he was working. And I believe him."

"Okay, Haley." Theodosia knew when it was time to back off. "I was just asking."

"Asked and answered," Haley said in a tight voice. She spun away from Theodosia and stood at the stove with her back to her. Finally she said, "I made a pot of squash bisque for lunch."

"You must have hit up the farmer's market."

"I did. And I'm doing chicken salad with apple and pineapple chunks, kind of a modified fruit salad, as well as a roast beef and Cheddar cheese sandwich."

"It all sounds wonderful," Theodosia said. She was pretty sure she'd offended Haley, even though they were both chirping away like nothing had happened. "I was also wondering if you'd worked out the menu for our Duchess of Devonshire Tea tomorrow?"

"I still have a couple of things to talk over with Drayton. I want all the food to complement his tea choices."

"Sure. I can see that."

Haley began peeling an apple. "We seem to be doing a lot more special event teas lately. You don't think we're doing too many, do you?"

"Not really," Theodosia said. "The teas are fun to do because they always revolve around an interesting theme. And they're a great marketing device. Our regular customers always bring guests along who get intrigued by our tea shop, and eventually become new customers. So it's really a win-win situation."

Haley shrugged. "If you say so."

Theodosia served lunch, packaged up take-out lunches, and greeted a group of women who'd driven in from Summerville. They called themselves the Summerville Tea Divas, and they pretty much adored every sweet and savory that was put in front of them. Of course, Drayton was called upon to expound upon the subtle differences between black tea and white tea, and he really got into it. For a while. Once lunch was concluded, he went back to being worrywart Drayton.

"I feel as jittery as a long-tailed cat in a room full of rocking chairs," he told Theodosia. They were both behind the counter, wiping out teapots and putting them away.

"You've got to relax," Theodosia said. "This is all going to play out. The FBI will do a thorough background check on your friend Rinicker, and I'm sure everything will turn out fine."

"And if it doesn't? If Rinicker really is this Count von Schmaltz . . . ?"

Theodosia smiled. "Count von Strasser."

"What if Rinicker really *is* an international criminal, and what if the FBI doesn't find out in time? What if something happens at the Rare Antiquities Show on Saturday?"

"Now you *do* think he's a criminal?"

Drayton looked depressed. "I don't know what to think, Theo. I need your help."

"What? You mean to investigate Rinicker? On our own?" She found the idea slightly unnerving.

"That would be the smart thing to do." Drayton looked hopeful. "Do you think we could handle something like that?"

"I don't know. Let me noodle it around. We wouldn't want to be *too* obvious when it came to asking him questions. Especially if we're coming in right on the heels of the FBI."

Drayton pondered her words. "I suppose you're right."

"But we could certainly, um, alert Timothy Neville."

"I was thinking the same thing. In fact, I think we almost have to. It's our duty."

"We? Our? Wait a minute. How did I get involved in breaking the bad news to Timothy?"

Drayton gave her a tentative smile. "I suppose . . . guilt by association?"

Just as Theodosia was about to beg off, the phone rang. Theodosia snatched it up. It was Brooke.

"Theo," Brooke said. "How's it going?"

"I'm working on a couple of ideas, Brooke."

"You are, really?" Brooke sounded jazzed and anxious.

"I've been talking to Detective Tidwell as well as those two FBI agents."

"I'd put more faith in Tidwell," Brooke said. "The FBI agents don't seem to have a handle on any of this."

"They're actually further along than you think they are."

"Really? That is good news. Can you . . . elaborate?"

"Not yet," Theodosia said. "But I promise, the minute I have something concrete you'll be the first to know."

"Bless you, Theodosia."

"I went by your shop last night when I was out jogging."

"Yeah," Brooke said. "What's left of it."

"You'll put the pieces back together. I know you will."

"Only if I don't cave under all the pressure that's being put on me by the various jewelers, collectors, and museums."

"I'm so sorry, Brooke."

"You know I'm counting on you, Theodosia."

Theodosia bit her lower lip as her heart did a slow flip-flop. "I know that, Brooke. I know you are."

9

❧

Once the lunch crowd had departed, once all the scone crumbs had been swept up and the teapots put back on their shelves, Theodosia and Drayton took off for the Heritage Society.

"We won't be long," Theodosia promised Haley.

"No problem," Haley called back.

Drayton tugged a brown ivy cap over his gray locks, then pushed the back door open for Theodosia.

A brisk autumn wind suddenly whipped in, scattering a pile of papers from Theodosia's desk and tossing her auburn curls against her cheeks.

"Gracious." Theodosia wrapped a light-blue pashmina around her shoulders, tugged it tight, and stepped out into the sun. Sheltered from the wind, it felt like a decent sixty degrees. But when the wind gusted in off the Atlantic . . . well, that was another story. Autumn in Charleston was sometimes two seasons jumbled together. The stubborn fingers of summer clung to each day with sheer Southern determination, while Old Man Winter rode into town at night and did his best to spread his chilly mantle. Currently, the two were at a standoff.

"Haley and I are already debating the Christmas tea menus," Drayton said as they stepped along Church Street. Ever the gentleman, he'd positioned himself on the outside of the sidewalk, tucking Theodosia safely between himself and the buildings. "She thinks we serve the same items every year and wants to rotate in some new scone varieties and entrées. But I think most customers look forward to our regular menu items. They're a fine tradition that folks can count on, like Christmas carols and wreaths hung on the door."

Theodosia smiled. She hadn't gotten her mind past Thanksgiving yet, but she was delighted that Drayton and Haley were thinking ahead. They were a powerful team, the perfect mix of creative passion and traditional wisdom. Now, if she could just keep them from killing each other.

"Have you started your holiday shopping yet?" Theodosia asked.

Drayton never broke stride. "Everyone gets tea."

"Of course."

As they followed the narrow walkway around St. Philip's Church, Drayton asked, "Are we absolutely positive we want to do this?"

"Don't tell me you changed your mind," Theodosia said. "You were the one who was so hot and bothered by the FBI showing up this morning. You were the one who decided we should go tell Timothy about Rinicker. To kind of warn him about the possibility of the Pink Panther gang."

"Yes, I suppose. I just hate to blindside Timothy."

"Think of it as a precautionary warning."

"Ah. That's a more reasonable way of putting it."

* * *

Tiny hurricanes of scarlet and amber leaves swirled past them as they headed into the cemetery, and Theodosia was hit with a twinge of anticipation. There was something so enchanting about this well-beaten path that wound its way between ancient headstones and linked one historic church-yard to the next. This was where the rich history of old Charleston enveloped you, this final resting place of elder statesmen, brigadier generals, fine Charleston ladies, and ordinary citizens. A great peacefulness pervaded this place, too, where Spanish moss draped the trees like lace on South-ern belles and live oak trees were bent and gnarled with age.

"So what's our plan?" Drayton asked as they strolled along. "I've been trying to figure this out but I think my train of thought left the station without me."

"There's no set plan," Theodosia said. "I think we have to just lay everything out for Timothy and let him draw his own conclusion."

"You don't think we should sort of help him along? Guide him?"

"Well," Theodosia said. "There's always that."

Five minutes later, they arrived at the front door of the Heritage Society, where a gardener poised with his trimming shears was sculpting two large shrubs into topiaries.

"What are they supposed to be?" Theodosia asked him.

The gardener just smiled. "It's a surprise."

Drayton opened the grand double doors with a flourish and ushered her in. "So we'll just meet with Timothy and sort of . . . spill the beans."

"Let's try to do it with a little more aplomb than that," Theodosia said.

The Heritage Society's foyer was elegantly appointed with a marble floor, an antique persimmon-and-blue Oriental carpet, and well-worn leather chairs. A magnificent crystal-and-brass chandelier cast rainbow prisms over the front desk.

The snapping of Theodosia's kitten heels echoed through the anteroom, raising the attention of a serious-looking young woman at the front desk.

Theodosia decided she was probably one of the many interns that the Heritage Society employed. Although most of the time they were paid only in college credits.

"We're here to see Timothy Neville," Drayton said.

The young woman lifted horn-rimmed glasses from a dainty silver chain and pushed them over the slope of her snub nose. Her black high-collar dress was almost as severe as her expression. "I'm afraid Mr. Neville is unavailable."

"But we have an appointment," Drayton said. "I called Timothy something like fifteen minutes ago."

Theodosia stepped forward. "Drayton is on the board of directors." She tapped the desk with a fingertip. "Here."

"Oh." The receptionist blinked rapidly, realizing she might have made a serious tactical error. "Then I guess you could . . . um . . . go right in."

"Thank you, we will do that," Theodosia said.

They walked down the hallway. "She seemed nice," Drayton said, barely able to keep a straight face.

"If your taste runs to rottweiler guard dogs," Theodosia deadpanned.

More Oriental carpets covered the hallway, and oil paintings and elaborate tapestries were hung on the walls in a patchwork of rich, dark colors. The Heritage Society was a testament to old-world elegance and luxury, almost a cross between a medieval castle and a baronial manor house. Before she'd purchased her own home, Theodosia had always thought she could happily live here. Ensconced in a four-poster bed in the cozy, leather-book-lined library, anyway.

They paused at a doorway with a two-story archway. An engraved plaque announced: GREAT HALL.

The sign didn't lie.

Wide, arching beams and stately columns marked the vast space with quiet authority. Natural light streamed through clerestory windows, illuminating dust motes and adding to the grandiose atmosphere. Workers in white overalls bustled about the room, arranging heavy wooden display cases and ornate library tables. Additional lights were being set up and tested.

A tall glass case stood pretentiously in the center of the room, as if to announce itself as being more important than any other.

"I take it that's the display place of honor?" Theodosia asked. A cluster of pinpoint spotlights shone down on the empty case, suggesting her hunch was right.

"For the Fabergé egg," Drayton said. "That's right."

"Are there any security measures in place?"

"Locks on all the doors," Drayton said.

"No laser beams, or thermal or pressure-sensitive alarms?"

"I don't think so. Not yet anyway." Drayton seemed to shrink back self-consciously. "I'm not sure I even know what those things are."

Theodosia walked in and circled the empty display case. "Well, this just isn't good. Sitting right out in the middle like this."

"There will be lots more treasures on display, too," Drayton said. "Some Early American paintings, Greek vases, Chippendale furniture, and some absolutely superb . . ."

"You're a bit early for the festivities, aren't you?" an authoritative voice suddenly rang out.

His train of thought broken, Drayton immediately spun around. "Timothy. Theo and I were just on our way to see you."

"Yes, yes, of course you were. Then, come along." Timothy Neville turned on his heel and gestured impatiently for them to follow him. He bopped along, a man extremely spry for his advanced age and diminutive stature. "We've been busy here. Busy, busy, busy," his voice floated back at them as they struggled to keep up.

When they reached Timothy's office, the octogenarian scurried behind a mahogany desk the size of a tennis court and gestured for them to take a seat. Of course, Timothy's desk chair was set at a much higher level than that of his guests. A sly little trick that brought him infinite pleasure.

Theodosia scanned the dramatically masculine office that was crammed with antiques, bronze statues, paintings, and trinkets from every era. She'd always teased Drayton that the Heritage Society looked like an overdone men's private cigar club, and that was precisely what Timothy's office looked like. Mahogany built-ins, oversized brown leather chairs, a freestanding globe, and never mind the clichéd drink trolley with its whiskey and bourbon decanters. All that was missing were the smoking jackets and pipe tobacco.

"What's up?" Timothy asked. His high cheekbones jutted sharply from his simian-looking face and his hooded eyes crackled with intensity. He was big on getting down to business with a minimum of fanfare. Or maybe he figured he just didn't have that many years left.

Drayton released a long breath. "I'm sure you've heard about the tragedy at Heart's Desire."

Timothy leaned back and folded his hands, clearly interested. "Yes, I read all about it in the newspaper and saw the various reports on TV."

"It was a smash-and-grab," Theodosia put in. "This crazy gang of thieves drove an SUV right through the window, stole every item of value, and disappeared in about two minutes." She paused. "I was there. And I want to tell you it was well orchestrated. Choreographed, almost."

Timothy's sparse brows shot up. "Indeed."

Theodosia continued. "We're worried the same type of robbery might happen at your Rare Antiquities Show this Saturday."

Timothy's hand stroked his narrow chin. "Why would you think that?"

"Here's the thing," Theodosia said. "Two FBI agents paid us a visit this morning to see if I could identify any of the perpetrators."

"They showed her a dozen different photos of known international jewel thieves," Drayton said.

Timothy continued to watch Theodosia carefully with eyes that were keen and bright.

"And what's problematic," Theodosia said, "is that there *was* a photo that may or may not have been an old photo of Lionel Rinicker."

"What!" he cried. Her words caught Timothy completely off guard. "That's the most preposterous thing I've ever heard. Rinicker is a learned historian, not some hooligan who goes about crashing trucks through jewelry store windows." Now his eyes sought out Drayton's. "Plus he's a valuable member of our board of directors."

"Which brings us to exactly why we're here," Theodosia said. "We don't want to slander the man any more than you do, but what if Rinicker is . . . is some sort of inside man?"

Timothy's smooth forehead dissolved into wrinkles and he shook his head. He was clearly in disagreement.

"Wait," Drayton said. He turned to Theodosia. "Tell him about the Pink Panther gang."

So she did. She told Timothy all about the high-end robberies all over Europe and the Interpol warnings.

Drayton scooted to the edge of his seat. "The gang members who've been caught have all managed to engineer daring escapes. Agent Zimmer told us they speak multiple languages and carry various international passports. Which means they could turn up anywhere."

Timothy steepled his fingers and inclined his head toward them. "Including right here in Charleston."

"It's certainly possible," Theodosia said.

"But . . . Lionel has become your friend, Drayton," Timothy said in a slightly reproachful voice.

"Yes. That's why this is so agonizing for me." Drayton gazed at Timothy. "It has to be for you, too. I mean, you were the one who introduced us."

"That's right," Timothy said. "I first met Lionel Rinicker last spring at an antiques auction. He impressed me with his verve."

Theodosia leaned forward. "How so?"

"We were both bidding on a Faulkner first edition," Timothy said. "And I overheard him misquote a famous line. Of course I couldn't help myself, I had to correct him. And that was that. We started conversing and he bought me a cognac. Despite the fact that he'd botched one of my favorite lines, I found him to be a charming and learned man. Since he'd already settled here in Charleston, one thing led to another, and now he's on our board of directors." Timothy's gaze shifted to Drayton. "You seconded his nomination."

"I did," Drayton said, looking almost miserable.

Theodosia decided to step in. "Despite all this good-old-boy camaraderie, I still think it's critical we keep an eye on Rinicker."

Timothy mulled this over for a few moments. "I suppose I could go along with that. We *watch* the man, but we do not move against him in any way. We are respectful of him. Agreed?"

"Yes, of course," Drayton said. "You know I'm just sick about this."

Timothy gazed at Theodosia. "Agreed, Theodosia?"

"Sure." Theodosia wasn't sick about the situation. Just extremely wary.

Timothy picked up a small bronze bust of Thomas Jefferson and creaked back in his chair. "My goodness, I find this hard to believe. Why, Lionel is even dating one of our rather prominent citizens."

"Who would that be?" Theodosia asked.

"Grace Dawson," Timothy said. "You probably know her. She's that peppy little blond-haired lady who lives in the old Burwick-Howell mansion on Tradd Street. You see her out walking sometimes with those two magnificent Doberman pinschers."

"Sultan and Satin," Drayton said. "Yes, they're beautiful dogs."

"They're dating?" Theodosia asked. Then she quickly waved a hand in front of her face as if to erase her words. "Wait, I didn't mean the Dobermans."

"I understand what you mean," Timothy said. "And, yes, the two of them *are* seeing each other. Keeping company, or whatever you choose to call it."

Theodosia smiled to herself. She'd call it dating, yes. Haley would call it friends with benefits. As for the dogs, Earl Grey and the Dobermans hadn't officially met yet. But she suspected it might be time to remedy that.

"So you've told the FBI about our upcoming show?" Timothy said. "About our Fabergé egg?"

"They're well aware of it," Theodosia said.

Timothy seemed to make up his mind then. He put Mr. Jefferson's likeness down and said, "I'll hire more guards for Saturday night. And do you have a phone number for that agent you mentioned? Ziskie, was it? I'd like to speak with him."

"Agent Zimmer," Theodosia said. She removed Zimmer's card from her pocketbook and copied down the information for Timothy. But she kept the card.

If she truly intended to help Brooke find some answers, Agent Zimmer just might come in handy.

10

Earl Grey lounged in front of the fireplace, looking lazy and content, as Theodosia bustled about the kitchen fixing dinner. Theodosia sometimes wondered who appreciated their harmonious evening routine the most. And judging by the peaceful, almost beatific look on her dear dog's face, she suspected it was him.

On warmer evenings, she'd have carried her plate out to the small patio in the backyard where decades of ivy crawled up a redbrick wall and a small fountain pattered away. It was a lovely Charleston pocket garden, green and lush, tangled rather than manicured. But tonight was way too cool and the fire much too inviting.

Theodosia moved briskly about the kitchen, dancing to Natasha Bedingfield's "Unwritten." Tonight was going to be salad night. She chopped and diced grape tomatoes, shallots, and parsley, then tossed everything into a bowl of bulgur wheat. She whipped some olive oil and red vinegar together and then poured it over her salad. Bits of crumbled goat cheese went on top, and there you had it. A Mediterranean grain salad. Haley would have approved. In fact, it was an adaptation of one of Haley's recipes.

Curling into a chair at the table, Theodosia tasted her creation. Mmn, it was delicious. As she nibbled her salad and glanced through the latest edition of *Charleston* magazine, her eyes were drawn to the pink orchid that sat on the dining room table. It had been a gift from Angie Congdon, her friend who owned the Featherbed House B and B.

Theodosia wasn't sure if she had a knack for the care and feeding of this particular *Phalaenopsis*, but she was willing to give it a try. Besides, it was nice to have something exotic in the house.

Earl Grey touched a nose to her knee and peered up at her.

"No," she said. "You've had your dinner. A delicious kibble entrée."

He continued to gaze at her, his sad brown eyes pleading for a bite.

"I know. If I give you a bite you'll never ask me again, right?"

"Rwww," Earl Grey responded.

"But you will. That's just how you are."

This time he rolled his eyes at her, which immediately tugged at her heart. And just as she was about to break down, to run into the kitchen and get him a dog cookie, the phone rang.

"Saved," she breathed, jumping up to snatch it. "Hello?"

"Hello, gorgeous," Max cooed into her ear. Her ex-boyfriend certainly knew how to get her attention.

"Hey there," Theodosia said. "How are things in Savannah?"

"Could be better." His teasing tone awakened a flutter of butterflies in her core. "You could be here."

"Oh, really?" Max was both charming and glib. He was a keeper, but one she couldn't keep.

His smooth chuckle rumbled over the line. "Definitely. In fact, I was hoping you might come down for the Festival of Lights in a few weeks. I know a great place you can stay."

"I'm sure you do. The thing is, the holidays are our busiest time of year."

"That sounds like a no."

"No, it's just a maybe."

"I could dine out on your maybes," Max said.

"Then I'll really try to make it down there."

"Can't ask for much more. How are things in Charleston?"

"Oh, fairly interesting."

"Don't tell me you let yourself get pulled into some sort of crazy investigation again."

"Then I won't tell you."

"I'm not sure if that sounds ominous or hopeful." Max chuckled.

"Probably a little of both," Theodosia said. She really didn't want to get into a hot and heavy discussion right now on how a ring of international jewel thieves might be operating in Charleston. It was just . . . too much.

"Are you still running?" Max asked. "Keeping up those eight-minute miles?"

"I'm still at it. In fact, I'm going to take a run tonight."

"Good girl. Just be careful. In the dark, you could twist an ankle on one of those pesky cobblestones. Or, you know . . ." His sentence hung unfinished in the air. He still worried about her. Theodosia wondered if that was a good thing or problematic.

"I'll be careful," she said. "I'm always careful."

"Yeah, right."

Theodosia hung up feeling a small void in her chest. Change wasn't exactly her favorite thing. But it was certainly in the air. Changing leaves, changing seasons, changing times.

* * *

By seven thirty, Theodosia and Earl Grey were bobbing down the back alley. The evening was beautiful, an inky blue-black sky scattered with shards of bright stars. Streetlights glowed like miniature beacons as she beat a path through the neighborhood, Earl Grey keeping pace at her side.

They bounced along, cutting through an alley or two, even running down Stoll's Alley, where narrow, rough-hewn stone walls closed in on them and a few withered ferns were attempting a heroic last stand.

As they hung a left onto Tradd Street, Theodosia experienced one of those serendipitous moments. There, up ahead of her, heading right for her, in fact, was a small woman handling two large Dobermans. It had to be Grace Dawson and her dogs.

Instead of giving the trio a wide berth, as she normally would, Theodosia stayed her course and gently slowed her pace. A few moments later, she and Grace were face-to-face, the dogs muzzle-to-muzzle.

There was the usual amount of sniffing and mingling, of doggy politics being played out. Then the dogs seemed to relax.

"You have a beautiful pair of Dobermans," Theodosia said.

Grace Dawson's brilliant smile was pageant-worthy. "Thank you. I totally agree. But, of course, I'm shamelessly biased. They're family." She patted her dogs' heads—one, then the other. "Sultan and Satin, meet . . ." She trailed off. "I'm sorry, you're both so familiar to me, I know I've seen you around . . . but I'm afraid I'm not very good with names."

"This is Earl Grey and I'm Theodosia Browning."

Grace beamed. "Of course you are. From the Indigo Tea Shop over on Church Street."

"You've visited us?"

"No, but I'm definitely planning to drop by. I've heard the most marvelous things about your tea shop. I understand you have your own pastry chef right there on the premises?"

"Haley bakes all our scones, muffins, bars, and brownie bites from scratch." *And she would adore being called a pastry chef.*

"Be still my heart," Grace laughed.

Assuming this woman eats anything sweet.

Theodosia studied Grace. She had to be in her early fifties, but was lithe and almost fashion-model thin.

Probably lives on kale and wheat shooters.

Her skintight black leggings and purple hoodie were definitely more Neiman Marcus than Sport Shack, and her sneakers were pure Gucci. With her blond hair pulled back into a sleek ponytail, she looked like an older, wealthier Barbie.

"You do a lot of running?" Theodosia asked.

"I try to take these energetic beasts out every morning and most evenings," Grace said.

Theodosia forced herself to focus. She needed to get serious before Grace continued on with her run. "You know, I was introduced to a friend of yours yesterday," she said. "Lionel Rinicker."

"Oh, Lionel!" Grace said with great enthusiasm. "Isn't he a dear? An absolute charmer?"

"I only met him for a few minutes, but he seemed like a very nice man."

"Oh, he is," Grace gushed.

Theodosia wondered if Grace might even mention something about the FBI coming to call on Rinicker. On the other hand, Rinicker probably hadn't told her. He was fairly new in town, had been lucky enough to make the acquaintance of a fairly well-to-do woman, so why would he want to screw things up?

Grace put a conspiratorial hand on Theodosia's arm.

"Let me tell you something, dear. Lionel's done a world of good for me since my husband passed away two years ago. He's made me feel alive again."

"That's wonderful," Theodosia said. Then, "What did your husband do?" she asked politely.

"Wilton owned a Mercedes-Benz dealership over on James Island."

"A lovely area. I take it you used to live there, too?"

"Yes, but now I really prefer in-town living. I bought my house a year ago and I honestly haven't looked back." Grace laughed, making a vague gesture at the neighborhood. "Look at this. Simply gorgeous. I can chug along on the beach or run through these amazing streets, admiring the history and architecture. The harbor and the yacht club are nearby and the air is always that heady oxygen-rich mixture of sea brine and freedom. And if I hadn't moved here, I never would have met Lionel."

"He did strike me as a charmer," Theodosia said.

"And very cultured. He's lived so many places I'm fairly green with envy. We met at the Coastal Carolina Flea Market, you know. I found a portfolio of sketches I thought might be Norman Rockwell originals and the seller agreed. Just as we were negotiating a price, Lionel came to my rescue. He knew right off they were just prints. Restrikes, I think he called them."

"So you didn't lose any money," Theodosia said.

"And I gained a boyfriend," Grace said as the Dobermans strained at their leashes.

"You know," Theodosia said. "My tea master, Drayton Conneley, and Lionel are on the board of directors together at the Heritage Society."

Grace's eyes twinkled. "So you're probably looking forward to the gala Saturday night. For all the Gold Circle members?"

"I wouldn't miss it for the world," Theodosia said.

*   *   *

Theodosia thought about her quick encounter with Grace Dawson as she jogged along. The woman definitely seemed enamored of Lionel Rinicker. So what did that mean? That he was a nice, okay guy, someone to be trusted? Or that he'd managed to pull the wool over Grace's eyes?

Theodosia dodged down a narrow alley that led between two enormous mansions, and then burst out into White Point Garden. Pounding across the dried grass, the blessed endorphins kicked in. There was nothing like the bliss of a runner's high at the end of a busy, stressful day.

"What do you think?" she asked Earl Grey. "Do you feel it, too, boy?"

They ran along a narrow ridge where the Atlantic crashed in on shell-strewn sandy shores. Finally, after a good half mile at a blistering pace, Theodosia slowed. Memories of romantic strolls along the shore with Max flitted through her mind. This part of Charleston, the very tip of the peninsula, was the most romantic and spirited. Here you could tumble back in time, surrounded by elegant homes and the whoosh and whisper of the eternal sea.

Earl Grey nudged her hand with a cool, wet nose, bringing Theodosia back into the moment. She was moving at a comfortable jog-walk pace now, ambling along, heading in the direction of the Charleston Yacht Club.

Theodosia had sailed out of the yacht club many times and always felt inspired and uplifted by the bobbing of the boats and the clanking of the halyards against the masts.

So elegant, she told herself as she surveyed the little fleet. All these posh blue-and-white vessels bobbing and nodding to one another, probably exchanging price points and pedigrees.

As she neared the clubhouse, she wondered if anyone was there.

But no, it was too late. All the lights were off and . . .

Her eyes flitted across a sign. An intriguing sign she'd never noticed before. It said: GOLD COAST YACHTS.

She'd almost forgotten about Sabrina and Luke Andros. She of the jewelry debacle and he of the fancy yachts.

Theodosia approached the small building that served as the office for Gold Coast Yachts and peeked in the window. In the dark, all she could make out were a large desk and a few chairs. Colorful posters of megayachts hung on the walls.

She checked her watch and was about to turn for home when a light way out at the end of the far pier caught her eye. She gazed through the mist that was starting to roll in now and saw an enormous one-hundred-and-twenty-foot yacht bobbing majestically.

One of the Gold Coast yachts? Had to be. All the other sailboats here were of the smaller variety. Ensigns and O'Days and a few Hobie Cats.

Curiosity pulled at her, dragging her toward that yacht like a moth to the flame.

And then voices floated across the sea air, muffled by the dampness.

Theodosia pressed a finger to her mouth, warning Earl Grey to be quiet. He turned his doggy gaze toward the boat, as if in complete understanding. And then they both tiptoed along the shoreline in the direction of the far dock. Together they stepped onto it and tread softly along smooth, wooden planks. Earl Grey's head bobbed sweetly as he seemed to make an effort to keep his toenails from clicking against the boards.

A voice grew steadily louder as they drew nearer the large craft, but Theodosia still couldn't make out any actual words. Could the voice belong to Luke Andros, the newly arrived, wealthy yacht broker? Was he the one who was doing all the talking?

Theodosia inched closer, straining to understand the murmurs.

Am I investigating now? Yes, I do believe I am.

She stopped at the edge of the dock where the boat bumped up against a dozen plastic fenders. Now it seemed as if there was more than just a single voice. There were four or five people on that boat.

She bent in closer. Could she peer through a porthole? No, that wasn't going to work. She was down here on the dock and that boat rode awfully high in the water.

Theodosia listened harder. Somebody with a deep voice was talking now.

Who?

She strained to pick up the words, but the incessant wind and lapping of waves made the voices sound like a bad radio signal that faded in and out.

". . . Four more days and then you guys can take off," the deep voice instructed.

Four more days? Theodosia straightened up and tried to think. What was going to happen in four more days?

Worrying that she'd overstepped her bounds, that someone would come out on deck and catch her eavesdropping, Theodosia backed up, gave Earl Grey's leash a tug, and hurried down the pier.

She was halfway back to shore when it hit her. The Rare Antiquities Show was in four days.

11

❧

Theodosia slow-walked the last couple of blocks to her home, settling her pulse and trying to process everything she'd learned tonight. There was a lot to think about. And a lot to worry about, too.

Now, in keeping with the theme of the night—strange encounters—she spotted a familiar burgundy-colored Crown Victoria parked at the curb in front of her house.

Tidwell. What does he want? She sighed. She was about to find out.

When Tidwell saw her approach, the dome light snapped on and he squeezed himself out from behind the wheel. "Good evening," he called out in his deep baritone.

"Staking out my home, are you, Detective Tidwell?" Theodosia asked. "See anything interesting? Stray cats? The neighborhood raccoons come to ransack my fishpond?"

He shut the car door and met her on the sidewalk. He was wearing slightly baggy pants and what looked like a frayed khaki fishing jacket that barely stretched across his weather balloon of a stomach. "I'm afraid I observed nothing out of the ordinary."

"Good." She smiled gratefully and motioned for him to follow her inside. "You might as well come in. I mean, you will anyway, right?"

"Thank you for your kind invitation," Tidwell said.

Theodosia snapped on the light in the small tiled entryway. Then ducked into her living room and turned on a lamp. Warm light flooded the room, showing off the fireplace, parquet floors, and chintz-covered furniture to advantage.

"Cozy," Tidwell said.

Earl Grey dashed into the kitchen and began to noisily drain his water bowl while Theodosia knelt in front of the fireplace. She added a handful of kindling and a new log, trying to coax the embers back into a robust flame. It seemed to be working. Finally, she dusted her palms together and turned to face Tidwell.

"Are you on or off duty?"

"Interesting question," he said. "On, I suppose."

"Then this is an official visit."

He smiled. "But perhaps we should call it an off-the-record visit."

"Off the record, then, would you care for a glass of wine?" Tidwell brightened. "I'd enjoy that very much."

Theodosia went into the kitchen, grabbed a half bottle of cabernet, and filled two glasses. She carried them back into the living room, to find Tidwell peering at a small, recently purchased oil painting that she'd hung above her fireplace.

"This is lovely," he said. "Who is the artist?"

"Josiah Singleton."

"Ah. Early American?"

"Well. Mid-eighteenth century, anyway." Theodosia handed him his wine and settled into a chintz armchair while Tidwell took a spot on the love seat opposite her. "What brings you by, Detective?"

"The FBI paid you a visit today," Tidwell said. He took a sip of wine and gazed at her expectantly.

"Yes," Theodosia said. "They wanted my firsthand witness account from Sunday night."

"Anything else?"

"They told me they're on the lookout for one or more European jewel thieves who might have been involved in the robbery at Heart's Desire."

"The Pink Panther gang."

"That's right."

"Doubtful," Tidwell said.

"They showed me a bunch of photos. Drayton and I thought one of the men bore a striking resemblance to Lionel Rinicker." She paused. "You know who he is?"

"I had much the same discussion with the FBI as you did. With a certain degree of reluctance on their part, they shared that same information with me and key members of my department."

"Okay," Theodosia said. "So you know what I know."

Tidwell took a gulp of wine. "They're very hot to point a finger at Mr. Rinicker."

"And you're not?"

"There's simply no concrete evidence against him."

"Other than the fact that he's relatively new in town . . ." When Tidwell made a face, Theodosia added, "You know what Charleston is like. You're considered a newcomer even if your parents were born here. You need to be able to trace your ancestry back to your great-great-grandpappy in order to be considered a dyed-in-the-wool Charlestonian."

"And then it helps if your ancestors were French Huguenots."

"That's always best," Theodosia said. "But getting back to Rinicker, there's also the fact that he managed to schmooze a number of influential people in a very short time and make his way onto the board at the Heritage Society."

"Probably a coincidence," Tidwell said.

"I thought you didn't believe in coincidences."

"I don't. Unless there are too many of them."

Theodosia drew a deep breath. "There's something I should probably tell you about. It might even be considered . . . a clue."

Tidwell cocked his head. "What is it? And why didn't you mention this before?"

"Because I didn't think of it. This information only bubbled to the surface when my memory was jogged by those FBI guys who came and interrogated me."

"They were forceful?"

"You mean did they drag me back to some deserted building and put me in handcuffs and leg irons? No, they did not. But they did project a certain, shall we call it, gravitas. In other words, I wouldn't want to play games with them."

"So what is it you remembered?"

"I remembered the hammer that one of the thieves used."

Tidwell sat forward. "Tell me."

"It was unusual-looking. Metallic and quite shiny. But not like any ordinary hammer I'd seen before. Not for pounding nails or anything like that."

"A specialized hammer," Tidwell said.

"Yes, but I don't know which specialty."

"If you saw a picture of that hammer, do you think you could identify it?"

"Maybe. I think it had a little claw on one side."

Tidwell shifted in his seat. "We received notice from the police over in Hilton Head about a fellow, at least we think it's a fellow, who is a kind of second-story guy."

"You mean like a cat burglar?" Theodosia asked.

"We don't call them that anymore. Anyway, a couple of homes on Hilton Head Island were robbed, but no one was ever apprehended."

"Robbed, you say. You mean they were robbed of jewels?"

"Jewelry, watches, a strip of gold Krugerrands. The thief even took two small oil paintings off the wall in one of the homes."

"Maybe that same guy is operating here," Theodosia said. "Maybe he's gotten himself organized and put together a gang." Fresh in her mind was the image of the robbers dressed in black and wearing red devil masks.

"That's a possibility."

Earl Grey wandered out and gave Tidwell an uninterested sniff. Then he walked over to the fireplace and curled up on a little rag rug next to the hearth.

"There's something else," Theodosia said. "Something I kind of stumbled upon tonight when I was out running."

"You do have the most productive jogs, Miss Browning."

"Listen." Theodosia took a quick sip of wine. "When I was jogging tonight, I happened to run past the Charleston Yacht Club and the office for Gold Coast Yachts."

"Is that supposed to mean something to me?" Tidwell asked.

"Yes and no. Gold Coast Yachts is owned by Sabrina and Luke Andros. They were both supposed to be at Heart's Desire that night, but only Sabrina showed up. After the robbery she seemed sort of . . . matter-of-fact about it. You know what I mean?"

Tidwell was studying her, listening to every word.

"Everyone was crying or walking around in a daze," Theodosia said. "But Sabrina was just kind of taking stock of the situation."

"Interesting," Tidwell said. "And you think this relates . . . how?"

"When I was at the yacht club, I walked out onto the dock where one of the Gold Coast yachts was moored. It was all lit up and a bunch of guys were talking onboard. I heard one of them say something to the effect of 'In four more days, you guys can take off.'"

"And what do you think that means?" Tidwell asked.

"Well, the Rare Antiquities Show happens in four more days," Theodosia said.

Tidwell finished his wine, set down his glass, and kneaded his hands together. "You've been busy."

Theodosia shrugged. "This all just kind of happened. It certainly wasn't planned."

"Do you intend to inform the FBI about the conversation you overheard?"

"Do you think I should?"

Tidwell thought for a moment. "Perhaps you should let me handle this particular aspect. At least for a day or two."

"Okay, if you say so." Theodosia peered at him. "Now that I've shared some information with you, how about a little quid pro quo?"

"What do you want to know?"

"Brooke told me there was a party crasher at her event. That you guys were going to try and make an identification."

"We did identify him," Tidwell said.

Theodosia waggled her fingers at him. "And?"

"Professor Warren Shepley."

"That's nice. What's a Professor Warren Shepley?"

"Professor of eighteenth-century Russian literature at Savannah State University," Tidwell said.

Theodosia frowned. "Savannah. That's where the stolen SUV came from. So why did this Professor Shepley crash Brooke's event? How do you think he figures into all of this?"

"We don't know. We plan to question the man tomorrow." Tidwell pushed himself up off the love seat, his knees making a popping sound as he stood up. He looked troubled. "The FBI is trying to block me, Theodosia. Trying to keep me out of the investigation. I don't like it one bit."

"So make a stink," Theodosia suggested. "You're good at that." Then, "Is there anything I can do to help?" She wouldn't mind getting Tidwell's blessing, especially since Brooke was counting on her to investigate.

"Just keep doing what you're doing," Tidwell said. "But please be careful."

"Always," Theodosia said, even though she was well aware that she was a risk taker and that she had a history of dashing in where angels feared to tread.

"I mean it," Tidwell said as they walked out to his car. "Listen to the rumors, keep an ear out for gossip, but do not take any unnecessary chances."

"Sure," Theodosia said as she followed him into the night, scuffling down her front walk. Rumors and gossip? She was going to need a lot more than that to resolve this case. To find closure for Brooke and justice for Kaitlin.

Tidwell stopped abruptly in front of his car and scowled. "Did you know that the Ford Motor Company stopped making Crown Victorias? It's a crying shame."

"What are you going to do when this one starts to fall apart?" Theodosia asked.

"Do the sensible thing, I suppose. Get it repaired."

Theodosia grinned. "Why do I have the feeling there's going to be a whole cadre of police detectives who are driving around in antique cars? It's going to be like all those cars from the fifties that the people in Cuba are still driving."

"Those are collector's pieces. Just wait until trade relations are finally normalized. All the classic car collectors and auto restorers are going to swoop in and strip that poor island bare."

12

❧

"Why are we not prepared for this?" Drayton asked. He was running around in a tizzy, an antique majolica blueberry teapot clutched in one hand, a box of white tapers in the other.

"Calm down, Drayton," Theodosia said as she surveyed the Indigo Tea Shop. "We've got time. We'll get it all done." She draped a long, black Parisian waiter's apron over her T-shirt and slacks and tied it in back.

"It's Wednesday morning," Drayton said. "Our Duchess of Devonshire Tea is scheduled to go off at twelve o'clock sharp. We have a million details to finalize and my floral bouquets still haven't arrived." This was all delivered with a certain *tone*.

"Did you call Floradora?" They were Drayton's favored florist and usually quite dependable.

"I called but they didn't answer. Which is why I left a very stern message."

"Good for you, Drayton," Haley said as she buzzed by. "That'll light a fire under them."

"If only we didn't have to contend with morning tea," Drayton fussed.

"Well, we do," Theodosia said. "We always do. So try to deal with it."

Drayton began fumbling candles into the half-dozen pewter candlesticks that he'd set out. "Maybe we'll get lucky," he said in a low voice. "And only a few people will drop by."

Theodosia snapped on her lighter and followed him around each table, lighting candles. "I'm right here, you know. I can hear you muttering."

Brooke was the first person to show up that morning. She poked her head into the tea shop and called out, "Are you folks open yet?"

"We are for you," Theodosia said, hustling over to give her a welcoming hug. Then she held her friend at arm's length and said, "Say, now, you're looking a little better today. You seem a little more upbeat."

"I'm feeling somewhat better," Brooke said. She was dressed in a fitted navy blazer and khaki slacks and looked a little like a real estate agent. It was a far cry from her usual silk tops and elegant slacks. "I think I'm starting to get a handle on things."

"Good for you."

"What I did was call up my accounting firm and have them put one of their people on this. You know, dealing with the insurance companies, getting the necessary police reports together."

"You're smart to outsource those things," Theodosia said.

Brooke gave a faint smile. "Like I did with you?"

"Well . . . I haven't accomplished all that much yet."

"You know I have the utmost faith in you, Theo."

"I'll try to live up to that." Theodosia drew a breath. "And I was wondering . . . is there going to be a funeral service for Kaitlin?"

Brooke's expression changed and she suddenly looked drawn and tired again. "Yes, but not until next week. Bullocks Funeral Home is shipping her body back home to her folks in Greenville. But I was wondering if we should have some sort of memorial service for her here." She blinked back tears. "What do you think?"

"That sounds like a lovely idea. I think we all want to say our good-byes." Theodosia touched Brooke's arm gently. "Would you like to sit down and relax? Maybe have a cup of tea?"

"I really should get back," Brooke said. "There's so dang much going on."

Theodosia smiled. "Takeout, then?"

"That would be wonderful. Fortifying even."

When Drayton saw Theodosia and Brooke at the front counter, he hurried over to help. "What can I brew for you?" he asked Brooke. "Perhaps a nice pot of oolong? Or some tasty rose hips?"

"I really enjoyed that stronger, slightly smoky tea you were serving here last week."

"The gunpowder green," Drayton said. "One pot coming right up."

Theodosia raided the kitchen and grabbed a half-dozen lemon scones for Brooke to take back with her. And by the time she'd done that, Drayton was pouring steaming hot tea into take-out cups and snapping on lids. Then he packaged up everything in an indigo-blue bag and handed it to Brooke.

"Thank you," Brooke said to Drayton. Then she gazed meaningfully at Theodosia. "And thank *you* for everything."

Theodosia walked Brooke to the door. "I haven't figured

things out quite yet," she said. "But I am working on a couple of different angles."

"I know you are. And so is Detective Tidwell. He's looking into the man who supposedly crashed my event."

Theodosia's brows shot up. "He told you about Professor Shepley?"

"Just this morning," Brooke said. "Says he's going to meet with him today and ask some tough questions."

"Good."

"Tidwell's been wonderful so far," Brooke said. "Very cooperative about keeping me in the loop on the investigation, but not pressuring me or making me feel overwhelmed." She gave a sad smile. "Who would have thought a big, brusque man like that could be filled with such kindness?"

Who indeed? Theodosia thought to herself.

Drayton got his wish. The Indigo Tea Shop wasn't as crowded as usual that morning. Maybe it was the cool weather settling in, or maybe it was Drayton's prickly vibrations projecting into the earth's atmosphere. So when eleven o'clock rolled around and most of the customers who'd stopped by for morning tea and scones had finally departed, he set to work like a fiend.

Tables were cleared and wiped clean, and then elegant white linens draped over them. Drayton pulled out a set of Staffordshire blue-and-white china in the Biddulph Castle pattern and placed the dishes and teacups carefully. Cloth napkins were folded and tucked beneath sterling Birks Saxon flatware, silver salt and pepper shakers were added. Drayton had also brought along a few Toby mugs from his small collection, so those went on the tables to add to his British theme.

Theodosia came over to inspect his work. "Your tables look lovely."

"But my flowers still aren't here."

"Oh yes, they are," said a voice. An enormous bouquet of tea roses, nasturtium, and heather was slowly advancing toward him.

Drayton peered at the flowers quizzically. "Haley, is that you behind all those blossoms and blooms?"

"It's me, all right," Haley called back. "Take these, Drayton, will you? Before I lose my grip and drop this whole thing."

He grabbed for the box of flowers. "Thank goodness they arrived."

"I think they've been here all along," Haley said. "There was this ginormous box of flowers just sitting out in the back alley. The florist must have delivered them, then dashed off. Like some kind of reverse trick or treat."

Drayton pursed his lips. "Just sitting there for anyone to steal."

"But nobody did," Theodosia said, grabbing a vase. "Here, let's just get these flowers into vases and onto the tables. And leave it at that."

They arranged the flowers, set the candles just so, and then stood back to admire their work.

Drayton held up a finger. "Place cards. We need to put out the place cards and favors."

Since they had taken advance reservations for their Duchess of Devonshire Tea, they knew exactly who was coming. Which meant Drayton had painstakingly written out everyone's name in a graceful calligraphic script.

"What did you come up with for favors?" Haley asked.

Drayton carried a cardboard box to the table. "I've got tea sachets and wands of French lavender."

"Let's talk menu," Theodosia said. "You two have been fairly secretive about what we're going to serve."

Haley pulled out an index card. "We didn't mean to be, but we were kind of fine-tuning things." She handed the card to Drayton. "Here, you read it to her." She spun away. "I've still got a ton of work to do."

Drayton put on a pair of tortoiseshell half-glasses and read: "First course, cranberry cream scones with Devonshire cream."

"Love it," Theodosia said.

"For our luncheon course, a prosciutto and fig butter tea sandwich and a smoked salmon and avocado on rye sandwich served with a citrus salad."

"Okay," Theodosia said. "Sounds good."

Drayton continued. "The scones and tea sandwiches will all be accompanied by our Lady London Ceylon tea. And our desserts will consist of English madeleines and shortbread squares topped with fresh strawberries. This will be accompanied by a vanilla chai."

"The menu is great," Theodosia said. "And the tea pairings are quite inspired."

"Thank you." Drayton smiled contentedly. "I thought so, too."

"Now I have a question."

"About the tea?"

"Not exactly. Have you ever heard of a Professor Warren Shepley?"

Drayton shook his head. "I don't think so. Why? Who is he?"

"He's a professor of Russian literature at Savannah State University. He also crashed Brooke's event on Sunday night."

Drayton looked puzzled. "Now, why would he do that?"

Theodosia narrowed her eyes. "That's precisely what we need to find out."

When the big hand and the little hand both hit twelve, the front door burst open and all their guests began to pile in. Hugs and air kisses were hastily exchanged, and then a mad scramble ensued to see who was sitting at what table.

Delaine showed up with a surprise guest, so an extra place

setting had to be squeezed in at the last minute. Then Lionel Rinicker showed up with Grace Dawson on his arm.

Theodosia hadn't even realized that Rinicker had reserved two seats, but she made up her mind to treat him like she would anyone else. That is, anyone else who could possibly be an international jewel thief on the run.

But as everyone settled in their chairs, and Theodosia and Drayton circled the tables with steaming hot teapots, Rinicker proved to be mellow and downright chatty.

"You'll never guess who showed up to talk to me yesterday," Rinicker said to Theodosia, a twinkle in his eye.

She knew darned well who'd shown up. A couple of special agents in charge. Steely-eyed guys in narrow ties. But she played it cool. Underplayed it, in fact.

"Tell me," Theodosia said. "Was it one of your European friends?"

Rinicker chortled heartily, then poked Grace in the ribs. "You think we should tell her?"

Grace laughed merrily. "I think you should definitely tell her."

Rinicker plucked at Theodosia's sleeve and pulled her closer. "The FBI," he said in a stage whisper. He chuckled again and said, "Can you believe it? Actual federal agents. Talking to *me*."

Theodosia could believe it. "What on earth did they want?" she asked, acting surprised yet knowing this conversation was veering into awfully strange territory.

"They wanted to quiz me about that robbery the other night," Rinicker said. He pointed at her. "The one at the jewelry store. The one you were right in the middle of, according to Drayton."

"The one where Brooke's niece was killed," Theodosia said, practically biting off her words.

"That's the one," Rinicker said. "It seems those FBI agents had me confused with some crazy jewel thief who robbed a shop in Cannes, in the south of France. Said I looked just like him."

"Isn't that the craziest thing?" Grace giggled. "We were just pulling my boat in from a run around the harbor, and there they were, standing on the dock, looking very grim."

"Amazing," Theodosia said. She switched her gaze to Rinicker. "But it wasn't you?"

"Of course not," Rinicker said. He gave his chest a hearty thump. "Can you imagine me masterminding some kind of daring heist?"

Yes, maybe I can.

"It does seem preposterous," Theodosia said.

With their guests enjoying the second course, consisting of tea sandwiches and citrus salad, Drayton clinked a knife against a water glass to gain everyone's attention. As soon as the conversation dropped to a low hum, he stepped to the center of the room.

"Welcome to our first ever Duchess of Devonshire Tea," he said. "As some of you history buffs are probably aware, there really was a duchess and she really did hail from Devonshire."

That brought a spate of polite laughter.

"In fact," Drayton continued, "this illustrious duchess that we celebrate today was the first wife of William Cavendish, fifth Duke of Devonshire. Her father was John Spencer, first Earl Spencer, which made her the great-great-great-great-aunt of Diana, Princess of Wales."

There was a spatter of applause and someone called out, "Wonderful pedigree."

"The Duchess of Devonshire attained a large amount of fame during her lifetime," Drayton said. "She was notorious for her catastrophic love affairs and her love of gambling." He stopped and smiled. "But she also had a softer side. Our dear duchess was also a socialite who gathered a large salon of literary and political figures around her, and she was one of the earliest campaigners for women's rights."

"Hear! Hear!" Delaine said.

"And then, of course, there's the Devonshire cream." Drayton smiled at Theodosia. "Theo?"

Now Theodosia stepped into the spotlight. "Devonshire cream, which is sometimes called clotted cream, is a thick cream made by heating fresh milk using a steam process, then allowing it to cool very slowly. During this cooling period, the cream content rises to the surface and forms 'clots.' This type of cream production is thought to have originated in the county of Devon, or Devonshire, where our illustrious duke and duchess resided." She smiled. "And while we didn't milk the cows or build up a head of steam, I can assure you that the Devonshire cream you're enjoying today is highly authentic."

There was a final spate of applause, and then Grace Dawson plucked at Theodosia's sleeve and said, "My goodness, that was so *interesting*."

The luncheon continued with lots more friendly banter, and Theodosia and Drayton were kept hopping. Pretty much everyone wanted seconds on scones, and they were definitely impressed with Drayton's own version of thick, rich Devonshire cream. In fact, halfway through the luncheon, Theodosia was forced to retreat to her office to quickly print out two dozen copies of his recipe.

When the luncheon finally drew to a close and guests began to wander about the tea shop, selecting tins of tea and perusing scone mixes and grapevine wreaths, Theodosia looked around for Lionel Rinicker. She found him deep in conversation with Drayton. Grace was listening in.

"I tell you," Rinicker was saying, "Timothy is worried sick."

"Worried about what?" Theodosia asked, trying her best to look innocent.

"He's convinced a gang of crazy thugs are going to come

storming into the Heritage Society's show and steal every precious object in sight," Rinicker said.

Drayton stared pointedly at Theodosia. "I wonder where he got that idea?"

Theodosia winced.

"And you know what I told him?" Rinicker continued.

"I can't imagine," Theodosia said.

"I told him it could happen," Rinicker said. "I said that if it happened at a local jewelry shop, it could certainly happen at an exhibition where a priceless Fabergé egg is being showcased." Almost as an aside to Grace, he said, "Smash-and-grabs are practically de rigueur all over Europe. And they're gaining in popularity here."

Grace touched a hand to her throat and looked pained. "Are you serious?" Then, before anyone could answer, she added, "Do you really think it could happen again?"

Rinicker bobbed his head, looking almost happy. "Absolutely, I do."

13

❧

"I'd say our tea was a smashing success." Haley beamed. She was still floating on air from what had seemed like an endless stream of compliments from their guests.

"A good time was had by all," Drayton echoed.

"Thank goodness," was all Theodosia had to say. She was delighted their guests had been charmed by the tea. And, for a few moments, she'd felt almost like Mary Poppins, flitting through the tea room, delivering sugar and smiles. But that was before Lionel Rinicker had voiced his opinion on the possibility of another theft. That notion had brought her crashing back down to earth. True, she herself had warned Timothy Neville of the very same thing. But, deep down, she wanted to be optimistic and assure herself that nothing else was going to happen. Of course, with the FBI scurrying about and the Charleston police on high alert, tension and danger seemed to hang redolent in the air. It just *felt* like something was going to happen.

"Who needs an afternoon pick-me-up?" Drayton called out. "I'm thinking of brewing a pot of Yin Feng green tea."

"Isn't that stuff, like, a hundred dollars a pound?" Haley asked.

"One hundred and fifteen dollars." Drayton allowed himself a self-satisfied smile. "But after all our hard work I think we deserve a special treat. And it is a superb green tea."

"You mean, like, green is the new black?" Haley asked.

"Precisely," Drayton said. He turned toward Theodosia. "Don't you agree, Theo?"

"Sounds good," she said in a distracted tone just as the phone rang. She snatched it up. "Indigo Tea Shop, how may I help you?" She listened and then handed the phone to Drayton.

He listened for a few moments and then said, "Ah, what a pity. But, I do understand. Perhaps another time, then." He hung up the phone, looking a little forlorn.

"What happened?" Haley asked. "Somebody cancel your subscription to *Bow Tie Monthly*?"

Drayton shrugged. "My opera companion just backed out on me."

"Ooh, too bad," Haley said. "And the season kicks off with *La Bohème* tonight. I suppose you still have those box seats?"

"Of course I do."

"Too bad I'm not an opera buff," Haley said. "Unfortunately, it's just not my thing."

Drayton lifted an eyebrow. "Theo? What about you? I know how much you love opera. Care to be my guest tonight at *La Bohème*?"

Theodosia cocked her head. "Let's see now, what were my glamorous evening plans? Slaving over laundry and sorting socks? Maybe cleaning out the vegetable drawer in my fridge?"

Drayton smiled. "Well, if you have something more important on your agenda . . ."

"I'd love to go!" Theodosia said.

"It's opening night," Drayton warned. "Black tie. You'll have to dress."

"I'll make the effort," Theodosia promised. "I can do glam."

"Long dress?"

"No problem." Well, she knew it might be a little bit of a problem, since she had to dash off to the TV station in a half hour or so. And if she didn't get home until late, then she'd have to fuss with hair and makeup and . . .

The bell over the front door *da-ding*ed noisily. Then it *da-ding*ed again even more insistently.

"What on earth?" Drayton said, turning.

Which is when Detective Tidwell blew in like a white squall. His heavy-lidded eyes took in the tea shop and then settled on Theodosia. Without preamble he said, "We need to talk."

"Certainly," Theodosia said. She pointed to a table that Haley had just cleared. "Let's take a seat over there."

Tidwell settled his bulk into a captain's chair and clasped his meaty hands together. "We have some important business to deal with."

Theodosia didn't like the look in Tidwell's eyes or the way he said *business*. His demeanor was about as charming as a hornet. Or maybe he just had low blood sugar.

She held up a hand. "Just a minute. Did you meet with Professor Shepley? Were you able to question the man?"

"Yes, I did," Tidwell said.

"Well?"

"Not much there, I'm afraid. Shepley claimed he was interested in looking at a necklace that was on display at Heart's Desire. Something made out of alexandrite?"

"I think that's the necklace that was plucked out of the case right before my eyes," Theodosia said.

"When you thought you saw a woman's hand."

"Right," Theodosia said. She let the image play in her

mind for a few moments. "But you don't believe this guy Shepley had any involvement at all with that gang?"

"Not that we can find. And he is a professor, for goodness' sake."

"Who hails from Savannah. The same place the black SUV was stolen from." It sounded suspicious to her. "So do we know what Shepley is doing here in Charleston?"

"He claims to be on sabbatical," Tidwell said. "Doing research for a new book he's writing."

"What's his specialty?"

"Eighteenth-century Russian literature."

"And he's doing research here?" It definitely sounded fishy to Theodosia. Tidwell had obviously decided to blow off Shepley as a noncontender, but Theodosia wasn't ready to let Shepley off the hook.

"Now," Tidwell said, "if I could please have your full attention." He slapped a leather attaché case onto the table, and then reached in and pulled out a stack of papers.

"What have you got?" Theodosia asked. "Some more suspect photographs for me to look at?" She reached over and flipped up the top two sheets. Ah, they weren't people photos at all. Tidwell had gathered images of a dozen different hammers. Every type of hammer known to man, from the looks of it.

"I had my people research and collect data on hammers," Tidwell told her. "You said you noticed a particular type of hammer being used during the Heart's Desire robbery?" He indicated the various images and downloaded pages. "I thought perhaps you might be able to identify one."

"I can try."

Tidwell held up the first page in front of her like a first-grade teacher with an oversized flash card. "Tell me if you recognize anything."

Theodosia concentrated on each image as it flashed by. A couple hammer images were vaguely familiar, a few were downright odd. She touched a finger to one page. "Is that even a hammer?"

Tidwell made a sour face. "I don't know what the female brain classifies as a hammer, so I brought a wide assortment."

Theodosia pursed her lips and decided to ignore the gibe. She chose to believe this particular rant was merely part of the gruff-detective persona he'd crafted and not necessarily his actual pinheaded beliefs.

"Anything?" Tidwell asked.

Two more images flashed by. "Nothing yet." Three more hammers flashed by. "Wait. That last one. What kind was it?"

Tidwell squinted at the photo. "It's a piton hammer by Petzl. A rock-climbing hammer. Note the stainless steel head that curves to a rather wicked-looking claw. Is that what you saw?"

"It's close. Very close. Who would sell this sort of thing?"

"There's only one store in Charleston," Tidwell said. "Triple Peak over on Maccorkle Avenue, near the university."

"Do you think they sold one of these lately?"

"I happen to know one was purchased there two weeks ago."

Theodosia stared at the rock-climbing hammer. It looked strong, agile, and serious. "So who's the person you think purchased something like this?"

Tidwell pursed his lips. "You know I can't divulge that information."

Theodosia blew out a small puff of air. Mmn. He was sharing some information with her, but not everything.

Drayton suddenly appeared at their table. "I took the liberty of brewing a nice fresh pot of Assam tea," he said. "Do I have any takers?"

"Thank you, yes," Theodosia said.

"And we still have some cranberry cream scones left over from lunch, if anyone is interested," Drayton said.

Tidwell's expression turned hopeful. "Scones?" His nose twitched like a bunny rabbit.

"With Devonshire cream, of course," Drayton said.

"By all means," Tidwell said.

"I'll bring your tea and treats out in a jiffy." Drayton spun on his heels and hurried into the kitchen. Two minutes later he returned, unloading a teapot, a plate of scones and madeleines, plus bowls of Devonshire cream and strawberry jam. He took great pains to arrange Tidwell's treats in a cluster, nearly spinning the detective into a joyful stroke.

"This is . . . too much," Tidwell said. But Theodosia knew that what he really meant was *Might there be seconds?*

"Enjoy!" Drayton whipped away the empty tray and tucked it snugly under his arm. The resulting puff of wind sent Tidwell's papers flying.

"Oh dear!" Theodosia said as she dove to collect the scatter of papers. Most had drifted gently beneath the table. A few had overturned in flight. As Tidwell reached for a scone, she clutched at the papers with the tips of her fingers. Gathering them up, she caught sight of the printout of the rock-climbing hammer. She flipped it over quickly and saw a name scrawled on back. Clement. Was that the name of the manufacturer? Or the person who purchased it? Never mind, she'd sort all that out later. She popped up like a manic gopher and tamped the papers back together into a stack. "Here you go—good as new."

Tidwell was wielding his butter knife like a samurai with his prized sword, spreading gobs of Devonshire cream and jam onto his scone.

Good, Theodosia thought. *He didn't notice a thing. Now, if he'll just eat and run, I can start my investigating.*

But it wasn't quite that easy. Nothing ever is. Because once Tidwell had said his good-byes and slipped out the front door, a few more customers arrived. And then Sabrina and Luke Andros came wandering in.

What?

Theodosia was a little stunned to see them in her tea shop. For one thing, she didn't really know Sabrina all that well. She'd talked to her for only two minutes the night of the robbery. And she didn't know Luke Andros at all, other than the fact that he owned Gold Coast Yachts and may have been the one talking on the boat last night.

But Drayton was chatting with them amiably and leading them to a table, so Theodosia figured she'd better make nice, too.

Sabrina waggled her fingers when she caught sight of Theodosia and quickly introduced her husband, Luke. She was dressed in tapered black slacks and a fashionable black jacket with gold trim. Luke, in a pink sweater, khaki slacks, and Top-Siders, looked like he'd just climbed down off a yacht. Which he probably had.

"I'm so sorry we missed your Duchess of Devonshire Tea," Sabrina said to Theodosia. "But when I called for a reservation, I was told all the tickets had been sold."

"So we came for afternoon tea anyway," Luke said. "If there's anything left."

"We always have tea and scones available," Drayton said. "But let me go and check . . ."

". . . with the kitchen," Theodosia finished. "Yes, why don't you do that while I chat with these two?" She was dying to talk to them, dying to ask a few questions. But they were both animated and distracted, gazing around the tea room, taking everything in.

"Your décor feels so cozy," Sabrina purred. "The pegged wooden floors, the stone fireplace, all the teacups and teapots arranged just so on shelves . . . I really love it."

"Reminds me of a tea shop you'd find in the UK," Luke said. "Maybe out in the Cotswolds."

Sabrina bent forward. "Do you have any other themed teas on your calendar?"

"Actually, we're having a Romanov Tea tomorrow and a Full Monty Tea on Friday."

"The Romanov Tea," Luke said. "Is it in honor of the Fabergé egg that's coming to the Heritage Society?"

"I hadn't planned it that way," Theodosia said. "But I guess that's how it worked out."

"We can't wait to see that Fabergé egg," Sabrina said. "We're big fans."

"So you'll be attending the opening?" Theodosia asked.

Luke patted his wife's hand. "As new members, we wouldn't miss it. Say, are these teas you're having just for women?"

Theodosia shook her head. "No, no, everyone is welcome."

"Then sign us up for your Romanov Tea," Luke said just as Drayton arrived with a pot of tea and a plate of scones.

"I hope you enjoy these lemon scones," Drayton said. "And I brewed a nice pot of Chinese Keemun tea for you."

"We're tea neophytes," Sabrina said. "So I'm sure anything you serve us is going to be wonderful."

While Sabrina and Luke enjoyed their tea and scones, Theodosia crowded behind the front counter with Drayton.

"What do you know about those two?" she asked him.

Drayton raised his eyebrows. "The Androses?"

"Yes."

"Not a lot. Just that he's the yacht guy. But we already gleaned that information from Delaine."

"They're also new members at the Heritage Society."

Drayton's nose lifted a notch. "That comes as a bit of a surprise. I had no idea."

"Yes," Theodosia said. "They work fast. In fact, they tell me they're planning to attend the Rare Antiquities Show Saturday night."

Drayton reached for a Yixing teapot and pulled it down.

"Then they must have made a sizable contribution, went right for Gold Circle membership."

"I need to tell you something," Theodosia said. "I . . . I was running down by the marina last night. And I happened to overhear a conversation on Luke Andros's yacht."

Drayton squinted at her. *"Happened* to hear?"

"Okay, so maybe I tiptoed out onto the dock." She made a fanning motion with her hands. "I couldn't help myself. There was this enormous yacht moored way out on the end, and it kind of pulled me toward it, like there was a tractor beam at work."

"Theodosia . . ."

"No, listen to me, Drayton. This could be important. I overheard a man talking to a group of people. I couldn't see who they were, but the conversation sounded serious."

Drayton stared at her intently. "Explain, please."

Theodosia leaned in and dropped her voice to a whisper. "The man was telling his group that they could leave town in another four days."

Drayton blinked. "Four days?"

"The Rare Antiquities Show is in four days. Or it was, anyway. Four days from yesterday."

"Oh." Drayton was still processing this information. "Oh my." His fingers crept up to his bow tie. "That does sound a little ominous."

"I think so, too," Theodosia said. "Which is why I made it a point to tell Tidwell about my eavesdropping."

"Good for you," Drayton said. He dipped his wooden scoop into a tin of loose tea and said, "But do you think Tidwell took you seriously? Is he going to investigate Luke Andros?"

Theodosia looked grim. "We can only hope."

14

❧

Theodosia arrived at Channel 8 studios with barely one minute to spare. She pulled her Jeep into the last available visitor's spot and gazed into her rearview mirror. Eek. An open window and an easterly wind had done a number on her hair, billowing and pillowing it into a mass of auburn curls that any Pre-Raphaelite angel would have been proud of. But not so great for a TV appearance.

Theodosia smoothed her hair and climbed out. She grabbed the cardboard box filled with tea, teapots, and scones that Haley had put together for her, and scurried toward the hulking white building that was ahead of her. It was hard to believe they produced all the area's lovely cooking, art, and local news shows inside all that stark architecture.

"Hello." Theodosia approached the expansive front desk, where a security guard and female receptionist sat in silence, transfixed by the glowing screens of their cell phones. "Excuse me." She tapped the desk gently with her knuckles. The reception area had the same white, sterile look as the exterior of the building, except for a bright-red rug in the middle of the floor.

The guard immediately hopped to his feet and stuffed the phone into his pocket.

The young woman glanced up at her and blinked. "Oh. I guess it's still windy outside, huh?"

"No," Theodosia said sweetly. "My car's still in the shop so I took a ride in the Large Hadron Collider."

"Huh?"

"I'm here for an appearance on *Charleston Today*. Theodosia Browning from the Indigo Tea Shop."

The receptionist frowned and touched a glitter-polished nail to her computer screen. "Let's see. Yup, here you are. And it looks like you're late." She shoved a plastic visitor's badge across the desk to Theodosia. "Put this on and head down the hall to Studio B, just past the room with all the vending machines."

Theodosia pinned the badge to her jacket lapel and grabbed her box. Halfway down the hall, the odors of popcorn and burned coffee wafted out to greet her. Could the vending room be far away? No, there it was just to her right.

She continued on down the hallway, bumped her way through swinging double doors into Studio B, and paused to take it all in. The enormous studio was dimly lit, with a smooth floor, lots of cameras and dollies parked everywhere, and klieg lights dangling overhead. A brightly lit set glowed at the far end of the studio. A kitchen set. Perhaps that was where she'd be taping her segment?

A blonde with wide eyes and a pixie cut bounded to Theodosia's side.

"Theodosia?" she asked.

Theodosia smiled. "Yes?"

"I'm Alicia, the production assistant for *Charleston Today*."

"Nice to meet you."

"Hmm." Alicia ran a practiced eye over her. "We might want to get you into hair and makeup."

"You think I need it?" Theodosia wasn't big on makeup. Just a touch of mascara and some lip gloss and she was good to go.

In answer, Alicia took Theodosia's box from her and propelled her into an adjacent room. "Tara?" she screeched. "We need you."

Tara materialized. A skinny young African American woman in low-slung jeans, a concert T-shirt, pink fauxhawk, and a fey smile. She whistled the sound of a falling missile, and then circled Theodosia like a critic. "Wind really got you, huh?"

Theodosia smoothed her hair again as she looked for the nearest exit.

"Whoa," Tara said, sensing that Theodosia was ready to bolt. "Take it easy. We're not gonna do anything radical. We're not gonna shave your head or anything."

"Thank goodness." Theodosia settled into the makeup chair and crossed her legs. She wasn't crazy about being fussed over.

Tara fingered Theodosia's wavy hair. "Where'd you come up with this crazy color?"

"Genetics." Theodosia smiled, thinking of her English-Irish ancestors.

"Okay, girlfriend. I can work with that."

Tara arched Theodosia's brows, lined her lips, and subtly rouged her cheeks. Then she grabbed a huge, round brush and combed her hair into loose waves. She placed her hands on Theodosia's shoulders and swung her chair toward a three-way mirror. "Now, what do you think?"

"Not bad." Theodosia studied her reflection. "What'd you do to my eyebrows?" She'd never seen them look so . . . manicured.

Tara shrugged. "Arched them and added a little eyebrow gel to keep everything in place. One of the tricks of the trade."

"I think I like your tricks," Theodosia said. Feeling a lot

more confident, she walked back into the studio where Alicia was waiting for her.

"Beautiful," Alicia said. "You'll be brilliant."

"Promise?" Theodosia said.

Alicia led her through the studio, dodging cameras and thick rubber cables that snaked underfoot, until they reached the brilliantly lit kitchen set. Her kettle had been put on to boil, the teacups, flowers, and candles were all arranged. A sound guy crept in and clipped a tiny microphone to Theodosia's collar, ran a thin wire down her back.

"You're on in thirty seconds," Alicia said, backing away.

"That soon?" Theodosia said. "Wait a minute, what do you mean 'on.' This is *live?* I thought we were taping."

But the show's genial host, a man with a gelled pompadour, suntan-colored pancake makeup, and a European-cut pin-striped suit was already slicing his way across the studio, heading right for her.

"Weston Keyes," the man said, his smile stretching tightly across his face. "Howja do, honey. Nice to have you as a guest. You stand on this mark here"—he grabbed her elbow and seesawed her into place—"and I stand right here."

"And we're doing this live?" Theodosia asked. "What we say and do just spews directly out to your audience?" She was having trouble wrapping her mind around this.

"Live TV always has a more immediate feel." His teeth were large and brilliant white. Like shark's teeth. He nudged her. "Ready?"

She straightened up. "I was born ready." *Actually, I'm terrified.*

Alicia, kneeling in front of them, held up five fingers and then silently counted down to zero.

"Welcome back to *Charleston Today,*" Keyes burbled to the camera. "I've got Theodosia Browning here from the Indigo Tea Shop, and she's promised to give us some insider's secrets on how to host a spectacular tea party." He turned toward her.

"Theodosia, what have we got here? It all looks so prim and proper."

"No, no," Theodosia said. "A tea party is all about having fun. Relaxing with friends and savoring the moment over a hot cup of tea."

"I'm a coffee guy myself," Keyes said.

"I'll bet the right tea can make a convert out of you," Theodosia said with a wink. She grabbed the kettle, poured a good draft of hot water into a fancy pink-and-green teapot, and swirled it around.

"Now why are you doing that?"

"To warm the teapot. Temperature is critical in brewing tea. Then we dump out this water, add our scoop of Darjeeling—always using the freshest tea leaves available—and add in our fresh hot water."

Keyes peered into her teapot. "Those leaves are jumping around like crazy in there." He gestured toward the camera. "Get a shot of this, Harry. Folks, take a look."

Theodosia tilted the pot toward the camera. "That's called the agony of the leaves. The tea leaves are twisting in the hot water, releasing their aroma and flavor."

"It certainly smells wonderful," Keyes said. "Very fragrant."

"I like to think of tea as aromatherapy," Theodosia said. "The scent of the tea, the lovely aromatic steam, it's all very conducive to relaxation."

Keyes pointed to her plate of scones. "Those biscuit things look pretty tasty, too."

Theodosia picked up a scone, dabbed on a puff of Devonshire cream, and handed it to Keyes. "Try one of our fresh-baked strawberry scones."

Keyes took a huge bite, bobbed his head, and said, in a muffled voice, "Absolutely delicious. Mmn . . . and we'll be right back once I polish off the rest of this scone."

"And we're out," Alicia said.

Still chewing, Keyes turned to Theodosia and said, "When

we come back from commercial break, you'll have twenty seconds to promote your event." He peered at her. "You do have an event to pitch, don't you?"

"Our Romanov Tea?"

"Sure, honey, whatever."

Tara was suddenly standing at Keyes's side, sponging at his makeup, spritzing on an extra layer of hair gel.

"Easy there," Keyes said, waving his hands. "You put any more of that tanner on my face and I'm gonna look like a bronze statue."

"Ten seconds," Alicia called, and then silently counted down.

Keyes stuck his face right into the camera and ratcheted up the charm again. "Tell me, tea lady, what marvelous event do you have coming up?"

"Our Romanov Tea is tomorrow and . . ."

"I'll bet it's in honor of that fancy Fabergé egg that's coming to town, right?"

"I suppose you could say that," Theodosia said.

"And there are still tickets available?"

"Yes, there are. And our Full Monty . . ."

"Thank you, Theodosia!" Keyes boomed. "And thank you, Charleston. I hope you're all having a Southern sunshiny day!" He leaned into the camera and said, in a conspiratorial voice, "Next up, a doggy fashion show you won't want to miss!"

That was it. Theodosia's TV career was over in the blink of an eye. She could barely remember what she'd mumbled, or if she'd even bothered to light a candle. She glanced back at the set. Alicia was haphazardly tossing everything back into her box, while a parade of poodles, schnauzers, and miniature collie dogs, all bundled up in colorful knitted sweaters, suddenly converged on the set.

"Here you go," Alicia said, shoving the box into Theodosia's hands. "Thanks so much." She backpedaled away. "Gotta set up for the next segment."

"Thanks for your help," Theodosia said. "Have a Southern sunshiny day yourself."

Outside, the wind had finally quieted down by the time Theodosia reached her Jeep.

Weird, she thought. What a totally weird experience. Like being in a car accident, but being so frightened you don't really remember getting hit.

A dose of chipper whistling caught her ear.

Theodosia shoved her box into the backseat, spun around, and scanned the parking lot.

"Hey there!" Lionel Rinicker called out. He was striding across the lot toward her, looking shockingly upbeat and dapper in a navy-blue suit and red rep tie.

"Mr. Rinicker?" she said, caught by surprise.

"Lionel, please," he said. "I thought that might be you with all that fiery auburn hair. You fit right in with this autumn day." He glanced at the building. "I bet you were here doing a TV gig."

"I'm afraid so. Although it felt more like riding a speeding roller coaster."

"Isn't that always the way it is when you have to appear in front of a camera or do some public speaking?" He stuffed both hands into his pockets and rocked back on his heels. "I'm doing a segment here, too."

"No kidding." This was a surprise.

"The Heritage Society is keen on publicizing the opening of our Rare Antiquities Show," Rinicker said. "Especially since it kicks off on Sunday for public viewing."

"Well, good luck with that." Theodosia wondered if Timothy had given his blessing to this bit of propaganda. Or had Rinicker set this up all on his own?

"My friend Grace says they'll try to put makeup on me," Rinicker said.

"Probably."

Rinicker tipped his head back and laughed. "Everything I've always wanted, then."

He certainly was a charmer, Theodosia thought.

A sudden puff of wind rattled dry leaves across the parking lot.

Rinicker blew into cupped hands. "The weather's started to shift. Temperature feels like it's really dropping."

"Autumn's like that in Charleston," Theodosia said. "One day it's eighty degrees and sunny and the azaleas are out, the next day, boom. The bottom drops out." She paused. "But you must be used to cool weather. You said you were from Luxembourg? That's what I'd classify as northern Europe."

"I lived there most recently, yes. For almost twelve years." His eyes took on a faraway look. "The Grand Duchy of Luxembourg."

"It must be a beautiful country. Lots of forests and mountains." Theodosia was thinking about the rock hammer Tidwell had shown her earlier.

"The Ardennes mountains," Rinicker said. "Spectacular, just nothing like them. Of course, there's the Kneiff and Buurgplaatz, too."

"I'll bet it's picture-postcard gorgeous." Theodosia glanced at her watch. She was running late. Probably Rinicker was, too. "You'd better get inside if you're appearing on *Charleston Today*," she told him. "They really like to hustle their guests along."

Rinicker stepped away and gave a friendly wave. "You're right. Gotta go drum up some big-time interest for our Rare Antiquities Show."

Theodosia smiled after him. She hoped that, when Sunday came, the collection would still be intact.

15

Theodosia knew she was definitely running late. She had to get home and do her makeup (thank goodness her brows were already in great shape), get gussied up, and then pick up Drayton at seven o'clock on the dot.

But first—well, she had to make a detour. Because ever since Tidwell had shown her that picture of the rock hammer this afternoon, ever since she'd seen the name *Clement* scrawled on the back of the paper, that nasty little tool had been percolating on the back burner of her mind.

She touched her brakes as she coasted down Maccorkle Avenue. There were lots of unusual stores over here that you didn't see in the Historic District, her regular stomping ground. Geo's Natural Foods, Power's Running Store, the Digital Café, Jelly & Craig's New Age Gifts. But where was . . . ? Oh, there it was. Up ahead on the left. Triple Peak. What Tidwell had told her was Charleston's only climbing store.

Theodosia pulled into a parking spot, plugged a quarter

into the meter, and danced her way across the busy street. Her heart gave a little thump-bump as she pushed into the shop.

And what an unusual shop it turned out to be. The first thing that struck her was the multitude of rope. One entire wall was covered with loops and coils of colorful nylon and cotton rope that, she supposed, was one of the most important tools a climber would ever need.

There was lots of other gear, too. Wicked-looking ice axes, fingerless gloves, chalk bags (whatever those were), carabiners, all manner of unusual shiny hardware, climbing shoes, nylon clothing, and an infinite array of safety helmets.

A clerk looked up casually from where he'd been pecking away at a computer terminal and smiled at her. He was probably twenty-three or twenty-four years old, all angles and long sinewy muscles, like a snake. His long hair was pulled back into a high, short ponytail in the style of a samurai warrior, and he had a thin scruff of beard.

"Help you?" he asked.

"I'm looking for a piece of equipment," Theodosia said.

"For rock climbing, ice climbing, big wall, or canyoneering?"

"Um . . . rock climbing, I guess," Theodosia said. She hadn't realized there were so many specialized aspects to climbing. To her it was just about ascending a scary-looking cliff. "I'm looking for a rock hammer."

The clerk gestured at the case in front of him. "We carry lots of different kinds. They're pretty much our bread and butter."

"The thing is . . . I'm looking for a particular type. I believe it's manufactured by Petzl?"

"Yeah," the clerk said, scratching his flat stomach idly. "We definitely carry that brand." He was dressed in Lycra leggings, a T-shirt that said ROCK AROUND THE CLOCK on the front of it, and some flat, rubber-soled shoes that Theodosia surmised were climbing shoes. "We keep them over here." He walked over to another glass case, bent forward, and slid open the back door. "Yup, here you go." He pulled out a Petzl hammer and handed it to Theodosia. "Pretty cool, huh?"

Theodosia hefted the hammer in her hand. It felt sleek, well balanced, and deadly. The kind of hammer you could whack someone in the head with and really get the job done. Or crack open a bunch of glass display cases in a hurry. Better yet, it looked like the one she'd seen the black-suited vandal wielding.

"This is perfect," she said. She was so excited, the hammer almost felt like it was vibrating in her hand. "I have a friend who had one just like this and then lost it up near Table Rock State Park."

"Oh yeah. That's some rad rock climbing up there. Jocassee Gorges is good, too. Right in the neighborhood. Lots of dudes I know climb up there."

Theodosia smiled at the kid. "I'd like to buy this one for my friend, to replace the one he lost." She dropped her voice to a conspiratorial tone. "But I want it to be a secret. You know, a surprise gift."

The kid nodded. "Sure. Cool."

"Which means I'd like to have it wrapped up and shipped out to him. You can take care of that, right?" She handed the hammer back to him.

"Send it out UPS today if you'd like." They walked back to the cash register, where the kid grabbed a pen and pulled out an order form. "What's the name?"

"Clement," Theodosia said. She fumbled in her handbag, searched around for a few moments, and then made a lemon face. "Oh, crumbs." She wobbled her head back and forth to reinforce her dingbat status. "I forgot the address at home." Then, "But I bet you have the address here. My friend has shopped here before, lots of times. So he's probably in your customer database, right?"

"Mmn." The kid stepped over to his computer terminal. "Let me take a look."

Theodosia followed him, staying on her side of the counter, but managing to get a good look at the computer screen.

"Clement?" you said.

Theodosia gave him a bright smile. "That's right."

The kid tapped a few keys and a name and address popped up.

"Here it is. Marcus Clement. Fifteen sixty-two Waverly Street. In North Charleston."

"That's it exactly," Theodosia said, committing the full name and address to memory. She pulled out her American Express card and handed it to the clerk. "Those are rock-climbing shoes that you're wearing?"

The kid nodded. "Yeah. La Sportiva."

She leaned over the counter to get a better look at his shoes. They were black and neon orange with two Velcro strip closures and a squishy-looking rubber sole. She decided they were probably the exact sort of quiet, easy-creepy shoe that a cat burglar might favor.

Theodosia was humming to herself as she hurried through her back door. She kissed Earl Grey on the top of his fuzzy head and let him scoot outside into the backyard. Then she bounded upstairs, taking two steps at a time.

Formal. Drayton had said she had to wear something formal tonight and she'd been tossing around a germ of an idea as she drove home. With the weather so nice and cool, maybe it was time to pull out that cashmere sweater she'd bought at Delaine's shop.

She found it still in a plastic Cotton Duck bag sitting on a shelf in her walk-in closet. Decided it was perfect.

Theodosia jumped into the shower, worked up a froth of bubbles, and jumped out again, feeling a lot more perky.

As she moved about her bedroom in her terry cloth robe, drying off, thinking about the evening ahead, her thoughts wandered to Max. She liked the idea of visiting him in Savannah at Christmastime. Really, there was nothing like celebrating the holidays in Savannah. Such a civilized city. She recalled going down there once for Christmas on the River with all its concerts, art festivals, and home tours.

As she retouched her makeup, she thought about the emotional aspect of their broken relationship. Did she miss Max? Yes, she did. Did she miss him a lot? She thought about that as she added a faint smudge of golden-beige shadow above her eyes. Mmn, maybe not as much as she thought she would.

And wasn't that surprising?

The blue-gray cashmere sweater felt soft and cloudlike as she slipped it over her head. But now . . . now to see if the outfit she'd envisioned would really work. She stepped into her floor-length silver crinkle skirt. She'd seen a photo spread in *Vogue*, where a supermodel wore something just like this, and loved the idea. The juxtaposition of a cozy casual sweater with a very formal, floor-length skirt appealed to her. It was a kind of . . . dichotomy.

Theodosia eyed herself in the full-length mirror. Did it work? Could she carry it off?

Her image shimmered back at her and she loved it.

In fact, the concept of high-low dressing definitely appealed to her. There was something very modern and today about it. She'd even noticed that celebrities were pulling off high-low with great aplomb. A Gucci blouse tucked into H&M khakis. A Burberry T-shirt worn with Target jeans. Fun.

Theodosia stood in front of her mirror and brushed out her hair. It snapped and crackled with a life of its own. But it was still fiercely windy out, so maybe she should wear her hair up?

Why not?

She brushed her hair into a thick ponytail and then twisted

it around a couple of times into what stylists today were call-ing a messy knot. She stuck in a couple of pins to anchor it.

Theodosia grabbed a silver beaded bag and tossed in her cell phone, lipstick, and a twenty-dollar bill. Then, for the pièce de résistance, she slipped into a pair of silver Manolo Blahnik heels.

Teetering slightly, she turned to look at herself in the full-length mirror again. And liked what she saw.

All that was left now was for Theodosia to let Earl Grey back inside, feed him, and grab a quick snack for herself. Maybe a piece of cheese and some fruit. Just something to keep her blood sugar up.

So, okay. She smiled to herself. *I'm all ready.*

She was poised to descend the first step when she had a quick afterthought. She shuffled back into her bedroom, pawed through the top drawer in her dresser, and found a comb. It was a tortoiseshell-patterned comb that was embedded with pearls. A comb that had once belonged to her mother.

She tucked the jeweled comb into her hair. It was a kind of talisman, she decided. A talisman that she hoped would guard against anything bad happening tonight.

16

❧

The street outside the Montagu Opera House teemed with shiny black limousines and town cars, all dropping off their passengers in front of the arched and beveled glass doors. Huge searchlights scoured the night sky, beaming their special welcome for opening night.

Theodosia paused just inside the front door, her feet sinking into the plush red carpet. She turned slightly to enjoy the scene, watching tuxedo-clad men and women in designer gowns greet each other amid a flurry of genteel hugs and spirited air kisses. Then she and Drayton swept up the grand circular staircase, passing under a glittering chandelier, in true Hollywood fashion.

"*La Bohème* is one of my favorites," Theodosia said as they sailed up, up, and up. "In fact, it's the first opera I ever saw."

"Ah," Drayton said. "Your first opera so often becomes your most favorite."

"From the moment the curtain went up, I was captivated. I knew I'd discovered my new passion." Theodosia inhaled deeply as they breezed along the mezzanine balcony. Ripples of excitement coursed through her and she was feeling what surely had to be a contact high from the crowd that swarmed through the theater. She tossed her head. "But I'm not sure I'll ever get used to the grandeur of this building."

"I hope you never do," Drayton said. "I hope there's always a little thrill to be had."

Theodosia was feeling very elegant and haute couture in her cashmere and silk. And Drayton certainly looked magnificent in a tuxedo that he'd had custom tailored in England a few years ago. His antique amber-and-gold cuff links flashed each time his wrists moved.

"I've always had a place in my heart for the character Rodolfo," Drayton said as he led Theodosia along, nodding to the occasional acquaintance. "There's something true and lasting in him. He pursues his dream with such fervor."

She smiled. "You mean he pursues Mimi."

Drayton turned toward Theodosia with a twinkle in his eye. "I meant that he was looking for true love." He hesitated, seemed to realize just where he was, and said, "My goodness, here we are at our seats already. Welcome to the rarefied world of the opera buff." He pulled open an ornately carved wooden door with a polished brass handle and stood aside for Theodosia to ease her way past him.

Which brought her into a dimly lit private box complete with four plush seats.

"These are our seats?" Theodosia asked. She was stunned. The box seats were basically a private and amazingly elegant perch situated high above the entire theater, with an unobstructed view of the stage.

"Two of the seats are ours, anyway," Drayton said. "I share this box with Edith and Howard Pinckney."

Theodosia took in the purple velvet seats, gold velvet draperies, and gilded walls. "I feel like we just time-traveled back a hundred years or so. To Belle Époque Paris or Emperor Franz Joseph's Vienna."

Drayton nodded. "Yes, well, do sit down and enjoy it." He sat down as well, only to spring up a few moments later when the Pinckneys arrived.

A flurry of introductions ensued, and then Theodosia had the distinct pleasure of leaning out over the brass railing to survey the crowd below. Everyone looked fabulous, of course, from the dazzling couples still streaming in, to the tie-and-tailed orchestra up front. And the buzz of conversation, mingled with occasional laughter and the low sound of musical instruments being tuned, ratcheted up her anticipation even more.

"This place is just remarkable," Theodosia whispered. She crossed her ankles and tried to settle in for the show, but her nerves were getting the best of her. Opening-night jitters? Yes! She couldn't wait for the opera to start.

"These seats are well worth the investment," Drayton whispered back. "What's life without a little splurge here and there?"

As the orchestra finished their warm-up, a zip of anticipation filled the air and a hush fell over the audience. Everyone could feel the pulse of energy in the theater.

Drayton set his Playbill aside and leaned forward expectantly.

The house lights dimmed until there was almost complete darkness.

Wonderful, Theodosia thought. *Magical.*

Then the stage lights flashed on, the curtain rose, and the orchestra's first vibrant notes shimmered high and sweet in the air. With that, Theodosia's heart took wing and she was swept back almost two hundred years to the Latin Quarter of Paris.

The arias, the music, the sets, all proved to be dazzling.

The opera singers who played Mimi and Rodolfo fairly mesmerized the audience. They danced across the stage, laughing, cajoling, singing their hearts out, and positively owning it.

This is it, Theodosia thought. *This is what makes people's hearts leap and quickens their spirit. This is what makes the arts so very special!*

Amazingly, the first act flew by. When the curtain was dropped and the applause thundered out, Theodosia let herself relax against her seat back for the first time that night.

"That was just magnificent," she said to Drayton. She was grinning from ear to ear.

Drayton was nodding and clapping with delight. "Absolutely transporting," he said. "Possibly the best I've seen."

Theodosia reached over and patted his arm. "Thank you," she said. "Thank you so much for inviting me tonight."

"It's not over yet," Drayton said. He rose to his feet and smiled. "Since we've reached intermission, would you care to indulge in a glass of sherry? Or, I suppose in this case they'll be serving wine or champagne."

They were indeed serving wine and champagne. Theodosia and Drayton braved their way to a temporary bar that had been set up on the second floor and ordered glasses of white wine. Then, as the glittering crowd surged around them, they stepped out of the way and sipped their wine gingerly.

"This wine is actually good," Theodosia said. "I was expecting something awful and puckery."

"Right," Drayton laughed. "Wine from a box. But this isn't half-bad, is it?" He took another sip. "See anybody you know? It's opening night, after all. The crème de la crème should be swanning about."

Theodosia peered over the crowd. "I don't know about the crème, but here comes Delaine."

"Who's she with?"

Theodosia shook her head. She didn't recognize the man who was escorting her friend. "Her boyfriend du jour?"

"Theodosia?" Delaine's sharp voice sawed through the low-key burble of the crowd.

Theodosia and Drayton both braced themselves. Delaine could be a little overpowering.

"Isn't this just *amazing*?" Delaine exclaimed. She hustled up to them, all wiggling pink shoulders and swishing skirts. "Aren't you thoroughly enchanted with this *production*!" When Delaine was excited, she loved to talk in exclamation points.

Delaine was not only over the top in her manner of speech, tonight she was dressed like a Greek goddess. Her cream-colored, one-shouldered long gown was strewn with gold accents, and matching gold and turquoise snake bracelets coiled about each wrist.

Versace? Theodosia wondered. *Has to be. Wow.*

Not surprisingly, Delaine was hanging on the arm of a very good-looking forty-something man. His dark, curly hair and architectural nose reminded Theodosia of a cross between a gigolo and an Italian count. Although, she giggled to herself, maybe they were one and the same. But Delaine was making introductions now, so she had to pay attention.

"Nice to meet you," Theodosia said politely to Delaine's date. He'd been introduced as Renaldo Gilles, an import-export agent.

But Delaine had gossip on her mind. She dropped her voice low and said, "You remember, Theo, you were asking me the other day about Sabrina and Luke Andros?"

"Yes?" Theodosia said. She'd been having such a wonderful time, she'd almost forgotten about them. Now, with just those few words, Delaine had spread a dark cloud over Theodosia's evening. Still, she leaned forward to listen. Maybe this was something important she should know about.

"I found out a few things about Sabrina and Luke from Tookie Carmichael," Delaine said. "You know her, she comes

into Cotton Duck all the time and is on the Spoleto commit-
tee this year?"

"Okay."

"Anyway," Delaine said, "Tookie told me that the Androses
used to live in Miami. Or at least that's where their yacht business was originally based."

"I wonder why they moved to Charleston?" Theodosia said.
"Or is their move permanent? Maybe they still have an office
in Miami, too?"

But Delaine was shaking her head. "No, no. Apparently
they felt there was just too much competition in Miami.
Just too many yacht brokers and wannabe's trying to elbow
them out of the way."

"But there's so much money in Miami," Theodosia said.
"International money, too. You'd think they could make a go
of it." *If they're good, anyway. If they can figure out how to market
themselves.*

Delaine rolled her eyes. "Goodness' sake, there's lots of
money here, too." She looked around, seemed to notice Gilles,
and snuggled close to him. "Hello, sweetie," she purred.

"Are you enjoying the opera?" Theodosia asked Gilles.
She felt like she should say something to him.

"I'm a huge fan," Gilles said, waving an arm enthusiasti-
cally, almost clobbering a woman with an overdone Throw-
back Thursday beehive hairdo. "I've actually had the pleasure
of seeing this particular opera performed in Paris."

"And how does it compare?" Drayton asked politely.

Gilles gave them all a slightly haughty look and shook his
head. "There is no comparison."

Theodosia smiled broadly and turned toward Drayton. "Well then, we should probably be heading back to
our seats."

"So soon?" Delaine looked disappointed.

"It was lovely to see you both," Drayton said, hastily backing away. "I hope you enjoy the rest of the opera. Or at least try to," he muttered under his breath.

Theodosia gave a little wave. "Nice meeting you . . ."

A few minutes later, the froth of the second act once again swept Theodosia up in its embrace. Her eyes fluttered shut as the music carried her from scene to scene. How could these singers simply open their mouths and fill this hall with such glorious mind-boggling sound? she wondered. She smiled as the music gained in intensity. She was devouring each note with her ears, anticipating the next.

And then, just as the mezzo-soprano was hitting her highest note, just as the chorus was really pumping out the backup chords, a scream suddenly rose up from somewhere in the audience. It mingled with the soprano's voice for a long moment, and then climbed to an even higher screech. Like steel wheels braking on rusted rails, it rose and fell and rose and fell until . . .

The soprano suddenly fell silent, a look of absolute shock on her face.

The orchestra faltered.

And still the scream continued, rising so high it ended in a horrible, guttural shriek.

Somewhere, a door slammed loudly, the noise reverberating throughout the entire hall, rattling everyone's sensibilities.

Now everyone on stage had stopped singing . . . the principal players, the chorus. Everyone glanced about nervously, unsure of what to do.

A few murmurs rose up from the audience. And then a hundred more people joined in.

The orchestra's frizzy-haired conductor turned around and stared at the audience with disapproval.

"What happened?" a woman cried.

"What's going on?" a man demanded.

Several members of the audience jumped to their feet.

Then, from the box seat next to them, Theodosia heard a plaintive voice call out.

"Help!" the woman cried. "Something terrible has happened to Abigail and Harold. Won't somebody please help them?"

As the screams continued, the house lights flashed on in a sudden blaze. Due, no doubt, to the quick thinking and fast action of a nervous usher.

It suddenly became very obvious that the screaming was coming from the private box that was closest to the stage. In fact, as Theodosia leaned forward, she could see a woman standing there, a look of utter terror on her face as she screamed bloody blue murder.

"Help!" the woman continued to scream, her voice drawing out the word in an awful, wrenching shriek. "Somebody please help me!"

Theodosia stood up. "Something's horribly wrong," she cried out to Drayton. Then, without thinking, without hesitating, she dashed into the hallway and sprinted down the row of box seats. If nobody else would help this poor woman, then she would do it!

She passed one, two, three doors that led to box seats. Ran past a curving stairway that led downstairs. For one brief instant it felt like she'd just missed seeing someone. That she'd caught a faint, ghostly image out of the corner of her eye. Then she was sliding to a stop in front of the last set of box seats where the screams were pouring out.

The door stood open.

Theodosia drew a deep breath and plunged inside.

Her eyes quickly took in the bizarre tableau. An elderly man in a tuxedo lay sprawled on the carpet, gasping for air. Blood poured from a cut on his forehead and had trickled down to soak through the front of his white shirt. An older woman—the screaming woman she'd seen before—was now bent over him and racked with sobs. A grim-looking theater manager crouched next to the man and barked sharp orders into his cell phone.

When the theater manager glanced up and saw Theodosia, he waved a dismissive hand at her. "Go away!" he cried.

"What's wrong?" Theodosia asked urgently. "What happened?"

The crying woman stumbled toward Theodosia, almost tripping on the hem of her long lilac-colored dress. "Help me," she gasped. Her shoulders shook and her body heaved with erratic sobs. "Somebody snu-snu-snuck into our box," the woman babbled. "They hit my husband over the head and then they . . ." Her right hand clutched at her bare neckline as her lower lip quivered wildly. "They stole the necklace right from around my neck."

Theodosia bent down to look at the elderly gentleman on the floor.

"Sir, are you all right? Sir, can you hear me?"

His eyes fluttered open. "I can hear you," he moaned.

"Stay down," she told him. "You've got a bad cut on your right temple and you might have a concussion." Why was she getting a terrible sense of déjà vu? Why did this suddenly feel like a replay of Sunday night at Heart's Desire?

"Did you call an ambulance?" Theodosia asked the theater manager.

He bobbed his head. "They're on their way. I'm talking to the police right now."

"Ma'am?" Theodosia reached a hand out to the crying woman. "You're white as a sheet. Come here and sit down. An ambulance is on its way. Help will be here in a matter of minutes." She was aware that a large crowd had gathered outside the door, that there was a high, insistent buzz, like the sound of a thousand cicadas.

The woman stumbled toward Theodosia.

Theodosia guided the distraught woman into a theater seat. "Here you go." The woman's legs buckled beneath her as she sat down heavily.

"Harold?" the woman sobbed.

"I'm here," the old man croaked.

"He's right here," Theodosia said, reaching down to pat the man's shoulder. "We're just going to keep him lying flat until the ambulance arrives."

The old woman nodded sadly. Then her fingers clawed helplessly at her neck again. "My emerald necklace." Tears streamed down her face. "I took it out of the safe just so I could wear it tonight." Her voice caught. "It was an heirloom."

Well, Theodosia thought. Of course it was.

17

It really did feel like the sad aftermath at Heart's Desire all over again. The EMTs arrived with a clanking gurney and a flutter of blankets. A half-dozen uniformed police officers came storming in. And, finally, Detective Burt Tidwell showed up as well.

Theodosia and Drayton watched the drama unfold from the security of their box seats.

"How are the police ever going to be able to question all these people?" Drayton asked.

Theodosia stared down glumly over the railing. "They're not. Take a look."

Drayton peered down. The audience was pushing and shoving and stumbling over themselves to escape from the theater. "Oh no," he said. "It looks like the last gasp on the *Titanic*. Right before the ship sank and all the passengers rushed to the Boat Deck in a blind panic." He shook his head. "This is definitely not good."

"None of this is remotely good," Theodosia said. She sat down, tapped her foot anxiously while she tried to think.

If only . . . No, that's not going to solve anything. I need to come up with a better idea than that.

"What's going to happen now?" Drayton asked. He'd worked himself up into a slight tizzy. "Who do you think stole that necklace?"

An idea was suddenly fizzing in Theodosia's brain. "We need to check on something right now," she said to Drayton. "Or, rather, check on someone."

"What are you talking about?" Drayton asked. "Who are you talking about?"

"We need to call your friend Rinicker. To see if he's at home."

"Because . . . ?" Drayton hesitated, and then comprehension slowly dawned. "Ah, because you suspect Lionel might have been the one who snuck in here, whacked that poor man, and stole his wife's necklace?"

"Her *emerald* necklace. And, yes, I think there might be a sliver of a possibility. If Rinicker really is a hotshot jewel thief, then he might have seen this place as easy pickings."

"So we're going to make an anonymous call to see if he's home. And then hang up if he answers?"

"Yes, we have to pretend that we're silly teenagers playing a prank."

Drayton pursed his lips. "You make it sound so appealing."

"Okay, let me rephrase my words. We're concerned citizens who are investigating a homicide and two robberies. There, does that make you feel any better?"

"Not really," Drayton sighed. "But I'm willing to play along with you. At least for the time being."

Theodosia and Drayton made their way down to the main floor and squeezed out a side entrance. Once they were out on the dimly lit street, they had to thread their way through a tangled web of honking cars as the horde of angry, disillusioned operagoers attempted to flee the area.

"It's gridlock," Drayton said, as they skipped across Wentworth Street.

"Never mind that," Theodosia said. "We have to concentrate on finding a phone somewhere."

"Why don't you just buzz Rinicker on your cell phone?"

Theodosia made a face. "Because if he's got caller ID, then he's going to know it's us."

"And that we're checking on him," Drayton said as they huffed along. "Good point. This sleuthing business isn't all that easy, is it?"

"No, it's not."

They finally located a battered pay phone stuck in the middle of a wall of colorful posters in an all-night mom-and-pop grocery store.

Theodosia fed a quarter into the phone and heard an old-fashioned *ding*. "This has to be the last pay phone in the tricounty area. Maybe in existence." She gazed at Drayton. "What's his number?"

"His . . . ? Oh, just a sec." Drayton pulled out his wallet and extracted a business card. He read Lionel Rinicker's number to her as she dialed.

"It's ringing," Theodosia told him. Anxiety nibbled in the pit of her stomach.

"He'll pick up," Drayton said.

But he didn't. The phone rang and rang until Theodosia was sick of hearing the dull ring at the other end of the line. If Lionel Rinicker was home, he definitely wasn't picking up.

"He's not home," Theodosia said.

"Now what?"

She shifted from one foot to the other, the arches of her feet keenly aware that she'd been dashing all over the place in designer heels. "I don't know."

"On the other hand," Drayton said, "Lionel could be with his lady friend."

"Grace," Theodosia said, pouncing at once on the idea. "We need to go check her out. We'll drive by her home and see if Rinicker's car is parked outside." She held up a hand. "Wait, do you know what kind of car he drives?"

"I'm pretty sure it's a BMW."

It took a good ten minutes for them to get Theodosia's Jeep out of the parking lot, and then another fifteen minutes to thread their way through heavy traffic and bump their way over to the Historic District. But finally they were cruising down Tradd Street.

Ten o'clock at night and the evening was dark as pitch. Only a few streetlamps glowed pink, giving the neighborhood an eerie, otherworldly feel. A few homes had lights on inside, but mostly it was a quiet Wednesday night. The weather had shifted, and the wind was gusting in from the Atlantic, stripping leaves from trees, whipping a few palmettos into a frenzy.

"That's Grace Dawson's home right there," Theodosia said.

"Where George Burwick used to live," Drayton said. "Before he died. Such a big place. And quite fancy, too."

"Take a look around. Do you see Rinicker's BMW parked on the street anywhere?"

"Not yet."

They cruised slowly up and down the street. Went around the block and checked the side streets. Came back again and double-checked. There was still no sign of a BMW.

"There are hardly any lights on in Grace's home," Theodosia said. "So I'm guessing she either went to bed early or she's not at home." Theodosia pulled over to the curb and put her foot on the brake. Sat there, tried to sort out her thoughts, listened to the engine's hum.

"Maybe the two of them went out together?" Drayton said.

"And maybe Rinicker is sitting at home fat and sassy with his brand-new heirloom necklace."

"You really have it in for him, don't you?" Drayton said.

"Not really. He's just at the top of my list of suspects."

"A long list. And getting longer."

Theodosia dug in her clutch and pulled out her phone. "Okay, now we have to call Haley."

"What? Why?"

"I want you to call her and, if she answers, if she's home, just ask her some silly question."

"It's okay to use your phone?" Drayton asked. "This call isn't supersecret?"

"No." Theodosia dialed the number and pushed the phone toward Drayton. "Just try to act normal."

"But what am I supposed to ask her?" He looked panicked.

"I don't know. Ask her if you left your hat in the kitchen."

"Hello?" Drayton stammered into the phone. "Haley?" He hesitated as Theodosia made a hurry-up spinning motion with her hands. "Did I leave my hat in the kitchen? You don't think so? Oh, you were? Okay, so sorry to have awakened you." He handed the phone back to Theodosia. "Okay, Haley's at home. She was sleeping. And she thinks I'm an idiot. So what does any of that prove?"

"We at least know that Haley's not out with her boyfriend du jour, Billy Grainger."

Drayton did a double take. "Now you think *he* was the one who robbed that poor woman tonight and hit her husband on the head?"

"I don't know. Maybe." Theodosia knew the connection was thin, but weren't all leads fairly tenuous? Wasn't that the hallmark of a good investigator? You had to be willing to search out every sliver of a lead?

But Drayton wasn't so keen on pursuing the Grainger angle.

"You think Grainger might be part of the gang that held up Heart's Desire, don't you?" he asked. "And it's all because he rides a motorcycle."

"I don't know, Drayton. It's possible. Grainger would have known all about the jewelry show at Brooke's because Haley had been tapped to set up the buffet and serve tea. So he could be playing her. She hasn't known him all that long."

"Still, wouldn't you call that circumstantial evidence?"

"I'm not sure it's evidence at all, but I'd sure like to know if Grainger's at home right now."

"So what do you want to do about it? Call him, too?"

"Actually," Theodosia said. "I'd like to drive over to his house and see for myself."

"Do you even know where Grainger lives?"

Theodosia affected a casual shrug. "I have his address."

"How on earth did you get that? Are you telling me that Haley willingly coughed it up for you?"

"Heck no," Theodosia said. "I did what any clever investigator would do."

"Which is?"

"I peeked at her cell phone when she wasn't looking."

Billy Grainger lived in North Charleston. On Fariday Street, which wasn't all that far from the airport.

They drove around for a while, hit a couple of dead ends, and then finally found the address. They parked three houses down and tried to take stock of things. The neighborhood looked okay, maybe a little shabby, but some of the homes looked like they were being rehabbed. It was also intensely quiet, with no sign of evening joggers or dog walkers. Probably too late for that, Theodosia decided.

"I didn't see any lights on inside Grainger's house," Drayton said. "Not even the telltale flicker of a TV."

"So he's either out for the evening or in bed for the night," Theodosia said.

"Should we call him, too? Or is this a straight-ahead stakeout?"

Theodosia gazed at him. "You think this is funny, don't you? You're amused."

The corners of Drayton's mouth twitched ever so slightly. "I think this is all a little strange. This is not exactly how I'd planned to spend my evening."

"Nobody back at the opera thought things would go sour, either," Theodosia said.

"Is that what happened? Things went sour?"

Theodosia had to giggle, Drayton looked so serious. "No, Drayton, only your mood."

He pretended to look outraged. "Wait a minute—I'm here, aren't I? I'm . . . what would you call it? Riding shot-gun for you."

"Yes, you are. And for that I'm eternally grateful. Because some of what we're doing tonight is a little scary." She reached over and clasped his arm. "So thank you for indulging me."

"You're welcome," he said. "And I didn't mean to be sour."

"You really weren't," Theodosia said. "I think I'm just unsure about what to do next."

"Theodosia," Drayton said, "of all the people I know, you're the most sure of themselves."

"You think?"

Drayton bobbed his head emphatically. "Absolutely."

They sat there for five minutes until Theodosia said, "I need to take a closer look." She reached up, turned off the dome light, and popped open the driver's-side door.

"If you're going to go creepy-crawl that house," Drayton said, "then I'm going with you."

"Oh dear," Theodosia whispered. "I think maybe I'm a bad influence."

They crept up a cracked cement sidewalk toward Billy's Craftsman-style home. Dim streetlamps overhead cast long shadows that ghosted along with them, a dog let loose a high-pitched yip from somewhere in a backyard.

"Creepy," Drayton said.

"You mean Grainger's house or our current situation?"

"Yes to all of the above," Drayton said.

They were standing in front of Grainger's bungalow now. The place had potential but an obviously unmotivated owner. A drainpipe hung askew, there were weeds in the dried-up flower beds, and the front porch sagged. They tiptoed up the front walk but were unwilling to go up onto the front porch, because that seemed a little too close for comfort. Instead, they snuck around the side of the house. Halfway down the length of it, they came to a low window.

"Let's take a look," Theodosia whispered.

Drayton cupped his hands together and peered inside. "I can't see a thing," he said.

"Shades drawn?"

"Hard to tell, it's so dark."

"You know what?" Theodosia said. "If a next-door neighbor looked out right now and saw us snooping, they'd probably call the police. Plus, we look strange. You're in a tuxedo and I'm wearing a long skirt."

"They'd just think we were high-class cat burglars," Drayton said, which set them both to giggling. Then Drayton pumped his arms and did a jaunty little quickstep. "Look at me," he said in a stage whisper, "I'm the gentleman bandit."

"Stop it." Theodosia batted him on the shoulder. "This is no laughing matter."

Drayton sobered up. "Then we should leave."

Theodosia held up a hand. "Not so fast. We've come this

far, so we should definitely check out the garage. See if his motorcycle is parked there."

They hunched their way quietly toward the garage, a single-car structure that looked like it was practically falling down.

"Is there a window?" Drayton asked.

"Mmn . . . I think maybe."

It was darker back there and the ground felt soft and squishy underfoot. Theodosia reached down and slipped off her shoes. No need to ruin them. They crept closer to the garage and found themselves stepping into some sort of flower bed loaded with mulch. Or maybe it was just dried-up leaves. Theodosia put a hand up against the garage wall and slid along to her left. Three steps later, her knee bumped against something hard. It was a wooden bench. And there was a small window set just above it.

"Help me up," Theodosia whispered.

Drayton put a hand out to help her. When she was balancing on the teetering bench, he said, "See anything?"

"No, it's too dark."

"Definitely time to go, then," Drayton said. "Before we really do get caught."

The words were barely out of his mouth when they heard a loud *rmm-rmm-rmming* sound.

Theodosia hopped noiselessly down from the bench and stared at him. "Was that a . . . ?"

"Motorcycle!" Drayton gasped.

A motorcycle was bumping down the alley, headed right toward them.

"Quick," Theodosia mouthed.

They both ducked low just as a single headlamp swept across the brittle, dry grass of the backyard. There was more loud, throaty revving from the engine, then the rattling sound of a garage door going up.

Run for it? Stay put? Theodosia wasn't sure. Then, suddenly, the engine switched off and the night went silent. Now it was too late to make any kind of move. They froze instantaneously, and then slowly, carefully, tried to crouch even lower in the bed of mulch. They waited, barely breathing, as they heard boots scuffle on the cement apron, and then the garage door rumbled down.

Theodosia's eyes were wide as saucers as Billy Grainger passed within ten feet of them, heading up his back walk. There was a jingle of keys, and then the back door opened. Seconds later, it snicked closed and a light went on inside the house.

Theodosia slowly let out a breath. A close call. Grainger was inside his house now and, thank goodness, he hadn't seen them creeping around like a pair of Peeping Toms.

"We have to get out of here." Drayton's voice was low and urgent.

Theodosia nodded. "I agree." Then she tiptoed toward the house. The lights were blazing inside now. "But not before we take one little look."

"No!" Drayton hissed.

But Theodosia was already creeping down the walk to the side of the house. Maybe something would be visible through that window now.

Drayton threw up his hands in frustration, but ended up following her anyway. When Theodosia pressed her nose to the window, he whispered, "Is Grainger in there?"

She nodded. "I think I saw him moving. But the window's so filthy it's hard to . . ." She rubbed a little circle on the window with her fist, trying to wipe away some of the grime.

"Now?" Drayton asked. "Now do you see him?"

Theodosia stared in again. "Oh jeepers." Her voice was urgent and low. "Oh crap."

"What? *What?*" Drayton asked.

Theodosia grabbed his hand and pulled him away from the window. Together they skittered toward the front of the house, then bent low and ran across the dry grass. Fifteen seconds later they were back safely in Theodosia's Jeep.

"What did you see?" Drayton asked. His curiosity was at a fever pitch; he knew she'd seen something strange.

"Billy Grainger," Theodosia gasped out. "He was wearing a white shirt with a black bow tie."

"What?" Drayton was practically dumbstruck by her words. *"What?"*

"I said Billy . . ."

"No, no, I heard you the first time," Drayton said. "What I meant was, what does that *mean*?"

"From the looks of things," Theodosia said. "From the starched white shirt and fancy bow tie that he was wearing, I'd say Billy Grainger could have waltzed right in to the opera tonight!"

18

❧

Midmorning on Thursday and the Indigo Tea Shop was filled with customers. Teakettles chirped and burped as Theodosia and Drayton worked at top speed. Drayton pumped out freshly brewed pots of Nilgiri, orchid plum, and English breakfast tea. Theodosia hastily delivered these pots of tea, along with Haley's cranberry bread and orange scones, to all their customers who were seated at tables.

Just as they'd reached their maximum tipping point, just when they couldn't seat one more person or accept one additional take-out order, a colorful horse-drawn jitney rumbled to a stop outside their front door and disgorged a load of passengers.

"Uh-oh," Drayton murmured. "Overload."

Eight people spilled into the tea shop, chattering and laughing and shrieking for tea.

Except for one.

A solid-looking woman in a bright purple dress put her hands on her hips and said, "I don't drink tea."

That brought the raucous group up short. They stood there, glancing about, shifting their feet.

Never wanting to turn away potential business, and seeing that a large table was about to become available, Theodosia stepped in to smooth things over.

"It's not a problem," she told the group. "We have a Tea Totalers menu."

Purple dress was not convinced. "What's that?" she asked, suspicion evident in her voice.

So Theodosia gave a quick explanation of teas and tisanes. How tea was brewed from the leaves of tea plants, but a tisane was basically a fruit or herbal infusion. She told her that a tisane might *look* like a tea and be served in a lovely china teacup, but it was really a brew made from plums or raspberries, peppermint or chamomile.

Once purple dress was satisfied that she could partake of a fruit tea, things settled down to a dull roar.

"Now, don't sneak any real tea into that lady's brew and make me a liar," Theodosia warned Drayton.

"Hah," he said. "After our sneak-and-peek excursion of last night, a little white lie is nothing. I ought to call and report you to Detective Tidwell for suspicious lurking."

She turned. "You wouldn't."

"No," Drayton said as he measured out scoops of chocolate mint tea. "But you've certainly got me thinking the worst about Haley's boyfriend."

"I hear you. But why would he be wearing a tux if he wasn't at the opera?"

Drayton poured a gush of hot water into a teapot, swished it around to warm the interior, and then dumped it out. "Oh, I don't know. Perhaps his chosen profession demands that manner of dress?"

"You mean he's either a headwaiter or a vampire?"

"Very funny. But what if we accuse Haley's boyfriend of being part of that awful gang and it turns out he's not?"

Drayton asked. "If she gets mad at us for thinking the worst, she just might up and quit." He glanced around at their roomful of customers. "Like right now. When we've got a full house."

Theodosia had to agree. "That would be awful in more ways than one. We both love Haley. She's part of our tea shop family."

"I completely agree," Drayton said. "Plus, we've got our Romanov Tea later today." He lifted an eyebrow. "You really wouldn't want to man the kitchen all by yourself, would you?"

Theodosia's eyes practically glazed over. "There's no way I could do what Haley does. Prepare all that food and get it out on time? Whip up actual blinis? I . . . well, I couldn't do it."

They gazed at each other.

"Then perhaps we'll let the issue ride for now?" Drayton asked.

As if on cue, Haley came dashing out with a second tray of fresh-baked orange scones. "What are you two whispering about?" she asked as she set her tray on the counter. Her brows pinched together. "You look positively conspiratorial."

"We were discussing you," Drayton said.

Haley looked more than a little curious as she lifted the lid on a glass pie saver and began stacking her scones inside. "Oh yeah? What were you saying about me?"

"We're worried that we're putting too much pressure on you with all these themed teas," Drayton said. "That you're possibly feeling scattered."

Haley dropped the lid, shoved back a hank of blond hair, and gave him a quirky look. "Scattered? Me? Haven't you heard? I'm a millennial so I'm *supposed* to be scattered." She struck a dramatic hand-on-her-hip pose. "And overly ambitious, too, don't you know? I'm supposed to be, like, this killer chef who has a hipster boyfriend and is studying

Mandarin Chinese while inventing new foodie apps for the iPhone. I'm supposed to want it all."

Drayton was taken aback by her little outburst. "Goodness, Haley, *do* you want it all?"

Haley raised a fist over her head and grinned. "Of course I do. World domination, one scone at a time."

At eleven o'clock, just as Theodosia was about to run into the kitchen and check on lunch, Detective Tidwell strolled into the tea shop. She glanced around, spotted an empty table, and ushered him to it.

"Tea?" Theodosia asked. She knew Tidwell had come to talk, but he didn't mind being fussed over, either. In fact, all men enjoyed being fussed over when food was involved.

Tidwell's jowls sloshed in the affirmative. "Tea would be grand. And I wouldn't mind a scone as well."

"Of course you wouldn't."

When Theodosia returned with a pot of Fujian white tea and two scones, Tidwell was smiling like the cat who'd swallowed the proverbial canary.

"I have news," he said, his beady eyes seeking her out.

Theodosia glanced about the tea room to see if she could spare a minute, and then slid into a chair next to him. "What? Is this about that poor woman last night at the opera?"

"No. My news involves the jewel heist at Heart's Desire."

Theodosia suddenly felt a flood of relief. "Oh my gosh, you broke the case? You found the jewels?" A girl could hope, couldn't she?

"Not exactly," Tidwell said. "But we have received word from the insurance company."

Insurance? What does that have to do with anything?

"Wait, does that mean they're going to pay off Brooke's claim?" Theodosia asked Tidwell.

"Not quite. It seems that United Insurance and Guaranty

received a rather mysterious phone call that our tech geeks have been unable to trace. Apparently, this band of rather opportunistic jewel thieves has expressed a willingness to ransom back part of the stolen merchandise."

"Ransom it back?" Theodosia had never heard of this before. "What does that mean? How does insurance ransom work?"

Tidwell explained, "It's not an uncommon practice, though you see it more often with stolen works of art. In this case, the thieves contacted the insurance company and presented them with the option of paying an enormous sum of money in order to get the jewels back in one piece."

"Really? That's how it works?"

"The insurer also has the option of just kissing the loot good-bye and paying off the policyholder. Eventually, anyway."

"Wait a minute," Theodosia said. "So you're telling me that the main thief, the ringleader of this gang, the whoever, actually *contacted* Brooke's insurance company?"

"That's right. And then the insurance company contacted the FBI." Tidwell picked up his knife and sliced one of his scones lengthwise.

"And then they contacted you," Theodosia said. She was stunned. "Will the insurance company do that? I mean, will they pay money to get the jewels back?"

"It's highly doubtful. Seeing as how there was a homicide involved."

"Wait a minute, how did the thief even know which insurance company to contact?"

"It was all spelled out in the newspaper. A pithy quote delivered by one of United Insurance's media-loving PR people. And one that our diligent robbers obviously picked up on."

"You said the robbers wanted to ransom back *part* of the stolen jewels? Which part?"

"That I do not know. Except that it probably doesn't involve diamonds. They're far too valuable and portable once they're pried from their settings."

Theodosia sat back in her chair. "That's just awful."

Tidwell slathered jam on his scone and took a bite. "Which part do you find distasteful?" He gave a perfunctory smile as he chewed.

"All of it."

"Well, it is crime. When you're dealing with a criminal element, you've got to expect a few rough edges."

"I get that," Theodosia said. She hated it when he played coy with her. "Okay, what about that lady last night? Do you think she'll ever get her emerald necklace back?"

"Probably not."

Theodosia shook her head. "Why not?"

Tidwell sighed. "Because the smash-and-grab at Heart's Desire was strictly business. While the robbery at the opera last night . . . well, it struck me as being slightly more whimsical. More like . . . sport."

She stared at him. "Whimsy. Sport. Explain, please."

"It's possible one of the thieves was toying with us," Tidwell said. "Taunting us."

"So you're saying that whoever struck last night might have been part of the same Heart's Desire gang?"

"I think it's possible. I also think that whoever is in charge of this gang, whoever masterminded the Heart's Desire robbery, might have decided to stick around Charleston for a while."

"Because the pickings are good," Theodosia murmured. She thought about all the wealthy people who lived in the area that was commonly referred to as Below Broad. In other words, the fat-cat district. This was where many of the pedigreed people lived, the descendants of Charleston's founders. They were the lucky ones who'd inherited great-*grandmère*'s jewelry, Dresden china, sterling silver candlesticks, Chippendale furniture,

French antiques, and oil paintings. And now it might all be at risk.

The other thing that haunted Theodosia was the fact that a priceless Fabergé egg was probably rolling into town right about now. A fancy, jeweled egg that would be on display at the Heritage Society starting this Saturday evening. Was it going to sit in its glass display case like a glorified magnet, attracting every petty thief or organized gang in the area? She was afraid that it just might.

Tidwell hadn't been gone five minutes when Brooke came in. She looked unsettled and a little scared. When she spotted Theodosia standing at the counter, she rushed over and said, "Have you heard?"

"About the insurance ransom? Yes," Theodosia said. "Detective Tidwell was just in here a few minutes ago and spilled the beans to me."

"I don't know what to make of all these new developments," Brooke said. "I mean, the thieves contacting the insurance company? And then that horrible robbery last night? At the opera, no less. Smack-dab in the middle of hundreds of people. I was just reading about it in the *Post and Courier.* And it's all people are talking about up and down Church Street."

"I know," Theodosia said. "I was there last night."

Brooke's eyes widened in surprise. "You were? Really?"

"With Drayton. Our seats were literally thirty feet away from that poor woman whose necklace was stolen."

"Ripped right off her neck, I heard. And then her poor husband got clobbered for trying to defend her. It's almost like the Heart's Desire robbery and Kaitlin's killing all over again! Oh, Theo, what's going on?"

"I don't know, Brooke," Theodosia said. "The robbery at the opera was horribly bizarre and daring. And now this ransom situation . . ."

Brooke nodded sadly. "It's unsettling . . . terrifying."

"Which pieces of jewelry did the thieves offer to ransom back to the insurance company—do you know?"

Brooke bit her lip. "Some vintage Tiffany and Cartier bracelets, a suite of Tahitian pearls, and some gemstone rings and necklaces. I think they're trying that tactic because those particular pieces might be more difficult to fence."

"And the other pieces?"

"Hah," Brooke said. "The really important pieces, a Van Cleef necklace and earrings set and a spectacular alexandrite necklace, were never even mentioned in the ransom offer."

"The alexandrite," Theodosia said slowly. Something had just pinged deep inside her brain. "What can you tell me about that piece?"

"Oh . . . well," Brooke said, a little flustered by the question. "I don't know if you're aware of this, but alexandrite is an extremely rare gemstone. It was named after Czar Alexander II. And the bluish-purple crystals that characterize the highest quality alexandrite were first discovered in the old emerald mines in Russia's Ural Mountains."

Theodosia gave Brooke a slightly crooked gaze. "What do you know about your event crasher, Professor Warren Shepley?"

Brooke shook her head. "Nothing, really. The police haven't told me a thing. Why do you ask?"

"Shepley's a professor of Russian literature."

"What!" Brooke's face contorted with a mixture of surprise and anger. "You don't think he was . . . Well, do you think Shepley was at my shop because he was after the alexandrite?" A tear slid down her face. "Do you think *he's* the mastermind?"

"I don't know," Theodosia said. "But I'm going to try and find out."

"How are you going to do that?"

"I don't know yet."

But Theodosia did know. Because even as she hugged Brooke again and gently ushered her out the door, a plan was beginning to form in her brain.

"Drayton," she said, leaning over the counter. "I have to run out for two minutes."

Panic filled Drayton's face. "You can't. You're not allowed. We're totally jammed and there's no way I can . . ."

She held up two fingers. "Two minutes. And I promise, cross my heart, that I'll be back in a flash."

Before Drayton could launch a more nuanced protest, Theodosia was out the door and running down Church Street. But she didn't have to run far. Her destination was just three doors down at the Antiquarian Bookshop. She ripped open the door and dashed inside.

Lois Chamberlain looked up from behind the glass counter that housed a few of her rare books, and a pleasant smile spread across her face. "Hi, Theodosia. You look like you're in a mad rush." Lois was a tidy-looking woman in her late fifties, a retired librarian who wore purple half-glasses and plaited her gray hair in a fat braid down her back.

Theodosia touched a hand to her chest. "I am a little crazed, Lois. Listen, I have kind of a strange question for you. Are you acquainted with a man by the name of Professor Warren Shepley? He's been doing research here in Charleston and I was wondering if perhaps he's dropped by your shop?"

"That's weird," Lois said. She took off her glasses and stared at Theodosia.

"What's weird?"

"He stopped in here yesterday."

Theodosia shot a finger at her. "Looking for books on Russian literature, right?"

"Eighteenth century," Lois fired back.

"So you know him." Theodosia couldn't believe her luck. Or karma or serendipity or whatever you wanted to call it.

"It's more like I know *of* him," Lois said. "He poked around in here for an hour or so, then bought a couple of books. One on Peter the Great, another on the poetry of Trediakovsky. He seemed like an okay guy, but a typical academic. A little standoffish, nose poked inside a book, asked just a couple of pertinent questions."

"What else do you know about him?" Theodosia asked.

Lois thought for a moment. "Hmm, not much at all. He wasn't exactly big on chitchat, if you know what I mean."

"Anything at all would be of help."

"Well, I do know that he's staying at the Rosewalk Inn."

"You," Theodosia gasped, "are totally brilliant. In fact, I'm going to buy you a fancy dinner at Poogan's Porch as soon as I solve this case." And she blew back out the door.

"Case?" Lois said in her wake. "What case?"

19

❧

Drayton was delighted to see that Theodosia had returned as promised. "You're back," he said. "Thank holy heaven. Haley's already popped out to take a few orders. It seems we have some very anxious and hungry customers." He glanced around the tea shop. "And lots of them, as you can plainly see."

"Then I'll run back and start grabbing luncheon orders," Theodosia said.

"Good. And please don't forget about Mrs. Biatek at table six. She brought in her daughter, Kristen, and two friends. They're waiting to place their order."

"Got it." Theodosia ducked into the kitchen, which was filled with the aromas of baking bread, stir-fry chicken, and shrimp gumbo. Haley had outdone herself yet again.

"Thank goodness you're back," Haley said. "We were beginning to worry."

Theodosia grabbed two shrimp gumbos. "These are for which table?"

"Table four." Haley added a Waldorf tea sandwich to each plate. "Then come right back here. By the time you serve those, I'll have a couple more luncheon plates all fixed up and ready to go."

Theodosia worked frantically for the next twenty minutes. Serving lunches, taking orders, pouring tea, serving more lunches. Finally, when every customer had been taken care of, she dashed up to the counter to tell Drayton what she'd learned.

"I found out where Professor Shepley is staying," Theodosia said, almost breathlessly.

His brows shot up. "Shepley, the mysterious event crasher?"

"That's right. He's got a room over at the Rosewalk Inn."

"The B and B that Tyrone Chandler manages. So now this Shepley character is on your short list of suspects, too?"

"My list's not that short anymore," Theodosia said. "I keep adding to it."

"So what do you plan to do about Shepley? Go over and accost this poor visiting academic? Demand that he confess to being an international jewel thief?"

"I've got a much better idea," Theodosia said. "I'm going to call over to the Rosewalk Inn and extend a complimentary invitation to Shepley. Invite him to our Romanov Tea tonight."

Drayton's face pulled into a slow grin. "My, aren't you a devilishly clever little investigator."

Just when Theodosia was clearing two tables at once, balancing a gray plastic tub of dishes on one hip, Delaine came sauntering in.

"Theodosia!" she exclaimed. She was wearing a cranberry-colored suede jacket, black pencil skirt, and had a half-dozen gold chains strung around her neck. She carried a black suede

Chanel bag that probably cost as much as a down payment on a house.

"Delaine," Theodosia said back. "Are you just slumming or did you stop by for lunch?"

Delaine cocked her head and considered this. "I suppose I could go for a nibble. As long as it's low carb."

"We can make that happen. At least Haley can." Delaine was obviously off her grapefruit juice and cider vinegar cleanse and back on her low-carb program.

"But that's not why I'm here," Delaine said.

Okay, why are you here?

Delaine offered Theodosia a cheesy grin. "I wanted to inform you that I've selected three very special dresses for you."

Wait, did I order three dresses? Was I shopping in my sleep? Did I drink and dial? Or maybe I have temporary amnesia because I sure don't remember ordering any dresses.

"Dresses?" Theodosia said, still racking her brain. "For . . . what purpose?"

Delaine tossed her head like a nervous show pony. "More like for what occasion." When Theodosia didn't respond, she said, "For Saturday night, you silly girl. To wear to the Rare Antiquities Show at the Heritage Society." When Theodosia's face finally registered surprise (if not dismay), she continued on. "We simply can't have you wearing that same old black cocktail dress again. I mean, haven't we all had our fill of that particular *dress*?" She said the word *dress* like she was referring to moldy cleaning rags.

"But I . . ."

Delaine gave Theodosia a sly smile. "Besides, you're back on the market, girlfriend. Which means you need to look sexy and sultry so you can attract one of Charleston's eligible bachelors."

"Really?" Theodosia said. "And here I thought that was your role."

"Well, dear, it often is," Delaine said smoothly, unfazed by the slight jab. "But it just so happens I'm seeing Mr. Gilles right now. Exclusively, I might add."

"But he doesn't actually live here, does he?" *So how exclusive can that be?*

"He does for the time being," Delaine said. "And that's good enough for me." She giggled. "A girl doesn't always have to settle for Mr. Right. Sometimes Mr. Right Now is better."

By the time Theodosia brought a salad, grilled chicken breast, and pot of jasmine tea to Delaine's table, she wasn't sitting alone. Turns out Grace Dawson had wandered into the tea shop and Delaine had invited Grace to join her for lunch.

"You finally made it," Theodosia said to Grace. She was delighted to see her. With or without the Dobermans.

"I surely did," Grace said with open enthusiasm. "I've heard so many people rave about the Indigo Tea Shop that I finally decided to drop by." She glanced at Delaine's lunch. "I hope I'm not too late."

"Of course not," Theodosia said. "What would you say to a bowl of shrimp gumbo, a tea sandwich, and an orange scone?"

Grace's eyes lit up. "I'd say, bring it on. It all sounds wonderful."

When Theodosia returned with a pot of tea and Grace's luncheon plate, the conversation had turned to the ill-fated opera last night.

"I was there!" Grace exclaimed to Theodosia and Delaine.

"You were there with Mr. Rinicker?" Theodosia asked. Here was her chance to nail down his whereabouts.

"No," Grace said. "I went with a friend. Lionel was busy with some sort of business. A meeting, I guess."

"Well, I was there, too," Delaine told Grace. "In fact, I ran into Theodosia and Drayton at intermission."

"So we were all there," Grace said. "Wow."

But where was Rinicker? Theodosia wondered. *Where was he really?*

"To tell the truth," Grace said, "that incident left me feeling a little heartsick. I mean . . . opening night with *La Bohème*, everyone dressed to the nines, and all that delicious anticipation." Her face shone with excitement for a few moments, and then her shoulders sagged. "Such a magnificent first act to be followed by that awful robbery. I think it rattled everyone to their core."

"That's for sure," Delaine said, all wide-eyed, as if she was practically reliving the event. "That robbery struck me as a bad omen, a harbinger of things to come."

Grace gave a little shiver. "Please don't say that, Delaine. It's hard enough living all by myself when the wind comes ripping off the Atlantic and the olive tree branches are tick-ticking against my bedroom window."

"Ooh," Delaine squealed. "You sound just like one of those scary stories by Edgar Allan Poe."

Just when Theodosia figured their luncheon service was over, just when she was gearing up to focus on tonight's Romanov Tea, the FBI came marching in.

Well, not the entire bureau, of course. Just Agents Zimmer and Hurley.

"I hope we're not interrupting," Zimmer said. He had the same clean-cut, sharp-eyed look that Theodosia remembered. An interesting-looking man, but a little intense. Maybe too intense.

"Of course you're interrupting," Theodosia said with a smile. "But come on in anyway. You can fill me in on what you've been up to."

Zimmer and Hurley followed her to a table and sat down.

"I'm afraid we can't really share any information with you," Zimmer said. "Agency policy is to remain fairly tight-lipped concerning ongoing cases."

"Well, you can at least tell me if there's anything new on the ransom offer," Theodosia said.

"You're not supposed to know about that," Hurley said.

Theodosia smiled. She'd detected a pinprick of surprise on his part. "Oh please. The copy desk at the *Charleston Post and Courier* probably knows all about it."

Hurley looked less than pleased.

"Okay, then maybe you can tell me where you are concerning Luke Andros," Theodosia said.

Zimmer and Hurley exchanged looks.

"How on earth do you know about him?" Zimmer asked.

"I'm the one who passed on some speculative information to Detective Tidwell," Theodosia said. "Who obviously passed it on to you."

Hurley glanced at Zimmer. "How is she getting this stuff?"

"Look around," Theodosia said. "It's a tea shop. People drink tea, let down their guard, and talk."

Zimmer managed a feeble smile. "Maybe we should be spending more time here."

"Maybe you should," Theodosia said. "And by the way, is there anything more on Mr. Clement and his rock-climbing hammer?"

Zimmer placed both hands on the table and pressed down. "Excuse me?"

"And what about Professor Shepley?" Theodosia continued. "I know for a fact that he crashed Brooke's jewelry show. Is he under investigation or am I the only one who thinks there might be more to him than meets the eye?"

"Miss Browning," Agent Zimmer said, a warning tone creeping into his voice. "I'm going to ask you to please not speak about these things to anyone."

"Even if they're just my personal suspicions?"

"Especially if they're just suspicions. It would be grossly unfair to all the people concerned."

"Okay," Theodosia said. "I guess I can see that. Just one more thing, then."

Both agents looked askance at her.

"What do you want to know?" Hurley asked in a tentative voice.

"Do you think the robbery of the emerald necklace at the opera last night is connected to the Heart's Desire robbery?"

"And you know about that robbery . . . how?" Zimmer asked.

"Because I was there," Theodosia said. "Me and about half of Charleston. So I suppose there are a whole lot of people wondering what's going on. If the two crimes might even be connected."

Red-faced and smarting, the FBI agents clammed up completely. Theodosia decided if they weren't going to play nice and share, then she wasn't about to grace them with complimentary tea and scones. They'd reached a mountain of an impasse and there was nothing that could be done. After a few minutes of conversation that was polite verging on brittle, she ushered them to the door.

"You certainly didn't show your warm and fuzzy side to those two," Drayton observed once Zimmer and Hurley had left.

"That's because they weren't particularly open with me."

"They're the FBI," Drayton said. "What do you expect? They have a long and storied history of not being open or friendly. Of demanding answers but never giving any in return."

"Still," Theodosia said, "they could have been a little more gracious."

"Maybe you should have invited them to the tea tonight," Drayton smirked. "You could have seated them next to Professor Shepley. Then sat back and watched the sparks fly."

"You know," Theodosia said. "I thought about that. But then I wouldn't have the fun of questioning Shepley myself."

20

❧

"Drayton," Haley sang out, "did you remember to bring in your Russian samovar?" She was standing in the middle of the tea shop, looking around expectantly.

Drayton leaned around the counter. "If you glance to your left, my dear Haley, you'll find that it's sitting right there on the pecan sideboard."

Haley looked over her shoulder and saw the elaborate silver-and-brass samovar. "Oh. I guess you did remember. Then how about the bouquets?"

"They're in my office," Theodosia said. "Gerbera daisies and red carnations. You can start bringing them out if you want."

It was five o'clock in the afternoon and preparations for their Romanov Tea were finally winding down. Haley had been rattling around in the kitchen for the last two hours, cooking beef Stroganoff in creamy mushroom sauce, as well as blinis and borscht. Theodosia had busied herself with decorating the tables, laying out blush-colored linens, and then setting out their Cobalt Net china by Lomonosov.

"You know I borrowed several sets of glass teacups," Drayton told her.

"Show me," Theodosia said.

Drayton promptly produced a small glass, and then popped it into a gilded metal holder with a lace design. "We have three dozen of these. Perfect for our Russian tea, yes?"

"And so authentic," Theodosia said. "Our guests are going to eat this up."

"Along with the food," Haley said. "Which really is the whole point." She looked around at the tables. "So what else?"

"Well, the flowers," Theodosia said. "And we borrowed some of those little Russian nesting dolls to liven things up."

"No bronze busts of Lenin or Trotsky?" Haley asked. "No Socialist posters on the walls?"

"Nooo," Drayton said, picking up a bright-pink box from the counter. "This is more of a czarist tea. Which is why I had the Toulouse Bakery make us a batch of cake and candy Fabergé eggs."

Haley reached out anxiously. "Ooh, let me see."

Drayton handed over the box. "Be careful, now. Those little cakes are fragile."

Haley flipped open the lid and gingerly removed one of the eggs. There were an even dozen pink, blue, and cream-colored eggs inside the box, all decorated with swaths of colored frosting and dots of candy that approximated pearls and gemstones. "These are absolutely precious. So I should just set a couple on each table?"

"That should do it," Drayton said. "Only let's display them in those enameled Khokhloma bowls we found at Ladybug Gifts down the street. It'll show them off better."

"Will we be serving Russian caravan tea?" Theodosia asked. "Or have you come up with something else?"

"I'm going to brew the Russian caravan tea in traditional teapots," Drayton said. "And then we'll serve a black tea spiced with cinnamon and cloves out of the samovar." He smiled.

"One to appeal to tea purists and one for those with more of a sweet tooth."

"Which is just about everybody," Haley said.

Theodosia squinted at Drayton. "Since we're calling this a Romanov Tea, how much are you going to say about the Fabergé egg that's going to be at the Heritage Society?" She'd been turning this question over and over in her mind. She'd nursed the desire to stage a Romanov Tea long before she'd even heard about the Fabergé egg. But now . . . now it seemed like the two were intertwined. So they almost had to mention it.

"When I introduce the menu," Drayton said, "I'll also talk about the Fabergé egg."

"But don't dwell on it too much," Theodosia said. "Because . . . well, you know why."

Timothy Neville was one of their first guests to arrive. Looking like a country squire in his dark-green Donegal-pattern tweed jacket, he shook hands with Drayton and said, somewhat nervously, "I've put on extra protection for Saturday night."

"I'm sure we'll be fine," Drayton responded.

Theodosia quickly inserted herself into their conversation. "Has the Fabergé egg arrived yet?"

"It showed up in an armored truck about an hour ago," Timothy told them.

"Then maybe that extra protection should start right now," Theodosia said.

Timothy focused on her. "Ah, but the egg's not at the Heritage Society."

"Where is it?" Theodosia asked.

"Locked tightly in a vault," Timothy said. "A bank vault."

"Smart idea," Drayton said.

"Too bad it can't stay there," Theodosia said as Drayton led Timothy to his table.

Much to Theodosia's surprise, Lionel Rinicker showed up next. And not with Grace Dawson, but with a man she'd never met before.

"I didn't realize you had tickets to our Romanov Tea," Theodosia said to Rinicker.

"I don't," Rinicker said. "My friend Robin Westlake bought tickets and invited me along. Have you met Robin, Theodosia?"

"No, I have not." She shook hands with a middle-aged, balding man with a slightly florid face. "Nice to meet you, Mr. Westlake."

"We're really looking forward to this tea," Westlake said with great enthusiasm.

"Glad to hear it. And your seats are right this way," Theodosia told the two men as she led them to their table. "I think you'll enjoy our food tonight. But I have to warn you, our menu is substantially more robust than just a cream tea or luncheon tea."

"That's fine with me," Rinicker said. "I'm a bachelor who rarely cooks, so this is going to be a real treat."

"How did your segment turn out yesterday at Channel 8?" Theodosia asked as the men settled into their seats.

"Fairly well," Rinicker said. "But I barely had time to mumble five words and . . . whoosh . . . the time was gone."

"I guess that's the nature of sound bites these days," Theodosia told him. "When I worked in marketing, we mostly produced thirty-second TV commercials; now you're lucky if you get to do a ten-second spot."

That was the last free moment Theodosia had, because their guests began pouring in like crazy. Many were friends from neighboring shops down the block, some were Historic District neighbors and tea regulars, and a few guests were brand-new to them. Theodosia and Drayton did quick meet and greets as they continued to usher guests to their tables.

When Professor Warren Shepley came in, Theodosia recognized him immediately. He was the guest with the quizzical look, baggy brown jacket with elbow patches, and a leather-bound book tucked under one arm.

"Professor Shepley?" she said.

He gave a slightly startled look. "Yes?" He was fairly short, with a shock of frizzy white hair and horn-rimmed glasses. His complexion was ruddy, as if he spent a lot of time outdoors, and his eyes were a watery blue.

"I'm Theodosia Browning. Welcome to my tea shop."

A smile touched Shepley's face. "You're the lady who invited me."

"Because I thought you might enjoy it." Theodosia knew he'd wonder about his invitation. "And because I thought our Romanov Tea dovetailed with your area of study." She gripped his hand, studying him. "And because my friend Lois, at the Antiquarian Bookshop next door, said you've been a good customer."

"Oh," Shepley said, his puzzlement starting to dissolve. "Okay, then."

Of course, Delaine showed up, clinging to the arm of Renaldo Gilles, her paramour du jour.

"Theodosia," Delaine exclaimed. "We're so thrilled to be here. I've been singing your praises sky-high to Renaldo." She squeezed his arm and fixed him with a starry-eyed gaze. "Haven't I, pumpkin love?"

"Yes, you have, sweet potato," Gilles murmured in return.

"I told him that you serve some of the finest food in Charleston," Delaine simpered. "Of course, that's not counting the Peninsula Grill, Beaumont's, Carolina's, and a few other notables."

"Of course," Theodosia said, hustling them along. "And I have a reserved table for the two of you right over here."

"Oh, we get our own special table," Delaine exclaimed. "How romantic. With flowers and candles and everything."

"Looks like we've got a full house," Theodosia said to Drayton as she surveyed the tea room.

Drayton consulted a clipboard. "I can't believe we packed forty-two warm bodies in here. I think it's a new record."

"Forty. We still have two empty seats."

"Oh dear, I wonder who hasn't . . . ?"

The door banged open loudly as Sabrina and Luke Andros came charging in.

"Looks like we won't be stuck with two empty places after all," Theodosia murmured.

"We're so sorry," Sabrina babbled to them. "We apologize for being late, but we had a last-minute meeting with a client."

"A prospective yacht buyer?" Theodosia asked as she took Sabrina's coat.

Luke nodded. "That's exactly right. It's a funny thing about wealthy people . . . as soon as they make up their mind they want something, everybody else has to instantly drop what they're doing and tend to their needs."

"I know the feeling," Theodosia said.

Once Theodosia and Drayton had filled everyone's teacups, once the air hummed with conversation and the candles flickered enticingly in the darkened tea shop, Drayton stepped to the center of the room.

"Welcome," he said, "to our Romanov Tea. Tonight we plan to turn back the clock to the romantic era of the Russian czars and dazzle you with a sampling of excellent food and tea."

Theodosia stepped forward to join Drayton. "I'm sure you've noticed that you've all been served tea in small glasses set in elegant metal holders. This is the traditional way tea was served back in that era." She paused as there were murmurs of approval. "We've also created a traditional Russian feast for you tonight. Our appetizers consist of hot beet borscht and blinis with smoked salmon. We have a chilled potato-and-herring salad for you, and your entrée will be a rich beef Stroganoff. For dessert we'll be serving Russian tea cake cookies as well as a tarte tatin, which is a caramelized apple tart."

"For those of you who chose our Russian caravan tea," Drayton said, "I urge you to also try our spiced tea served from a traditional Russian samovar. I think you'll definitely find it to your liking. For, as an old Russian saying goes, 'Where there is tea, there is paradise.'"

As Drayton's melodic words hung in the flickering light, with the strains of balalaika music playing over the sound system, Haley suddenly appeared carrying an enormous silver tray. Drayton whisked it from her hands, and then he and Theodosia circled the tables to serve their first course.

"This is traditional borscht," Drayton told the guests. "Served with a cool dollop of sour cream to compliment the soup's heat and zest."

From that point on, Theodosia and Drayton were frantically busy. Even as they accepted high praise from their guests, they removed dishes, served the blinis and salad course, and then took those dishes away and moved on to the entrée.

"This is a madhouse," Drayton said when he met up with Theodosia at the counter. "We can barely keep up."

"We should have asked Miss Dimple to come in and help," Theodosia said.

"Let's at least get the old girl in here tomorrow night for our Full Monty Tea."

"You'll get no argument from me," Theodosia said. "And who was the genius who decided to hold three event teas in one week?"

Drayton pointed a finger at her. "You."

"Well, you have my permission to smack me upside the head if I ever suggest it again, will you? Because this is down-right crazy."

"Hold that thought," Drayton said. "While we hurry up and serve dessert."

Their desserts, Russian tea cakes and tarte tatins, were met with a chorus of praise and compliments. And as forks clinked against china plates, as more steaming tea was sipped and enjoyed, as conversations became ebullient, Drayton stepped in to say a final word.

"In the year 1638," Drayton said, "a Russian ambassador purchased one hundred and thirty pounds of fine black tea from a Mongol khan. He delivered that tea to Czar Aleksey Mikhaylovich, where it became an instant hit in the royal Russian court. In fact, the czar was so taken by this excellent beverage that he sent the khan one hundred sable skins as a token of his gratitude." There were murmurs of approval and a spattering of applause. Drayton continued. "In keeping with the spirit of our Romanov Tea, I want to remind you all about the precious Fabergé egg that will be on display at the Heritage Society this coming weekend."

As Drayton continued speaking, Theodosia began to worry. She worried that Drayton might be hyping the Fabergé egg too much. She worried about Sabrina and Luke Andros, who were sitting right there, listening with rapt attention. Professor Shepley, whom she still wanted to question, also seemed completely agog. But mostly she worried about a repeat performance, of thieves storming the Great Hall and smashing the cases and getting their hands on that precious jeweled egg.

That simply cannot happen, she told herself.

Theodosia wasn't sure how she was going to thwart a gang of international jewel thieves, she just knew she had to. If she could do that, she could also exact a small token of justice for Brooke.

"Theodosia?" Drayton said for a second time.

She pulled herself back into the here and now. "What?"

Now there were bursts of giggles from the guests.

Drayton looked at her expectantly. So did many of the guests. "You were going to say a few words?"

"Yes. Of course." Theodosia snapped to, her heels clicking sharply against the wooden floor as she hurried over to join him. "Yes. I just wanted to thank everyone for coming tonight. When one plans a special event tea like this, you never know how well it's going to be received." She turned in a circle, a smile on her face. "Or if anyone is even going to show up."

"We love you!" Delaine called out.

"But it looks as though my fears were unfounded," Theodosia continued. "So thank you all for coming. I hope you enjoyed the food, and I hope you decide to join us at the Indigo Tea Shop for our next special event tea."

Thunderous applause rocked the tea room as Theodosia and Drayton smiled their appreciation. Then all the chairs screeched back as the guests seemed to jump up at once for a group mingle.

"It's gridlock," Drayton chuckled as they were quickly enveloped by the crowd.

"We can't possibly clear these tables with everyone milling around like this," Theodosia said with a shrug.

"Then we'll just let them go. We'll bid everyone good night and do our work later."

"You'll grab the coats?" Theodosia asked him. "The ones that are stashed in my office, anyway?"

"Yes," Drayton said. "But you better grab that professor of yours while you can and start shaking him down."

"I will."

Theodosia collared Professor Shepley just as he was about to slip out the front door. "I'm so sorry we didn't get a chance to talk," she said, grabbing hold of his sleeve and reeling him in like a struggling redfish on a hook.

"It was a lovely dinner," Shepley told her. "And I'm pleased to say I made the acquaintance of some of your wonderful Charleston neighbors."

"We're a friendly bunch, that's for sure. But you probably know that already. I understand you've been staying at the Rosewalk Inn?"

Shepley nodded. "Yes, but not for much longer. My work here is almost finished."

Theodosia smiled as she hung on to him. "What work is that?"

He looked slightly disconcerted. "I'm writing a book on the influence of the baroque and rococo on eighteenth-century Russian literature."

"Uh-huh, that's nice. And when are you leaving?"

"I was planning to drive back to Savannah on Monday. Possibly Sunday."

"Do you have any plans for Saturday?" Theodosia knew she was pressing him, maybe even scaring him a little, but didn't much care.

"Well, um . . . yes, I suppose I might. I just now learned about the Fabergé egg that's going to be on display at the Heritage Society."

"Really."

"I hadn't heard about it until your man mentioned it. Drayton? Is that his name?"

Theodosia ground her teeth together. "That's right." She pinched Shepley's arm even more tightly.

"I was thinking I might drop by for the opening party. Try to wangle an invitation. A sort of quid pro quo, one academic institution to another."

"Wouldn't that be lovely," she spat out.

"But I . . ." Shepley gave a vigorous tug and broke free,

his jacket finally slipping through Theodosia's fingers. "Now I really must be going."

Theodosia waved after him. "Bye-bye, I'll be looking for you." *Will I ever.*

"How shall I put this," Drayton said. "It was an event to remember."

They were standing in the darkened tea room, candles guttering in their pewter holders, dirty dishes littering the tables. The flowers looked peaked in their glass vases and most of the candy Fabergé eggs had disappeared. Walked out the door with the guests. Theodosia hoped petty theft wasn't a bad omen.

"I'd say our tea was a huge success," Haley said. She was puttering around at one of the tables, stacking dishes. "I mean, our guests ate everything we put on the table. Seemed to enjoy it, too."

"It *was* a success," Drayton said. He glanced at Theodosia, who hadn't said anything. "Don't you think so, Theo?"

"Smashing," she said. Then winced. Maybe *smashing* wasn't the best word for it. *Smashing* brought back memories of . . .

"Are you okay, Theo?" Haley asked in a tentative voice. "You had kind of a funny look on your face for a moment."

"I'm just tired," Theodosia said. She wasn't really tired, she'd just been thinking about Brooke and Kaitlin.

"You're not, like, mad about anything, are you? Mad at me?"

Theodosia turned and touched a hand to Haley's shoulder. "Not in the least. In fact, I should be thanking my lucky stars that we have you on our team. You're the one who was in the kitchen today, cranking it out like crazy right up to the bitter end."

Haley ducked her head. "That's okay. It's what I do. What I love to do."

"And now I think you'd better run upstairs and take it

easy while Drayton and I clean up." Haley had moved into the apartment above the tea shop, where Theodosia used to live.

Haley looked surprised. "Are you sure? You don't want me to stick around and help with the cleanup?"

"Absolutely not," Theodosia said. "You take off, okay?"

"That's right," Drayton chimed in. "We'll handle it from here."

"Well . . . okay," Haley said. "Hey, thanks a bunch."

"So what did you find out about Professor Shepley?" Drayton asked. Haley had finally gone upstairs, and he and Theodosia were stacking dishes into the dishwasher.

"He's sticking around here until Sunday or Monday," Theodosia said.

"Because . . . ?"

"Because he said, and I quote, he's going to try to 'wangle an invitation' to the Heritage Society's big show. He also claims to have been unaware of the presence of a Fabergé egg until you so helpfully brought it up tonight."

"Maybe he's telling the truth."

"And maybe he's not," Theodosia said. "Which is why Shepley is blipping on my radar screen like an errant satellite that's suddenly dropped out of orbit."

"But you're also suspicious of Sabrina and Luke Andros and Lionel Rinicker," Drayton said. "And let's not forget Billy Grainger from last night. Good old Motorcycle Billy."

"There's another person I'd like to take a closer look at, too."

Drayton looked surprised. "You can't be serious." And then, because Drayton really was the curious sort, he said, "Who is that?"

"The rock-hammer guy," Theodosia said. "A fellow named Marcus Clement."

"This is because of those hammer images that Tidwell showed you?"

Theodosia nodded. "That's right. Clement's a rock climber. He supposedly owns one of those rock-climbing hammers like the thieves used to . . ."

"Smash open the cases," Drayton said.

"Yes."

"How did you come by this person's name?"

"I have my ways."

"Theodosia." Drayton half closed one eye and fixed her with a disapproving look.

So Theodosia gave him the rundown on Clement. And how Tidwell had already checked on the fact that he'd recently purchased a rock hammer.

"Wait a minute," Drayton said. "You're losing me. Who bought the hammer?"

"He did." She paused. "Clement did. And then I did, too."

"*What?*"

She explained how she'd gone to Triple Peak and bought a rock hammer that was identical to the one Clement had purchased. And then had it delivered to his home.

"And you did this, why?"

"Well . . . so I could clandestinely obtain his address."

"Of course, silly me. So now that you have Mr. Clement's home address, what do you plan to do about it? Or shouldn't I ask?"

"You can ask. But I'd rather you just come along quietly with me."

"With you." Drayton rolled his eyes, looking more than a little exasperated. "You want me to . . ."

"Snoop around Clement's house," Theodosia said. "That's right."

Drayton smoothed a hand across the top of his head. "I'm getting too old for these ridiculous capers."

"Don't say that, Drayton. You're my voice of reason."

"How could I be? Since you rarely heed my advice. Or warnings."

Theodosia stood with her hands on her hips, a mischievous smile playing at her lips. "So. Are you coming with me or what?"

"Yes, but for one reason only," Drayton said. "I might have to post bail if you get caught."

21

It *was almost* ten thirty when they rolled past Marcus Clement's home. Theodosia checked the address she'd jotted down against the numbers on the house. Then she checked it again. They were in a neighborhood with a mixture of clapboard, stucco, and ubiquitous Charleston single houses. The asphalt streets were pitted, and the lawns and trees looked a little bedraggled.

"This is it?" Drayton asked.

"Yup. And thanks for coming, by the way. I appreciate having your company."

"Not that I had much say in the matter."

"Oh, come on, Drayton. Where's your sense of adventure?"

"Back home in my sock drawer, if you really must know."

"But what if this guy turns out to be the ringleader of the gang that stormed Heart's Desire and ended up killing Kaitlin?"

Drayton pursed his lips.

Theodosia gripped her steering wheel. "Well?" She was fired up and ready to explore.

"Then I'd prefer he be hunted down by a federal agency and appropriately charged with robbery and murder. Not tracked by Nancy Drew and an aging Hardy Boy."

Theodosia opened the driver's-side door. "Come on, let's go take a look."

Drayton got out carefully. "I think we should just stroll casually past his house. But no prowling the premises like we did last night. Agreed?"

Theodosia's whisper floated back to him in the darkness. *"Come on."*

They strolled past a drab-looking little bungalow that had probably once been painted a Caribbean blue. But wind, heat, humidity, and rain—all the elements present in typical Charleston weather—had ground it down to silvered wood. No lights shone, it looked like no one was home.

"Charming," Drayton remarked in a droll tone. "Homey. All it needs is an old-fashioned washing machine on the front lawn. Broken, of course."

"Don't be snobby," Theodosia said.

They walked past the house, turned the corner, and then walked back via a gravel alley.

"I want to take a closer look," Theodosia said once they were standing directly behind the house.

"Not a good idea."

"Just a peek." Theodosia tiptoed up to the back porch, a screened-in affair, and looked in.

"You see," Drayton whispered loudly. "Nobody's home. I think we should go."

"Clement isn't here, but look," Theodosia said excitedly. "There's a package tucked inside. Looks like it was left by UPS."

Drayton walked up and pressed his face to the screen door. "What do you suppose it is?"

"I'm guessing it's the rock hammer I ordered for him."

Drayton pulled back. "Wait a minute, you really did do that? I thought you cooked up some shaggy-dog story to lure me over here."

"I'm gonna go in and look. See if it is the rock hammer."

Drayton grabbed her arm. "Please don't."

"You worry too much."

"You don't worry enough."

"Think of it as part of our investigation."

"You're acting just like the FBI, you know that?" Drayton said.

"Not on your life," Theodosia said. "I don't believe in wiretapping or trampling all over people's rights."

"You just don't mind trampling your way onto their back porch."

Theodosia pulled open the screen door. "I really wish you hadn't said that." And ducked inside.

"Theo!" Drayton whispered.

"Shhh, I'm checking the package." She bent forward and scanned the label. "Yup, it's the one I sent."

"Get back out here."

"I just want to . . . look around." She wondered if maybe her rock climber had left a key somewhere. Rock climbers were casual, trusting sorts, weren't they? Maybe hanging near the door . . . ? She ran a hand up the doorjamb to check. No luck. Or under the mat? She flipped back a rubber mat and saw the glint of something shiny. A key. "I found a key, Drayton." *Do I dare?*

Drayton turned his back to her and fiddled nervously with his bow tie. "I don't want to know what you're going to do."

"Then at least give me your hankie."

"Fine," Drayton said. He pulled a hankie from his jacket pocket and passed it to her. "Blow your nose and let's get out of here. Because I really don't care to participate."

"The hankie's so I don't leave any fingerprints," Theodosia said. She slipped the key into the lock. "And I don't need you to participate, Drayton. I need you to be my *lookout*."

"This really is insanity."

Theodosia turned the key in the lock and heard a soft *click*. Just like that. Open sesame, quick and easy, no big deal. "I'm going in," she whispered, a faint, eager smile on her face.

"Please don't," Drayton whispered back. But she was already gone.

Inside, Theodosia paused in what was a small kitchen. A mélange of cooking odors hung in the air. Fried hamburger, some fried onions and potatoes. The place was warm, dark, and claustrophobic, but there was a small light on above an old Hotpoint stove that made it a little easier for her to get her bearings. In fact, as she looked around, it felt as though she'd stepped inside a vintage kitchen.

No, not vintage, Theodosia told herself. A kitchen that's never been updated. Old appliances, old curtains. Everything just . . . sad and tired.

She pulled herself back to the task at hand. Look around, she reminded herself. See if there might be something that points to Clement being a jewel thief.

Okay. If there are jewels, where would he hide them?

Her eyes went to the freezer compartment above the refrigerator. She stepped briskly across the kitchen and pulled open the freezer door. There wasn't much in there. A tray of crusty ice cubes, two frozen spaghetti dinners, a half loaf of garlic bread, and a carton of strawberry gelato.

She grabbed the gelato and pulled off the top. It was nothing but a swirl of pink dessert. With a touch of freezer burn at that.

Theodosia put the gelato back, closed the freezer door,

and spun around. What else? Where else? She stepped hesitantly across the linoleum, hearing it crackle softly beneath her feet. Felt her way along and ended up in a small living room. There was an ugly overstuffed sofa, the kind that sold for two hundred bucks at some awful furniture-barn-type place, a coordinating chair, a flat-screen TV mounted on one wall, and a small desk.

She moved to the desk and started riffling through the drawers.

There wasn't much there. Paper, pencils, a few stamps, a map of South Carolina, an envelope filled with canceled checks. She leafed through the checks, saw nothing that seemed strange or out of place. No big payoff from a fence in Miami.

"Theodosia," came a strangled voice. Drayton was calling to her.

She went back to the kitchen and found him peering nervously through the screen door.

"Let's go," he hissed. He tapped at his wristwatch. "Time's running out. It isn't safe."

"Hang on a minute." Theodosia was reluctant to give up so easily. Then her eyes fell upon a door. She stepped over and pulled it open. A dark stairway led down to a cellar. "One minute," she called again, then flipped on the cellar light, started down.

The cellar was surprisingly clean and well lit, with climbing and camping gear strewn everywhere. But it was organized chaos. A pegboard for rope, shelves for tents and backpacks and cooking gear.

But where's his rock hammer?

Theodosia poked around, opened boxes, and dug through a backpack, but couldn't find it.

If Marcus Clement had used his rock hammer to smash the glass cases at Heart's Desire, would he have disposed of it? Would he get rid of evidence that might contain microscopic particles of telltale glass? She knew it was a possibility. And as far as jewelry went, it could have already been fenced, buried for safekeeping, or stuck in any number of lock boxes across the state.

Or Marcus Clement might be completely innocent. Which meant her trip here had been in vain. A projection of her overactive imagination.

Okay, Drayton was right. She should get out of here. Quick, before somebody came home. Before they were both tagged as intruders and the police called in to investigate.

"I can't believe you stayed inside for so long," Drayton said. "You realize that was an actual home invasion." They were back in Theodosia's Jeep, sitting in the darkness, nerves positively frayed. "Probably a felony offense."

"I thought maybe . . ." Theodosia stopped. What had she thought, really? That an amateur rock climber was also a professional jewel thief? Was she grasping at straws or diligently chasing down leads? She turned on the ignition, put her Jeep in gear, and coasted slowly down the street. Just because a lead didn't pan out didn't mean . . .

"Watch out!" Drayton screamed.

Theodosia jammed her foot down on the brake and rocked to a stop. "Now what?"

Drayton was craning his neck, peering through the windshield, and then twisting and turning to look out the side window. "I think we almost hit a dog."

Theodosia's heart leapt into her throat. "Oh no. I didn't see him." It was her worst nightmare come true. She had been distracted and not concentrating on what was in the road ahead of her. And now she'd run down a poor, innocent creature. "Where is . . . ?" She followed Drayton's gaze.

"There it is," Drayton said.

Theodosia blinked. There, cowering at the edge of her headlights, was a small brown-and-white fuzzy dog. The creature looked scared, half-starved, and had apparently been wandering right down the middle of the street. "Dear Lord, do you think it's okay?" she asked.

"Poor thing," Drayton said. He immediately jumped out of the car and ran over to the dog.

"Drayton." Now Theodosia had leapt from her car, too. "Is he okay? Or she?"

"I think so." Drayton was on his hands and knees in the street, seemingly not caring that his trousers were getting filthy. He gently gathered the dog into his arms. "Poor little thing. No collar. And, look, her coat is completely matted and filthy. I do believe the little thing is a stray, that she's been trying to get by living on the street."

Theodosia knelt down and gently put a hand on the little dog's head. It was small, maybe fifteen pounds soaking wet, with floppy ears and enormous brown eyes. "It kind of looks like a King Charles Cavalier," she said.

The little dog looked at Theodosia with baleful brown eyes and shivered. Then it looked at Drayton and snuggled deeper into his arms.

"Looks like you've got a friend," Theodosia said.

"I want to take her home and give her a bath," Drayton said. "Try to figure out what to do."

"Sure," Theodosia said. "Of course."

Drayton's kitchen was warm, cozy, and well-appointed. He'd made considerable upgrades over the years, adding a countertop of reclaimed pecan, a hammered copper sink, and vintage hardware. A pair of Chippendale highboys held tins of tea and displayed part of his extensive teapot collection.

Drayton ran warm water into the sink, tested the temperature, and then gently eased the little dog into the water. "There you go. Not too hot, I hope. Just right?" He reached over and grabbed a small squeeze bottle of dish soap. "Do you think this soap is okay? I don't have any dog shampoo."

"What kind is it?" Theodosia asked.

"Dawn. The kind they use to clean seabirds with when they've been caught in an oil spill."

"Should be okay, then."

Drayton squirted soap into the water and fluttered a hand, producing a mound of suds. "When we're done here," he told the dog, "we'll find you something tasty to eat."

"She is awfully skinny," Theodosia said.

"Probably just been scrabbling through trash cans for scraps." Drayton picked up one of her front paws and scrubbed it gently, like he was doing a doggy pedicure. "We've got to plump this little lady up."

"When we're done here, I suppose we should take the poor thing to one of the local shelters."

Drayton drew back, looking horrified at the thought. "And let them incarcerate her in some dreadful cement cell? Not on your life. Honey Bee isn't going to end up in a place like that."

"I was thinking more along the lines of a rescue shelter, not San Quentin. Wait a minute . . . Honey Bee? You've already *named* her?" Theodosia had always felt that once you named an animal you assigned a certain de facto personality to it. And along with that came serious responsibility. In other words, that animal was yours. For life.

Drayton was smoothing soapsuds on the dog's back, talking quietly to ease her nervousness.

"You named her," Theodosia said again.

"That's right." Scrub, scrub. "Because I'm going to keep her."

"You're going to keep this dog?"

Drayton gave Theodosia a sideways glance. "I'm offended that you would find that so out of character for me."

A slow smile spread across Theodosia's face. "Imagine that. Drayton with a dog. Our Drayton has a soft spot in his heart after all."

Drayton touched a sudsy finger to his mouth. "Shh. Don't you dare tell a soul."

22

"*Ask Theodosia what* she did last night," Drayton said. It was Friday morning and he was standing behind the front counter brewing a pot of Madoorie Estate tea. It was a special Assam that Haley had put in a request for.

Haley looked interested. "What did you do?"

"Oh no," Theodosia said. "We're not opening that can of worms. Better you should ask Drayton what *he* did last night."

"What have you two got going on?" Haley asked. "Is there some big hairy problem I should know about?"

"Theodosia broke into someone's house," Drayton said.

"Drayton rescued a lost dog," Theodosia said.

Haley shook her head. "You guys. Always trying to get my goat and top each other with your crazy stories. Well, it's not gonna work today. We open in, like, twenty minutes and I'm way too busy to play games." She waited as Drayton filled her teacup, then she cupped a hand over it and scurried back into her kitchen.

"That didn't work out quite the way you planned, did it?" Theodosia asked.

"Do you think Haley's been a trifle overly sensitive lately?" Drayton asked.

"Haley's still upset about Sunday night. She bonded with Kaitlin and then basically saw the poor girl get killed right before her eyes. She's still processing the robbery and the death." Theodosia thought for a moment. "I think young people have a harder time handling death."

Drayton poured out cups of tea for the two of them. "And what about you? Not that you're not still young."

"I passed being upset last Tuesday," Theodosia said. "Then I dove into angry and am now veering into revenge territory."

Drayton handed her a cup of tea. "Isn't revenge one of the seven deadly sins?"

Theodosia took a sip of tea. "I don't think so. But it probably should be."

They worked together then, readying the tea shop. Lace place mats were laid down, their Royal Albert Country Roses china set out along with the Alexandra pattern silverware. Drayton had salvaged a few red carnations from the previous night and was arranging them in smaller bundles to go into crystal vases.

"You know what your professor Shepley said to me last night?" Drayton asked.

"Now he's *my* professor Shepley?" Theodosia said.

Drayton snipped at a flower stem. "That's right."

"What did he say?"

"Shepley told me that red carnations are a symbol of war and military might in Russia."

"No kidding," Theodosia said. "Did you know that when you placed your order?"

Drayton snipped another stem shorter. "Of course not." He had the faint trace of a smile on his face.

Most mornings the Indigo Tea Shop served a cream tea and today was no exception. Haley had baked lemon poppy seed scones and Drayton was preparing small dishes of Devonshire cream and strawberry jam. In the UK, a cream tea always consisted of scones, Devonshire cream, jam, and tea, and was most often served in the afternoon. But, hey, it was a morning favorite at the tea shop, so nobody was standing on ceremony.

"You think we'll be busy today?" Drayton asked. They'd already seated and served a half-dozen people.

"I do," Theodosia said. "Fridays are often our busiest days. Plus there'll be lots of tourists pouring into Charleston for the Lumiere Festival tonight."

"I've never gone to that. Is it fun?"

"The Lumiere Festival is your basic overstimulation for the eyeballs and the mind," Theodosia said. "There are light shows splashed against buildings, dancers cavorting with light sticks, colored light projections, light sculptures, LED installations by artists . . . you name it."

"So, definitely worth seeing?"

"I'd say so, though it's not to everyone's taste."

"Meaning mine," Drayton said.

Theodosia hesitated. "Well . . . your tastes can be a bit rarefied."

"Nonsense. I'm as down-to-earth as the next person."

"Hah," Theodosia said. But it was said with kindness.

Grabbing a cloth, Drayton polished a spoon until it shone. Then he laid it down carefully. "Will there be light installations around here?"

"Oh sure. And I know there are supposed to be a whole

bunch of them over in White Point Garden. Near the yacht club, too. I know that some of the boats will be lit with strings of lights."

Drayton looked interested. "Yachts, too?"

Theodosia immediately caught the gist of his question. "Interesting you should ask about that. Maybe we should walk over there tonight and take a look."

"At Gold Coast Yachts."

"You took the words right out of my mouth."

Drayton pulled down a tin of orange pekoe tea and peered at it suspiciously. "Did you ask Miss Dimple to come in today and help?"

"First call I made this morning. She said yes and that she'd be thrilled."

"Good, because I can't say I'm looking forward to presiding over our Full Monty Tea this afternoon."

"I'm about ready to lose my good humor, too," Theodosia said. "Never again; never will we schedule three major event teas in one week."

"What were we thinking?" Drayton responded. He flapped his arms like a hapless crow. "It feels like we've been jammed up all week long."

"At the time, we didn't know there was going to be a huge robbery at Heart's Desire. Or that Brooke's niece would be killed," Theodosia said. "And we didn't know that a crazy band of international jewel thieves would swoop into our city."

One of Drayton's eyebrows twitched. "Plan for the unexpected. Expect the worst?"

"That sounds fairly dour."

"I'm a fairly dour person."

"No, you're not," Theodosia said. "That's just an act. And by the way, how was Honey Bee this morning?"

Drayton's eyes lit up and he beamed. "She was *so* much better. Especially after some nourishing food and an exploratory sniff in my backyard garden. When I left, the little sweetheart was curled up fast asleep on my living room sofa."

"The antique Victorian sofa that you overpaid for at Sotheby's?"

"That's the one."

Just as Theodosia was making the rounds, a teapot filled with Irish breakfast tea in one hand, a teapot full of jasmine tea in the other, Miss Dimple toddled in. Barely five feet tall, beyond plump, and with a cap of pinkish-blond curls, Miss Dimple was seventy-something and spry as ever. She'd started out as their bookkeeper—in fact, she still came in twice a month. But what she really loved and adored was helping out at the Indigo Tea Shop.

"Thanks for calling me," Miss Dimple said, putting a hand on Theodosia's arm and giving it a friendly squeeze. "You know how I just *love* working here." She spun on the stubby little squash heels that gave her an extra inch in height, and grinned at Drayton. "Hello, Drayton, long time no see."

"My dear lady," Drayton said in his courtliest manner. "Thank you so much for taking time out of your busy day to come in and assist us."

Miss Dimple gave an airy wave. "I wouldn't pass up this opportunity for the world. When you live with your bachelor brother and a pair of old cats named Samson and Delilah, you take your fun where you can find it."

"And you're implying that we're fun?" Drayton looked mock-startled. "Horrors." Then he smiled and said, "Perhaps you'd better come over here, lovey, and let me put an apron on you."

Satisfied that the tea shop was in capable hands, Theodosia retreated to her office to take care of a little business. Not tea shop business, mind you, but investigation business on behalf of Brooke. She spent the next half hour running a number of Internet searches on her list of suspects. And came up with several photos and articles about Lionel Rinicker, Sabrina and Luke Andros, Marcus Clement, and Professor Warren Shepley.

Humming to herself, she printed everything out and stuffed the pages into her leather messenger bag. Her plan was to take it all to Brooke and see if any of this information rang a few bells.

"You're leaving us?" Drayton asked as she slipped into her suede jacket. "Right in the middle of tea service? Again?"

"I have to run something down to Brooke," Theodosia told him. "But you'll be fine. You've got Miss Dimple."

Miss Dimple patted Drayton's arm reassuringly. "That's right. You've got me, sweetie. Not to worry."

"He always worries," Theodosia told her.

Miss Dimple nodded sagely. "I think that's part of his charm."

Heart's Desire was still all boarded up, but Theodosia walked across a few clattery planks, located the temporary wooden door, and thumped on it loudly.

"Hello? Just a minute," Brooke's voice floated out to her. "Who is it?"

"It's me, Theodosia."

The door popped open and Brooke was standing there. She was dressed in blue jeans, a navy T-shirt, and had a red bandana tied in her hair. She looked youthful, perky, and, best of all, more in control of the situation. The tension lines that had etched her face a few days ago seemed to have eased.

"Come into our construction zone if you dare," Brooke said. "I'm sorry I don't have a hard hat to offer you."

"That's okay." Theodosia stepped inside the shop and looked around. All the glass had been swept up, the broken cases discarded, and the old carpet ripped out. New rolls of carpeting were stacked in the corner and a single display case—probably the only one that had remained intact—was shoved to the back of the shop.

"We're putting the pieces back together," Brooke said.

"You repainted the walls."

"The painters came and did it yesterday," Brooke said. She looked around, pleased. "Yes, I decided to freshen the place up. Eventually we'll be good as new." Then her smile faded. "Well, almost as good as new."

Theodosia gave her a warm hug. "You'll come through this. I have faith."

"I *have* to come through it. I mean, what are my options?" Brooke waved a hand. "But you didn't come here to listen to me grump. Dare I ask how you're coming with suspects? The police and FBI still don't seem to have a whole lot going. Or, if they do, they're no longer sharing it with me."

"I might have a little too much information for you."

Brooke looked pleased. "Information overload? I doubt that."

So Theodosia carefully detailed her list of suspects— Lionel Rinicker, Billy Grainger, Sabrina and Luke Andros, Marcus Clement the rock climber, and Professor Warren Shepley. As she went through her list, she laid out for Brooke exactly *why* she viewed each one as a potential suspect.

Brooke was stunned by Theodosia's list. And maybe a little overwhelmed, after all.

"I knew the police were taking a look at Rinicker and Shepley," Brooke said. "But I never heard boo about them seriously investigating Sabrina and Luke Andros. And those other people you mentioned, Grainger and Clement, I never even *heard* of them. Wait a minute, tell me again why you see those two as suspects?"

"I'll give you the short version," Theodosia said. "Grainger rides a motorcycle and Clement owns a rock hammer."

"Ah." A smile flitted across Brooke's face. She lifted a hand and touched it gently to Theodosia's cheek. "You're a very smart lady."

"Thank you. But realize, please, that I could be completely off base. I probably *am* off base with most of these guys. But"—she dug into her messenger bag and grabbed her stack of papers—"I'd like you to look at all this stuff I pulled off the Internet."

Brooke inclined her head toward the papers in Theodosia's hands. "What is all this?"

"Press releases, newspaper articles, photos, you name it. I'd like you to skim through them and tell me if any of these people ring a bell with you. Maybe you've run into one of them before, or they've come into your shop, or you vaguely recognize one from the attack the other night."

"You want me to go through this right now?"

"Sure. If you could."

They went back into Brooke's office. Brooke sat down behind her desk and Theodosia took a chair across from her.

"You did a lot of work here," Brooke said as she paged through the printouts.

"If anything pays off, it'll be well worth it."

Brooke went through the stack of papers, studying everything. Then she went through it a second time. When she'd finally turned the last paper over, she said, "The only ones I really recognize are Sabrina and Luke Andros, Lionel Rinicker, and Professor Shepley." She gazed at Theodosia. "But Rinicker, only because I've seen him hanging around at the Heritage Society, never at my shop. And, of course, Shepley, because he crashed the party." She tapped a grainy photo of Rinicker. "He looks . . . interesting, though. Do you think he could he have been part of the robbery gang?"

"Maybe," Theodosia said. "If anybody could get away

with it, I have a feeling he could." She remembered how Rinicker had chortled about the FBI dropping in on him. Who did that? Who was that brazen and calm?

"So how are we going to resolve this?" Brooke asked.

Theodosia gave a faint smile. "Eeny, meeny, miny, moe?"

"Seriously."

"I don't know yet," Theodosia said. "There are a lot of suspects, but only circumstantial evidence. I guess I have my work cut out for me." She also had a nervous inkling that things might just shake out at the Heritage Society tomorrow night.

Back at the Indigo Tea Shop, Theodosia decided it was time to stop dancing around Haley. In fact, she decided that she had to be open and honest and lay everything out for her.

"Haley," Theodosia said, ducking into the kitchen. "Can we talk?"

Haley had just removed a pan of popovers from the oven. They were golden brown and super puffy, looking almost like miniature chef's hats. "Sure. About today's menu?"

"Actually, it's a little more serious than that."

Haley set her pan down. "Uh-oh."

"You know Brooke asked me for help."

Haley nodded. "Sure. I was there, remember? I seconded the vote."

"Yes, of course. And you know Drayton and I have been whispering about a few suspects . . ."

Haley picked up a jar of strawberry jam and wiped the top of it with the edge of her apron. "That's all you two have been doing. Pretty much all week long."

"And one of our suspects . . . mind you, he's kind of on the periphery."

Haley leaned in closer to her. "Yes?"

Theodosia took a gulp.

"Just spit it out, Theodosia."

"Okay, I will. One of our fringe suspects happens to be your new friend Billy Grainger."

"I knew it!" Haley slapped a hand down hard on the butcher-block table, jarring a bowl of frosting and sending a spoon clattering to the floor. "I just knew you were still suspicious of him. Even though you kind of told me you were going to drop the whole thing. It's because Billy rides a motorcycle, isn't it?"

"That and a couple of other things," Theodosia said.

"But you're wrong about him," Haley said. "You're so far off base it's ridiculous." She wasn't so much angry as she was insistent.

"I'm actually glad to hear you say that."

"In fact, you are so wrong that I'm not even going to worry about this," Haley said. She smiled, but Theodosia thought that she saw hurt behind Haley's smile.

"Then I won't say any more," Theodosia said. "We'll just let this whole thing play out."

"I think that might be best."

"No hard feelings?" Theodosia asked.

Haley shook her head. "No. Well, one question. Did you tell Detective Tidwell that you considered Billy a suspect?"

"No, I did not."

"Really?"

"You have my word on that, Haley."

"Okay, then," Haley said. "That's one small load off my mind. I'd hate to think that Tidwell was dogging Billy's every footstep."

"So we're good on this?" Theodosia asked.

Haley held up a finger. "As long as we never mention this again."

"If that's the way you want it."

Haley nodded vigorously. "It is. Pinky swear you're not going to bring it up again?" She held up her little finger.

Theodosia hooked fingers with her. "Pinky swear."

"Okay," Haley said. "Now. Do you want to know what's on the menu for lunch?"

Theodosia breathed a sigh of relief. Haley wasn't mad. In fact, she just wanted the subject dropped. "Yes, Haley," she said, "I'm dying to know."

23

❧

"*We'll be serving* a mixed green salad, pepper jack quiche, and crab salad on a croissant," Theodosia told Drayton and Miss Dimple. "Plus cinnamon apple scones and chocolate cake for dessert."

"Perfect," Drayton purred. "I'm delighted to see that Haley's come up with a slightly more manageable luncheon menu since we have to turn things around fast for our Full Monty Tea later on."

"What time is that supposed to start?" Miss Dimple asked.

"Two o'clock," Theodosia said.

"And what's the menu for that?" Drayton asked.

"Haley says it's going to be a variation on lunch with a few extras tossed in."

"Goody," Miss Dimple said, practically clapping her hands.

"So in order to get our tables set up, we need to send our luncheon guests merrily on their way by one thirty at the latest," Theodosia told them.

Miss Dimple nodded. "What should we do? Just shoo them out?"

"Nothing quite that obvious," Theodosia said. "But it works wonders if we send Drayton over to glower at them."

"Drayton doesn't glower," Miss Dimple said. "That's just his serious look. He's a serious sort of gent."

"Gent." Theodosia was amused. "That's a funny word. Kind of old-fashioned."

Miss Dimple looked pleased. "But that's exactly what Drayton is. Courtly and polished and a little old-fashioned."

Drayton popped the top on a Brown Betty teapot. "If you say so."

Theodosia spent most of the lunch doing the heavy lifting. That is, running back and forth, grabbing luncheon plates, then clearing away dishes. She let Miss Dimple wander through the tea room with a pot of tea, dispensing compliments, advice, and refills.

"Have you decided which teas to serve this afternoon?" Theodosia asked Drayton. She knew he liked to ruminate over what might be the most suitable teas for all their events.

"I'm thinking a Prince of Wales tea and an Irish afternoon tea," Drayton said. "Prince of Wales is always such a popular choice in England and it has a light, slightly delicate flavor. And the Irish afternoon tea is more full-bodied and brisk."

"And both work well with milk or sweetener. Good choice."

Theodosia pulled out their set of Staffordshire dishes as well as two Limoges porcelain figures. There'd been no need to worry about the luncheon guests leaving on time, because they simply had. By one thirty they'd all cleared out, as neatly as if Haley had swept the leaves away from the front door.

"Let's put out the glass teapot warmers," Theodosia told Miss Dimple. "And I'll grab a box of votive candles."

"What about these flowers?" Miss Dimple asked. "What if I cut the stems and popped them into your short, white ceramic vases?"

"Go for it."

Theodosia was pleased with how the tea room was shaping up. They had . . . what? Maybe twenty-eight people coming today? Not as big a group as last night but still enough guests to keep them hopping. And keep them in business, too, since that was the whole purpose of serving tea.

Oh, is it really? she thought to herself. *Is that why I do this?*

Well, no. Theodosia knew her purpose was really to be master (or mistress) of her own destiny, enjoy the freedom of being a small-time entrepreneur who reported only to herself, and do something that she was passionate about.

And she was definitely passionate about the Indigo Tea Shop. She loved it more than anyone would ever know. This was what dreams were all about. Have a vision, build on that vision, and work hard to make sure it all came to fruition.

The front door creaked open, pulling her out of her introspection. It was Detective Tidwell.

He peered around, his broad face registering surprise at seeing the tea shop empty, yet all set up for tea service. "Are you open?" he asked in a bold voice that seemed to resonate a little too loudly in the empty shop.

Theodosia tucked one hand on her hip. "It depends. Are you here for a late lunch or are you arriving early for our Full Monty Tea?"

Tidwell's eyes glowed expectantly and he was suddenly interested. "There's a special tea? A . . . excuse me, what did you call it?"

"A Full Monty Tea."

"Ah. You must have named your event in honor of the venerable field marshal Bernard Montgomery."

"That'd be about right."

"I believe I might enjoy your Full Monty Tea."

"I'm sure you would, since Haley's come up with quite an extensive menu."

Tidwell did everything but smack his lips and tuck a napkin down his shirtfront. "I understand old Monty always enjoyed a full complement of rations at breakfast."

"And at teatime, as well," Theodosia said. "Even when he was in the field commanding his troops."

"Or sitting safely at the rear," Tidwell said.

Theodosia led Tidwell to a table and pulled out a chair for him. "Am I to surmise you're a student of history?"

"Most definitely. In fact, I'm a bit of a World War Two buff."

"I would have pegged you for more of a Civil War buff," Theodosia said. "Maybe even one of those fellows who wander around old battlefields with a metal detector, looking for uniform buttons and minié balls."

Tidwell's jowls sloshed. "That's definitely not my style."

Theodosia brought him a cup of tea and then sat down next to him. "So what's new? What do you hear about the rock-hammer guy?"

Tidwell added a lump of sugar to his tea and then another. "Your FBI friends sniffed him up and down for about two minutes."

"You're telling me they don't see him as a viable suspect?"

Tidwell looked smug. "If they do, I'd say they're grasping at straws."

"Because there isn't enough hard evidence?"

"My dear, there really isn't any evidence at all."

"I'm sorry my information about the hammer didn't pan out," Theodosia said. "*You* seemed to think there might be something there."

"Investigations are like living, breathing things. They're fluid and the information changes constantly."

"Like how?" Theodosia asked. "Has something else changed?"

"Not really," Tidwell said.

"Then tell me about the other suspects. Is the FBI hot on the trail of anyone?"

"Not as hot as this tea is."

"Okay, if *you* could point me in someone's direction, who would it be?"

"You know I can't do that."

"Of course you can," Theodosia said.

"I don't want you charging in and getting into trouble."

"I wouldn't do that." Theodosia sat for a couple seconds with her hands in her lap, and then said, "Of course, you could drop a subtle hint. Or even a very broad one."

"You're body punching now. You don't give up easily, do you?"

"Never. Not until the bitter end."

Tidwell considered her words for a few moments and then said, "They've tried to downplay this, but I know the FBI is still moderately interested in Professor Shepley."

Theodosia pounced on his words. "Because Shepley crashed Brooke's jewelry event? And possibly had an interest in the alexandrite necklace?"

"That and the fact that he's studied all things Russian."

"You mean not just Russian literature?"

"The man spent time in Russia," Tidwell said. "He's probably well versed in art, culture, and . . ."

"Politics?" Theodosia said. "Has the FBI got their underwear in a twist over his politics?"

Tidwell leaned back in his chair. "I doubt Shepley subscribes to the Communist Manifesto, but I'm sure he's not unfamiliar with its precepts."

"We're back to the days of the Cold War again, are we?" Theodosia asked.

"That and the fact that many of today's more daring and brash jewel thieves hail from Eastern European countries."

"That is interesting," Theodosia said. "So you're saying Shepley might have had the wherewithal to recruit a gang?"

"No," Tidwell smiled. "*You* said it."

Their Full Monty Tea kicked off at two o'clock sharp with the menu being, in Drayton's words, "Terribly, terribly British."

Haley pulled out all the stops and arranged their offerings on silver four-tiered serving trays. Fruit scones sat on top, squares of mini quiche on the second tier, cream cheese and cucumber tea sandwiches occupied the third tier, and small slices of chocolate cake topped with fresh raspberries were on the bottom tier.

Miss Dimple bustled around, serving tea and cooing happy hellos to all the people she knew, which turned out to be pretty much all of the guests.

While their guests enjoyed their first course of fruit scones, Theodosia did a little song and dance about the origin of the term *the full monty*, and then it was Drayton's turn to take the floor.

He strode to the center of the tea shop, looking spiffy in his Harris Tweed jacket, cleared his throat, and said, "I thought since you were enjoying a proper British tea today, that you might also enjoy a poem. The one I've chosen to recite was penned by an anonymous London poet, and I think it speaks well to the great British tea tradition."

A hush fell across the tea shop and then Drayton began:

> *Ambrosial plants! that from the east and west,*
> *Or from the shores of Araby the blest,*
> *Those odoriferous sprigs and berries send,*
> *On which our wives and government depend.*

Kind land! that gives rich presents, none receives,
And barters for leaf gold its golden leaves.
Bane of our nerves, and nerve of our excise,
In which a nation's strength and weakness lies.

"Bravo!" Tidwell called out. "Excellent." He was seated at a table for four, with two women. He'd basically done his best to ignore them and, after their initial overture at friendliness, the women had decided to ignore him, too. It was a nonaggression pact of sorts.

As the applause rose and then fell, the front door suddenly popped open and Delaine rushed in. She gazed about, a look of concern clouding her lovely face. Then, once she'd spotted Theodosia standing behind the counter, raced over to talk with her.

"Theodosia!" Delaine said. "There you are."

"Did you think I'd be someplace else?" Theodosia asked. She lifted an eyebrow as she popped a blue-and-white chintz cozy over a teapot. "Wait a minute, am I supposed to be someplace else?"

Delaine shook her head. "No, no. It's just that I'd planned to attend your tea and somehow—I have no idea how—the time completely slipped away from me." She waggled her head back and forth, her eyes going purposely wide. "Things have been cray cray you know?" For some reason, Delaine had begun using texting phrases, like cray cray (for "crazy, crazy") and sup (for "What's up?") in her everyday conversation.

"So you really are here for tea?"

"Oh yes," Delaine said. "In fact, I'd say it's a celebratory tea."

"The occasion being . . . ?"

Delaine grinned like a Cheshire cat and batted her eyelashes. "Renaldo has decided to stay in Charleston for a few more days!"

"Lucky you."

"Aren't I? He said he wants to take me out tonight for a fancy dinner and then escort me to the Rare Antiquities Show tomorrow night."

Theodosia looked at her sharply. "Where did you say your boyfriend was from?"

"I didn't actually specify," Delaine said. "But since you're interested, I'll tell you. Renaldo hails from near Nice, in the south of France. He has a chateau in a small town by the name of Beaulieu-sur-Mer."

"Is that anywhere near Monte Carlo?" Theodosia asked. It had just occurred to her that Renaldo Gilles was new in town, too. That is, new in town since just before the robbery.

"I suppose it probably isn't all that far from Monte Carlo. It's in that ooh-la-la French Riviera vicinity, anyway."

As Delaine drummed her fingers on the counter, her rings caught the light and flashed. Theodosia was momentarily reminded of the butterfly brooch at Heart's Desire. Before all the broken glass, before all the heartbreak. Then she pulled her thoughts back to the here and now.

"And you've known Renaldo for how long?"

"It's only been a few weeks," Delaine said. "But when you've finally discovered your true soul mate in a world filled with treacherous, barbarous creeps, it feels as if you've been together forever." Delaine clutched her hands together, then touched them to her heart and beamed.

"Your soul mate," Theodosia said. "My, that is major news." Delaine had been discovering her soul mate for as long as Theodosia could remember. First there'd been Cooper, then Charles, then Roger, and wasn't there someone named Bentley? But no need to dredge all *that* up. "Now that you mention it, you do have a certain glow about you."

Delaine touched a hand delicately to her cheek and moved

closer to the counter. "I just had a caviar facial at the Silver Moon Spa. So I'm feeling positively *incandescent*."

"I hope it's not catching." Theodosia chuckled.

"Silver Moon is such a gorgeous spa," Delaine babbled on. "Fresh flowers everywhere, a mineral springs hot tub, architecture like a Grecian temple, and absolutely *everyone* caters to your slightest whim. It's absolutely decadent, my kind of place. While I was checking out, I even ran into Grace Dawson. You remember her, don't you? The two of us sat together at lunch yesterday."

"Sure, the nice lady with the Dobermans." But Theodosia really remembered Grace Dawson as the wealthy woman who was dating Lionel Rinicker.

"Do you know that Grace employs a personal assistant?" Delaine asked, seemingly enraptured. "Isn't that amazing? He was there with her today, this wonderful little person who actually takes notes and runs errands and does her complete bidding. Just like the movie stars have."

"Sounds great." Theodosia knew having someone at her beck and call would just make her anxious. She'd have to hustle up busywork for them to do.

"Grace is an extremely classy person," Delaine said. "She knows that *blue chip* isn't just something you dunk in a bowl of guacamole." She idly fluffed her hair. "Anyway, I wanted to hit the spa so I'd be in tip-top shape for my evening with Renaldo."

"Wait a minute," Theodosia said. "What exactly does Renaldo do for a living?"

"Renaldo is in the import-export business," Delaine said. "A little of this, a little of that." She gave a vague wave of the hand. "French perfumes, Italian shoes, silks, what have you. You know, high-end luxury goods."

"And where did you meet him?"

"A fashion trade show in Miami."

"Interesting. I look forward to getting to know him a little better."

Renaldo Gilles might be Delaine's soul mate and an import-export agent, but Theodosia sincerely hoped the man didn't plan to export any luxury goods from the Heritage Society over the next couple of days.

24

❧

It was the perfect evening. An inky black sky lit with a random scatter of twinkling stars. The breeze off the Atlantic carrying a hint of salt and sea brine. Temperature still hovering in the low sixties. And twenty-five dancers, all clad in black leotards with tiny lights running up and down their arms and legs, dancing and leaping to a blast of rock music. The Lumiere Festival was well under way, and Theodosia and Drayton were standing on the front steps of the Charleston Library Society, watching the dazzling presentation that was taking place on King Street.

"Those young ladies certainly know how to twirl," Drayton remarked.

"They're little sprites," Theodosia said. She figured she'd get fall-down dizzy if she ever tried that sort of manic gyration. Still, it was great fun to watch. "And did you see what's happening down the street at the Gibbes Museum?"

Drayton nodded. "The images they're projecting on the

outside of the building remind me of an underground movie from the sixties. Still, I think it's rather clever that they chose slides from their own collection. It's almost like . . ."

"Art for the people?"

"Something like that, yes. Though I suppose putting it that way sounds a bit condescending."

"Just a bit," Theodosia said. "But the supersized paintings and sculptures might help bring a few more folks through their doors, which is always a good thing."

"You see," Drayton said, "that's where the Heritage Society differs."

"How's that?"

"We really don't want any more people flocking through our doors."

Theodosia stared at Drayton, who managed to keep a straight face for all of five seconds. Then she punched him in the arm and said, "Let's see what else is going on."

Turns out, there was a lot to be dazzled by. Searchlights arced in the sky, more light shows splashed against fine old buildings, and LED installations buzzed and hummed all around them. There was even an interactive light tube on the front lawn of the historic Reese-Parker home.

"I had no idea that light had become such a highly regarded artistic medium," Drayton said. "I guess I have to catch up with the times."

"You're out tonight," Theodosia said. "That's a good start."

They'd wandered down King Street and turned onto Archdale. Here, magnificent Georgian, Italianate, and Victorian-style homes, all deemed "architecturally significant," by those who made such decisions, sat cheek to elegant jowl. All privately owned and rarely seen by the public, these homes were a vision in grandeur and sumptuous luxury and served as time capsules for Charleston's history, taste, and décor.

"You see that sign up ahead?" Theodosia pointed.

Drayton peered ahead through darkness that was punctuated by glowing streetlamps. "Yes, it says 'Fire Garden.' What on earth is a Fire Garden?"

"I'd say we're about to find out."

They picked their way through throngs of strolling people and stopped in front of a large redbrick mansion that featured tall white columns, a wide veranda, and was surrounded by a genuine Philip Simmons wrought-iron fence.

"This is the Rosewalk Inn," Drayton said. He cocked an eye at Theodosia. "Did you bring me here to spy?"

"You said you wanted to attend the Lumiere Festival. I'm just obliging you."

"I have to admit, I'm a little curious about their Fire Garden installation."

"So am I. Let's go in."

Tyrone Chandler, the manager, greeted them on the enormous front veranda. He was an African American man in his late fifties, quite distinguished-looking with his salt-and-pepper hair and infectious smile. Tonight he wore an elegant camel hair jacket with a white shirt and charcoal-gray slacks.

"Drayton, is that really you?" Chandler asked. He stuck out a hand as Drayton greeted him. "And Theodosia, too." He chuckled merrily. "Have you come to see our Fire Garden?"

"We're trying to figure out what a Fire Garden is," Drayton said.

"It's an idea that Marcella came up with," Chandler told them. Marcella Soliere was the owner of the Rosewalk Inn. "She saw something like it in Perugia when she was traveling through Italy last summer. Couldn't wait to re-create one here."

"We're intrigued," Theodosia told him as they were ushered into the inn.

"Just head straight through the breakfast room," Chandler said. "And then step out the sliding doors and onto the patio. The Fire Garden is just beyond our rose garden."

"Thank you," Theodosia said.

* * *

The Rosewalk Inn was named for the multitude of rose-bushes that graced its back garden. Though most of the floribundas, polyanthas, and English roses were no longer in bloom, there were a few pink Chinese roses standing tall.

"Mr. Chandler must have grown these in a hothouse," Drayton said. "Then transplanted them here especially for tonight." His eyes traveled down the rosebush to study the area around the roots. "Yes, that's exactly what that sly fox did."

"Can't put anything past you, Drayton," Theodosia said. Then her eyes caught sight of what had to be the Fire Garden and she said, "Oh my, take a look at this."

Theodosia and Drayton stepped past the expanse of rosebushes and onto the back patio. A huge circle of enormous rocks, à la Stonehenge, had been arranged in the middle. Inside were concentric circles of rocks that stepped up to form a large rock pyramid in the middle. Every one of the rocks had an enormous flaming candle on top of it.

"This looks like an image straight out of Dante's *Inferno*," Drayton said, though he was clearly intrigued.

"It's a gorgeous display," Theodosia said. "It really is a Fire Garden." Flames danced and licked atop red, yellow, and orange candles that dripped rivulets of wax down the stones. But the arrangement didn't look one bit hokey. It looked almost . . . sacrificial.

"There's a bar over there," Drayton said, gazing across the dozen wrought-iron tables and chairs where guests were camped out. "Should we grab a table and have ourselves a cocktail?" He gestured toward the bar. "Or maybe a glass of wine?"

"Chardonnay, if they've got it. Or anything dry."

Drayton sped away. "Coming right up."

Spotting a table that was unoccupied, Theodosia hurried to grab it. Just as she pulled out a chair, someone clamped a hand on the chair adjacent to her. She glanced up quickly, surprised to see the two FBI agents who'd been practically haunting her shop.

"Hello," she said. "I was wondering when I'd see you two again."

Agent Zimmer nodded politely to her while Hurley actually smiled.

"Still working the case?" Theodosia asked, even though she pretty much knew the answer. Of course they were. They were jackhammering away like crazy.

"Absolutely we are," Zimmer said.

"That's good to know," Theodosia said. She glanced around. Drayton was still standing at the bar ordering glasses of wine, and nobody else had taken notice of the two agents, even though they were dressed like a couple of G-men in a made-for-TV movie. "I assume you're here because you've been talking to Professor Shepley? Interviewing him because he crashed the Heart's Desire event?"

"You knew he was staying here?" Zimmer asked. "At this particular inn?"

Theodosia smiled demurely.

"If you had knowledge that he was staying here, that means you've been meddling," Hurley said.

"She sees him as a suspect," Zimmer said.

"I don't really know if he is or isn't," Theodosia said. "I'd have to defer to your judgment on that."

Zimmer exchanged a knowing glance with Hurley and then said, "We've done a careful assessment of Shepley and don't believe he poses any immediate threat."

"That's good to know," Theodosia said just as Drayton arrived with two glasses of wine.

"Gentlemen, if I had known . . ." Drayton indicated the wineglasses he held in his hands.

Zimmer put up a hand as the two of them backed away. "No, no. Thanks for the offer, but we have to get going."

"Nice to see you again," Theodosia called after them as she and Drayton sat down.

"What were *they* doing here?" Drayton asked as he slid a glass of wine in front of her. "Oh, and it's Chablis rather than Chardonnay, if that's all right with you."

"Just fine. And it seems our FBI friends have cleared Professor Shepley of any wrongdoing. If their story can be believed."

Drayton frowned. "Shepley? I just ran into him at the bar. He was ordering a Dubonnet."

"He's here?" Theodosia spun around in her chair. "Where?" Her eyes searched what had turned into a sizable crowd on the patio. "Oh, I see him."

"We should probably leave the man in peace," Drayton said.

At which point Theodosia jumped up and waved at him wildly. "Professor Shepley," she cried. "Over here. Come on over here."

Shepley noticed her waving and visibly flinched. Then, head down, he all but reluctantly strolled toward their table. The three of them exchanged somewhat formal greetings, and then Shepley didn't waste any time mincing words.

"I'm leaving Charleston," he told them. "Driving back to Savannah first thing tomorrow."

"We're sorry to hear that," Theodosia said. "I take it your research here is finished?"

"Not at all," Shepley said. "But I no longer feel welcome."

Theodosia felt a flicker of guilt. Had she contributed to driving Shepley out? Probably. She'd sicced both Tidwell and the FBI on him and it had probably unnerved the man to no end. Yes, she felt guilty, but a little relieved, too. Her list of suspects was gradually being whittled down.

"I hope your research was at least successful," Drayton said diplomatically.

"Yes . . . well . . ." Shepley edged away from their table. "That remains to be seen." He held up a hand. "Good night."

"You drove him out," Drayton said in a low voice. He sounded mildly accusatory.

"I didn't mean to," Theodosia said as they watched him retreat. "I was only trying to help Brooke."

"You were well-intentioned. But"—Drayton stared after Shepley—"I think you scared the pants off the old boy."

They sat at their table for a while, enjoying the evening and the buzz of activity going on around them.

"Are we going to view any other light installations?" Drayton asked.

"I hadn't planned on it," Theodosia said. "But if you want to . . ."

Drayton raised a hand. "No, I think it's been a fine evening. Let's just leave it at that." He looked around. "Though I would like to ask Mr. Chandler a question about his Chinese roses."

"Go," Theodosia urged, picking up her glass. "Go ask him." She'd already spotted Grace Dawson across the patio and had decided to go over and say hi. Grace was looking very sporty tonight, in black leggings and a supple black leather jacket. Theodosia decided that if she had to attach a name to Grace's distinct style, it would be *sport couture*.

"If you don't mind," Drayton said, starting to get up. "I mean, I don't want to leave you sitting here."

"You're not," Theodosia said, getting up from her chair, too. "In fact, I've got people to see and questions to ask." She strolled past the bar, sipping her glass of Chablis (it really was quite nice, very buttery and light), and strolled over to where Grace was standing. Coming up behind her, Theodosia said, "Where are your beautiful dogs tonight?"

Grace spun around, caught sight of Theodosia, and smiled broadly. "I would have loved to bring them, but I was afraid they'd jump out of their skin with all the lights popping and strobing."

"Probably would."

"Lovely to see you again," Grace said. "But I have a bone to pick with you."

Theodosia took a step back. "Uh-oh, what's that?"

"You've got me positively hooked on tea and scones."

"That was my plan," Theodosia laughed. "To turn you into one of my regulars so we can see you again and again."

"And make me gain five pounds!" Grace exclaimed. "I swear, I'll probably have to do an extra hour of Pilates to compensate for all the sugar I imbibed this week. Or go on a low-carb diet."

"Like Delaine," Theodosia said.

Grace's eyes lit up. "Say, I ran into Delaine this morning."

"She told me."

Grace looked surprised. "How did you . . . ? Ah, you were at the spa, too?"

"Don't I wish," Theodosia said. "No, Delaine popped in for a late lunch and mentioned that she'd run into you there."

"That Delaine is such a little jitterbug. Running all over town, her fingers stuck in all sorts of different pies. You know, she's been putting pressure on me to join the board of directors of one of her animal rescue groups. Apparently she's a big wheel in two or three different ones?"

"Probably because she's such a successful fund-raiser," Theodosia said. "I think Delaine single-handedly raised something like a million dollars just to get Madison's House Small Animal Rescue built."

Grace let loose a low whistle. "Very impressive. I take it Delaine's a confirmed dog lover?"

Theodosia shook her head. "Delaine thinks all critters are wonderful, but she's seriously into cats. She thinks cats are smarter and way more esoteric."

"Cats *are* great," Grace laughed. "Even Sultan and Satin love cats."

"Sure they do," Theodosia said in a tone that implied *No, they don't*; the two women laughing together at her little joke.

"You know what?" Grace said. "We should all get together for a spa day sometime. Really do the works—nails, hair, massages, sea scrubs, you name it."

"That sounds like fun."

"We could invite Sabrina Andros along, too." When Theodosia fixed Grace with a quizzical look, she explained. "I also bumped into Sabrina this morning while I was getting my mani-pedi. I understand she's a regular there." Grace dropped her voice. "Please don't ever tell Sabrina I said this, but I think she was getting her roots done."

"She stopped by for tea a couple of days ago," Theodosia said. "Along with her husband, Luke."

"The yacht guy," Grace said. "I hear he's doing a gang-buster business. Sabrina mentioned that he received a call from some big muckety-muck bank president in Rio de Janeiro who's hot to buy a custom yacht. So Luke is cruising one of his yachts down there tomorrow night."

"Is Sabrina going along?" Theodosia asked.

Grace waved at someone sitting across the patio. "I don't know. Maybe." She waved again. "Probably." Then she pulled away. "Excuse me, my assistant is looking positively frantic. He probably has six calls holding and a couple of last-minute invitations." And she was gone. Poof.

Theodosia pondered this new information about Sabrina and Luke Andros. Tomorrow night, for all intents and purposes, they would be leaving the country. Sailing into international waters.

Snapping her head around, Theodosia quickly located Drayton. He was standing near the makeshift bar, talking to Teddy Vickers, the man who managed the Featherbed House just down the block. Well, she would just have to interrupt him.

"Theo," Drayton began when he saw her. "Teddy was just telling me that . . ."

"I'm sorry," Theodosia said to Drayton. "But we have to go. Like . . . now."

"What was so all-fired important that we had to leave poor Teddy standing there like that?" Drayton asked as Theodosia propelled him across the patio and into the Rosewalk Inn. She glanced around hurriedly, looking for a private spot to talk, and then yanked him into a side parlor. Painted a soft robin's-egg blue and decorated with a rag rug, the room featured some loosely rendered watercolor paintings as well as a pale-blue love seat with needlepoint cushions.

"Sabrina and Luke Andros are sailing to South America tomorrow night," Theodosia told him a little breathlessly.

"What?" Drayton's reaction was one of stunned surprise. He grabbed one of the cushions and gave it a squeeze.

Theodosia slowly related everything Grace had revealed to her.

"Are they leaving before or after the Rare Antiquities Show?" Drayton asked.

Theodosia shook her head. "I have no idea, but that's a very good question."

Drayton looked thoughtful. "Well, the timing matters."

"It certainly does. But just how are we supposed to find out their exact departure time? I don't expect it's noted in any maritime log."

"Maybe," Drayton said, looking thoughtful. "Maybe we should just go and ask them? Not flat out, but in a kind of casual way?"

"Huh," Theodosia said. "Why didn't I think of that?"

Drayton beetled his brows together. "Because I did."

"So maybe Sabrina and Luke are over at the yacht club right now," Theodosia said, warming to the idea even more.

"Getting ready to . . ." She broke off her words. "You know what, Drayton? Asking them point-blank is kind of in-your-face, but it's also a smart way to put them on alert."

"Exactly," Drayton said. "We let Sabrina and Luke know that *we* know they're planning to leave town."

Theodosia nodded. "If they're guilty, they'll figure we're keeping an eye on them."

Theodosia had left her Jeep parked nearby, so it was a simple matter of hopping in and driving over to the Charleston Yacht Club.

"Not so much going on over here," Drayton observed as they drove along.

"I don't know," Theodosia said. "The yachts are all supposed to be lit up."

"Well, I don't see . . ." Drayton did a sudden double take as they spun around a corner and the harbor came into view. "Oh my, you're right. The boats are all lit up." He smiled, a smile so heartfelt and genuine that Theodosia knew he was utterly charmed. "Look at them, just gliding back and forth across Charleston Harbor. Like pirate ships sailing off to Neverland."

About three dozen sailboats had been lit, stem to stern, with multiple strings of white lights. And, just as Drayton had said, they appeared to glide gracefully across the surface of the gilded moonlit water.

"Now all we have to do is find Sabrina and Luke Andros," Theodosia said, turning into the parking lot at the Charleston Yacht Club.

But that was going to be a piece of cake. Because the very last pier, where two enormous yachts tugged at their moorings, was lit up like a Christmas tree. And so were the yachts.

"Two yachts," Theodosia said. "He's brought another one in."

"It would appear there's a party going on," Drayton said as music and the hum of many voices floated toward them. "And judging from all the people on deck, it looks like Gold Coast Yachts is having a fairly large shindig. Do you think it's a going-away party? Or should I say anchors aweigh?"

"This will make it even easier for us," Theodosia said. "It means we can waltz in, hop on a boat, mingle with the crowd, and ask our innocent little question."

"Sounds like a plan."

But the best-laid plans often went awry. Or at least were met with serious obstacles. Because halfway down the pier, Theodosia and Drayton were stopped in their tracks by a very burly man in an ill-fitting navy-blue blazer.

"Sorry," the man told them as he crossed his arms and blocked their way. "But this is a private party."

Theodosia offered him a winning smile. "We know. We're good friends of Sabrina and Luke."

The security man touched a hand to the velvet rope that stretched across the pier, blocking their passage. "In that case, you folks probably have an invitation?"

"Not exactly," Theodosia said.

"Are your names on the guest list?"

"We just thought we'd drop in and say a quick hello," Theodosia said.

"Or a quick good-bye," Drayton added with a hopeful note. "Since we know that Sabrina and Luke are leaving tomorrow."

"For South America," Theodosia said.

The behemoth simply shook his head. "Sorry," he growled. "If you're not on the list, I can't let you by."

"Really?" Theodosia said in a slightly wheedling tone.

"I don't make the rules," the security guard said.

"Sheesh," Theodosia said. They turned and headed slowly

back down the dock. "I'm disappointed. And what's with that velvet-rope crap?"

"Pretentious," Drayton said. "Just like the old Studio 54."

Theodosia turned to look at him sharply. "What do you know about that place?"

Drayton gave a shrug. "I wasn't always so buttoned-up. And I *did* reside in New York for a time."

Theodosia grinned. "Well . . . *Drayton.*"

25

❧

Theodosia wasn't exactly in the mood to try on dresses. But Delaine had been so insistent about it the other day that her defenses had pretty much crumbled. So here she was, on a cool, slightly overcast Saturday morning, standing outside Cotton Duck, hoping like crazy that Delaine wasn't inside to harangue her and make the process even more painful.

"Hello," Theodosia called out as she entered the boutique. "Anybody here?"

"I'll be right with you," a voice called back.

Good, Theodosia thought as she recognized the voice. Janine, Delaine's overworked, overstressed assistant, was here. But it would appear that Delaine wasn't. So, blessed be, there'd be no nagging, rolling of eyes, or overwrought hysterics.

Theodosia couldn't help smiling as she gazed around the sparking jewel box of a shop and slowly fell under its spell. Racks of long gowns hung next to circular racks jammed with silk tops and suede slacks. Peekaboo camisoles and demi bras were nestled in satin boxes that sat on antique highboys. Strands of opera pearls mingled with gold necklaces, turquoise and coral pendants, and clover necklaces made of gold and mother-of-pearl. Glass shelves displayed reptile and supple leather handbags. Even though Theodosia wasn't a dyed-in-the-wool fashionista, she found it all wonderfully enticing.

"Janine?" Theodosia called out as she perused a rack of leather bomber jackets. "It's me, Theodosia." She reached out and touched one. It was soft as butter. "I think Delaine pulled some dresses for me to try on?"

Thirty seconds later, Janine came huffing toward her.

"Yes, yes," Janine said. She was red faced and always seemed to be in a perpetual state of distress. "Delaine phoned me first thing this morning and gave strict instructions to put the dresses in a fitting room for you."

"Great," Theodosia said, not really meaning it.

"Three cocktail dresses, right?"

Theodosia shrugged. "I guess."

Janine smiled warmly at her. "Must be nice to get all dressed up and go to fancy parties." Janine was short, slightly stooped, and had wavy brown hair and large brown eyes. She was wearing a skirt that covered her knees and her blouse was untucked.

Theodosia suddenly felt horribly ungrateful.

"Some of those events *are* nice," she told Janine, then put an arm around the woman's shoulders. "In fact, you should come along sometime."

Janine brightened as if the sun had suddenly burst out from behind the clouds. "Really?"

"Yes, really. In fact, if you'd like to come to the opening at the Heritage Society tonight, I can certainly get your name on the list." Theodosia knew that Drayton wouldn't mind one bit.

"I can't make it tonight," Janine said. "But maybe some other time?"

"Sounds like a plan." Theodosia was starting to feel more and more upbeat by the minute. Being kind to people, having a charitable attitude, was good for the body and the soul. "Now, where are those dresses you have for me?"

Janine pushed back a plum-colored velvet drapery and led the way into a fitting room. "Hanging up right here." She reached out and smoothed one of the dresses. "And I have to tell you, Delaine was very insistent that all the dresses be short and black."

"Cocktaily," Theodosia said.

"That's right."

"Okay, I'll give them a try."

Janine pulled the privacy curtain across and said, "Once you're changed, Theodosia, be sure to come out and give us a fashion show."

But the first dress Theodosia tried on was so wrong. A clingy jersey number that was too short, too tight, and had a flouncy skirt that looked like it would blow up and reveal everything with just a paltry puff of wind.

No way.

The second dress wasn't terrible, but it wasn't great, either. A one-shouldered gown with a wrap-around shrug that reminded Theodosia of something a Sicilian widow might wear.

Two strikes against me so far.

The third dress didn't look like much on the hanger, but when Theodosia put it on, the black silk slithered over her beautifully. It flattered her midsection and hips, while the modified sweetheart neckline made her neck and shoulders look positively swanlike.

Okaaay. This is more like it.

Theodosia slipped into a pair of strappy black high heels that Janine had put in the fitting room and walked out into the shop. She knew the real proving ground would be the three-way mirror.

"Oh, Theodosia," Janine exclaimed when she saw her. "That dress fits you perfectly."

Theodosia tiptoed up to the three-way mirror and peered into it. And smiled at her reflection. The sheath dress did look pretty good on her. Very sophisticated.

"You look like you should be posing in front of a stone fireplace in some ginormous mansion, getting your picture taken for the society section of *Charleston Trends* magazine," Janine said.

"Oh no," Theodosia murmured.

"Oh yes." Janine crept forward and adjusted the neckline slightly. "If this dress is your first choice, and I'm hoping it is, I bet Delaine is going to be jealous of how great you look."

"Delaine? Jealous?" Theodosia said. *Hah!*

But Janine was dead serious. "You have no idea how head-over-heels crazy in love Delaine is with that new boyfriend of hers," she said, whispering, as if the walls had ears. "Every day Delaine practically drives herself crazy trying to look and dress her best. She's been spending a fortune on facials and manicures. I think she's so paranoid about looking young and cute that she's even had Botox."

"She doesn't need that stuff. Delaine always looks great."

"No, this is different," Janine said. "Delaine is constantly pushing herself to up her game. She claims that's what you have to do when you're madly in love. To, you know, keep the attraction going."

"Maybe she really is madly in love, then," Theodosia said. She'd figured this guy was just another guy in a long string of guys. *So maybe I should take a little time to get to know her boyfriend? That is, if he really is her one true love.*

"Have you met him?" Janine asked.

"Just briefly. For all of about two seconds."

"I've met Mr. Gilles," Janine said, "and I'd have to say

he's very handsome." She gave an appreciative shiver. "Mysterious, too."

Theodosia turned toward her. "Mysterious? In what way?"

"I suppose because he's European, with such a lovely accent and fine manners."

"But he's leaving to go back home in a week or so," Theodosia said. "He's going back to France."

Janine nodded sadly. "I know, but Delaine is hoping and praying she can convince him to stay here forever."

"You mean she wants to *marry* him?"

"I think she does, yes."

"For her sake then, I hope he stays."

Janine nodded briskly and said, "So . . . shall I wrap your dress or do you want to wear it out? Or is there something else you want to try on?"

Theodosia twirled back to face her image in the mirror. "I guess I have to make a decision, don't I? Well, I love this sleek look . . . and I've got some black heels that should go perfectly." She touched a hand to the neckline. "But is it just the teensiest bit plain on top?"

"Maybe it could use a necklace or a colorful pin?" Janine said.

"You think?"

"A pin would definitely glam it up," Janine said. "Especially if you have one with tons of sparkle."

Theodosia eyed her reflection in the mirror again. As far as finding a stunning piece of jewelry went, she was pretty sure she knew who to ask.

When Theodosia rushed into Heart's Desire, Brooke was standing in the middle of the shop directing a bevy of carpenters and rug guys. A ladder was set up at one end of the shop and, way at the tippy-top of it, a man was installing a row of pinpoint spotlights.

"Theodosia," Brooke said when she spotted her. "Tell me some good news."

"Professor Shepley is out of the running," Theodosia said. "I spoke with the FBI guys last night and they claim they've cleared him completely."

Brooke cocked her head to one side, considering this. "I guess I never believed the professor was any kind of criminal mastermind. From what you told me, he was an odd duck, yes, but probably not a jewel thief." She sighed. "So it's back to square one?"

"No, we left square one days ago. Now we're playing an advanced game of cat and mouse."

That brought a faint smile to Brooke's face. "You being the cat?"

"Hopefully."

"Theodosia, you are a dear soul. And I know I asked for your help . . . well, I actually *begged* for your help. But the more I hear about international jewel thieves, the more I worry that you might be in danger. That you might put yourself out there a little too far."

"That's exactly what I wanted to talk to you about."

Brooke looked puzzled. "What do you mean?"

"What if I wore an exotic piece of jewelry to the Heritage Society show tonight?"

"Well, sure," Brooke said. "It's no problem if you want to borrow something. I've still got a few choice pieces stashed in my safe."

Theodosia decided she should probably clarify her request. "I mean I want to wear a spectacular piece of jewelry as bait."

"Bait?" Now comprehension dawned on Brooke's face. "Oh no, honey, there's no way I could let you do that. You flash some major jewels around and it really could put you in danger. I mean, what if this guy or gang who robbed me crashes the party? Or the same person who robbed that woman at the opera? If they see that you're wearing a particularly tasty piece of jewelry, they might decide to go after you!" She shook her head. "No, it's simply too dangerous."

"But don't you see, that's exactly what I want to happen. I want this guy or gang or whatever they are, to be enticed and then . . ."

Brooke lifted an eyebrow. "Rob you? Hurt you?"

"I was thinking more like they'd get swarmed by the police and arrested."

"I see the method to your madness. But still . . ."

"Listen, this might be our only chance of catching these guys," Theodosia said. "They might be moving on soon. To better pickings in another city. Please, I really want to do this."

"Yes, I'm getting the idea," Brooke said. "I see the determination in your eyes."

"Then let me do it, for goodness' sake." Theodosia drew a deep breath. "For Kaitlin's sake."

"Theodosia . . ."

"Timothy Neville has assured us there'll be plenty of security present."

"Sure there will," Brooke said. "Did they hire armed guards from Fort Knox? Or, better yet, is SEAL Team Six standing by?"

When Theodosia didn't reply, when she continued with her slightly imploring look, Brooke took her hand and squeezed it. "Okay, Theo. You win. This is against my better judgment, but we'll find something fabulous for you to flash around tonight. But I want you to swear on a stack of Bibles that you'll be super careful. That you'll promise not to take any unnecessary risks."

"I promise," Theodosia said, even though she figured she might be taking a huge risk. But she was tired of chasing after shadows and anxious to make something happen. Exactly what, she figured she'd have to wait and find out.

* * *

When Theodosia finally swung into the Indigo Tea Shop it was almost eleven o'clock.

"There you are," Drayton said. He looked up from behind the counter, where he was packaging up two dozen chocolate chip scones in indigo-blue boxes for a take-out order. "We haven't been terribly busy with morning tea service . . . we're about half-full as you can see. But the phone has been ringing off the hook for take-out orders. It seems like every coffee shop, B and B, and anxious hostess in a ten-block radius wants to get their paws on a dozen of our scones. Like immediately. So Haley had to ramp up and bake another four dozen."

"Was that a problem?" Theodosia asked.

"No. Haley pretty much took it in stride. You know what a little trouper she is. And the kitchen's all toasty warm and smells heavenly. Like somebody blended sugar, chocolate, and cinnamon to concoct some kind of delicious foodie perfume."

"Nothing wrong with that," Theodosia said. "But I think I'll go check on Haley and see how she's doing."

"You want to hand me that aluminum mixing bowl?" Haley asked abruptly as Theodosia stepped into the kitchen. As Drayton had predicted, it was toasty warm and smelled heavenly. If chocolate was your idea of heaven.

Theodosia glanced sideways. "The big one on the top shelf?"

"Yup. That's it."

Theodosia grabbed the bowl, bobbled it slightly in her hands, and then passed it over to Haley. "Drayton said you had to whip up a few more pans of scones?"

Haley gave a quick nod. "Yeah, we've been crazy-busy with take-out orders. So I baked another four dozen chocolate chip scones and now I'm going to whip up three dozen mara-schino cherry scones. Once that's done, I'm going to collapse and call it a day." She grabbed a canister of sugar and popped off the top. "We're still planning to close early today, right?"

"One thirty or two o'clock. As soon as we can gracefully get everyone out of the tea shop without ruffling any feathers."

"Sounds like a plan," Haley said. She grabbed a scoop and began measuring out sugar. "You know, I've been thinking about the Rare Antiquities Show tonight and I decided that I'm actually looking forward to it."

"That's great to hear. I'm glad you decided to join us." Haley wasn't always gung ho about black-tie events. Espe-cially the ones at the Heritage Society, which she deemed to be a little too stuffy for her bohemian sensibilities. "Have you figured out what you're going to wear?"

Haley glanced up. "I thought I might wear that mid-night blue dress you let me wear last time. Would that be okay with you?"

"Absolutely it would. Especially since it's still hanging in your closet."

"Well . . . yeah. But if it's a problem . . ."

"It's not," Theodosia said. "Besides, I already made a run to Cotton Duck and picked up a new black dress. Though it was done under duress and Delaine technically picked it out for me."

"Was she there? Futzing around the shop?" Haley asked.

"No, thank goodness."

Haley chuckled. "Delaine's kind of an ankle biter, isn't she?"

"Hmm?"

"You know, like one of those little teacup dogs that's always jumping around and yapping at your ankles."

"I doubt Delaine would see it that way."

"So," Haley said, "what'd she pick out for you? A cool dress or a gag-me dress?"

"It's cute. I think you'll like it."

"But the big question is will I fit into it?" Haley asked. "At a later date, I mean."

"You probably will. If you don't snarf down too many of your own scones."

"I know," Haley chuckled. "I gotta be careful about that. I don't want to be a product of my own success."

"Speaking of which, what's on the docket for lunch today?"

"I made it easy peasy," Haley said. "Tomato bisque soup, egg salad tea sandwiches, and mini chicken Wellingtons."

"*Chicken* Wellington? We've never served that before," Theodosia said. "In fact, I've never heard of it before."

Haley grinned. "You wouldn't. Since I just invented it."

After relaxing at home for the afternoon, Theodosia took Earl Grey for a nice long walk and then came home and slipped into her tub for a bubble bath. As she unwound and luxuriated in the hot, silky water, her thoughts predictably turned toward the evening. She ruminated about the Heritage Society's big coup in obtaining a genuine Fabergé egg for their show, and all the well-to-do patrons who'd be in attendance.

There was also the possibility, of course, that coyotes might sneak into the chicken coop. That uninvited guests might infiltrate the show, with hungry eyes and theft on their brain.

Of course, someone with a proper invitation might also be biding their time to grab the Fabergé egg. Lionel Rinicker came to mind, as did Sabrina and Luke Andros. She didn't think her other two suspects—Billy Grainger and Marcus Clement—would be there. But you never know. It could turn out to be an anything-can-happen night.

Toenails clicked against the bathroom tile and Theodosia glanced up to see Earl Grey peering in.

"I know," she said. "I'm turning into a prune and probably making myself late. I'll kick it into high gear."

Earl Grey curled up on a plush cushion in Theodosia's upstairs turret room as she bustled about in her slip, getting ready. Delaine had once urged her to wear more eye makeup, so tonight she dutifully stood before her mirror and dabbed on a smidge of beige eye shadow, applied a coat of brown mascara, and then added a second coat.

There. Enough. I don't need to have tarantula eyes.

Lipstick was just a touch of Chanel's Imaginaire lip gloss.

Theodosia reached up and removed the plastic clip from her hair. Her auburn locks tumbled down around her shoulders, giving her the look of an angel in a romantic painting by Raphael. She grabbed a fat brush and tried to tame her curls and fierce waves. But the more she brushed, the more her hair crackled and came alive.

At least it's not doing its high-humidity double-volume thing.

In a world of upper-crust women who wore sleek designer bobs and sophisticated pixie cuts, she would just have to go au naturel tonight.

"Woof."

Theodosia walked out of the bathroom and said, "What?" Earl Grey was standing at the window, his nose pressed hard against the glass, staring down into the backyard. "What do you see, fella?"

"*Rrrrw.*" His hackles were up and his tail was down.

"Somebody in the backyard?" Theodosia came to the window and looked down. "Are the raccoons back?" But she didn't see anything moving. No bright eyes staring up, no bushy tails. "I think we're okay," she said. "You can probably stand down." But like a good guard dog, earnest and unperturbed, Earl Grey remained at his post.

Theodosia slipped into her new black cocktail dress and squiggled her feet into black velvet high heels. She brushed back waves of hair and put on a pair of diamond stud earrings that her aunt Libby had given her. The last thing she did was attach the pin that Brooke had loaned her. When she was ready, when she finally glanced at herself head to toe in the mirror, her dress and all her other preparations seemed like background noise. The sparkling ruby-and-diamond flower pin clearly took center stage. Sitting high on her dress, the multitude of jewels sparkled and danced, projecting a thousand points of light.

And as Theodosia turned to leave, the dazzling shards glimmered seductively and seemed almost to whisper, *Come and snatch me if you dare.*

26

❧

"Theodosia," Drayton exclaimed. "You look positively radiant tonight." He looked and sounded appropriately awestruck.

"Thank you," Theodosia said. She had just stepped into the Great Hall at the Heritage Society and been enveloped in a swirl of elegantly gowned women and tuxedo-clad men. Waiters carrying silver trays plied the crowd with crystal flutes filled with French champagne, and over in the far corner a string quartet played the sprightly notes of Vivaldi. Drayton himself wore a one-button Fitzgerald tuxedo with a red cummerbund.

"As you can see," Drayton said, looking pleased, one arm sweeping the crowd in a rather grand gesture, "the Heritage Society has had a record turnout."

Theodosia glanced about at the well-heeled mob, where society ladies exchanged air kisses, men shook hands and congratulated each other on business deals and golf scores, and singles were on the prowl. "Heavens," she said, "how many people are here, anyway?"

"At last estimate, a tad over three hundred guests."

"I don't know if that's good or bad."

Drayton's brows knit together suddenly. "Like you, I still worry about some disaster befalling our Fabergé egg."

"Humpty Dumpty had a great fall," Theodosia murmured softly. "So . . . are there extra guards? Has added security been put on?"

"Timothy says yes, so I have to believe him. Though most of the security detail seem to be dressed in plain clothes and are mingling anonymously."

"And where's the guest of honor?" Theodosia asked. "Where is this amazing Fabergé egg?" She glanced around, saw fine oil paintings, marble sculptures, and some sterling silver pitchers that were probably genuine Paul Revere. But no egg.

"At the last minute, Timothy had the display case moved to the rear of the Great Hall," Drayton said. "Instead of keeping the Fabergé egg front and center, he thought it would be safer if it was back by the wall, easier to guard." He gave her a knowing look, then put a hand on her shoulder and steered her through the press of warm bodies. "Come along, I'll show you."

When they were within fifteen feet of the Fabergé egg, Theodosia began hearing appreciative murmurs. The cacophony of words that rang in her ears included such words as, "spectacular," "amazing," and "I wonder how much it's worth?"

"How much *is* it worth?" Theodosia asked Drayton as they jostled their way to the front of the line.

"Take a look and then you tell me," Drayton said.

Theodosia edged forward two more steps and then, suddenly, there it was. A dazzling, ruby-red, jewel-encrusted imperial Fabergé egg. Gracefully encased in delicate swirls of 24-karat gold, it was one of the most amazing pieces of art that Theodosia had ever seen.

"Oh my goodness," Theodosia exclaimed, completely taken aback. "It's beautiful." She'd never set eyes on a genuine Fabergé egg before. She'd only seen photos of them in a Sotheby's catalog. Clearly, even glossy photos couldn't do the eggs justice because this particular Fabergé egg was take-your-breath-away stunning.

"Isn't it a honey?" Drayton was smiling unabashedly now. "You see how the middle of the egg is set completely with rubies?"

"I see that," Theodosia said.

"With a dozen rows of diamonds at both the top and bottom?" Drayton flicked his hand just so.

"Amazing." Any one of the many diamonds would have made a girl swoon.

"And do you see the design of the gold work? How the imperial Russian eagle morphs seamlessly into that lovely swirl pattern." Drayton waggled a finger. "Do you see how the design almost anticipates the Art Deco movement?"

Theodosia nodded again. "I suppose it does."

"Fascinating, yes?"

"Yes," Theodosia agreed. She knew that everyone else found it just as fascinating, since all eyes seemed to be focused on the egg.

A moment later, Drayton turned his attention to her. "Wait a minute." His eyes narrowed and he took a step back. "What, pray tell, do you have pinned to your dress?"

Theodosia's hand fluttered to her ruby pin. "You mean this?"

"Yes. Of course I'm referring to the pin you're wearing. The one with more diamonds and rubies than the crown jewels. It looks like it's worth an absolute fortune. It looks almost like . . . well . . ." He glanced sideways at the egg. "It looks almost like a mate to the Fabergé egg! The jewelry equivalent, anyway, done in rubies and diamonds."

Theodosia grabbed Drayton by the sleeve and pulled

him out of the scrum of admirers. "It is expensive," she told him. "Brooke loaned it to me."

"How interesting." Drayton was acting a little twitchy now. "I thought all her jewelry had been stolen in last Sunday's heist."

"She had this particular Bulgari piece stashed in her office safe. Probably because it *is* so rare and pricey."

"Okay," Drayton said, focusing a stern gaze on her. "Now tell me why *you* happen to be wearing it? Why you're attempting to stick out like a sore thumb?" Before Theodosia could answer, he touched a hand to his forehead and said, "Oh no. Silly me. You're wearing that piece on purpose, aren't you? You're parading around with it on your person, winking and blinking like a homing beacon, so you can catch the eye of any would-be jewel thieves."

Theodosia pursed her lips. "I'm not parading around."

Drayton's eyes bored into her. "Yes, you really are."

"Okay," Theodosia said. "So the piece is going to get noticed. Is that such a bad thing?"

"It's terrible," Drayton said. "If those awful jewel thieves happen to show up here tonight, you could get smashed and grabbed yourself!"

"I don't think that's going to happen," Theodosia said. When Drayton continued to stare at her, she decided she'd better come clean. "Okay, maybe I *did* think my pin might possibly attract the attention of the jewel thieves. But if it does, isn't that a good way to flush them out?"

"It's not good at all," Drayton said. He was almost beside himself. "In fact, it's an insane plan. Which is why we're going to get you out of here. Right now. This instant."

Theodosia pulled away from him. "Drayton . . ." She wanted to at least give her plan a chance to work.

"And I can't believe Brooke loaned it to you," Drayton spat out. "What was she thinking?" He shook his head, baffled.

"Well, she wasn't thinking, that's for sure. Good thing *I'm* the one with the clear head."

"I'm not leaving this party, if that's what you're saying." Theodosia was a little shocked. She'd never seen Drayton quite so insistent before.

"Then we'll lock that thing up in Timothy's office for the time being. Come on."

Theodosia's shoulders sagged. "Oh no . . . seriously?"

But just as Drayton tried to propel her away from the crowd, Lionel Rinicker loomed directly in front of them. Tall and gawky in his black tuxedo, he looked like an ominous scarecrow.

"Drayton!" Rinicker exclaimed. "Can you believe this marvelous turnout?" He smiled a lopsided grin at Theodosia and said, "Hello, Miss Browning, it's lovely to see you again."

"Hello, Mr. Rinicker," Theodosia said. She was actually delighted to see Rinicker. One, because now she could keep a keen eye on him. And, two, because now Drayton couldn't drag her off like a sack of potatoes to Timothy's office.

"Lionel," a woman's voice purred. "I grabbed a glass of champagne for you." Grace Dawson suddenly joined them, looking petite and elegant in a strapless black dress with fluffy black ostrich feathers around the hem. She had a glass of champagne clutched in each hand. "I'm not usually a two-fisted drinker," she chuckled to Theodosia and Drayton.

Theodosia and Drayton greeted her warmly and then Theodosia said, "Have you seen the Fabergé egg yet?"

Grace handed one of the glasses to Rinicker and said, "Have we ever. I think we were among the first ones here tonight."

"Impressive, isn't it?" Drayton said. He was fidgeting, glancing at Theodosia, still trying to pull her away.

"I saw a blue Fabergé egg at a fancy auction in Miami once," Grace said. "It came from one of the old Palm Beach estates. It was gorgeous, all blue enamel and gold fretwork.

But it was nothing of this caliber. This is"—she seemed to search for just the right word—"this is a prize."

"Coming through! Coming through!" called a loud voice. Theodosia, Drayton, Rinicker, and Grace all quickly stepped out of the way as two technicians from Channel 8, one carrying a video camera, and another juggling a large light and wearing a battery pack around his waist, pushed their way brusquely through the crowd.

"TV people have arrived," Rinicker said.

"What?" Drayton jerked his head toward him.

"Oh, didn't you know?" Rinicker asked. "Channel 8 is here to cover the show. They're going to do some interviews and, I think, maybe even a live remote for their ten o'clock news."

That was when Weston Keyes, the host of *Charleston Today*, suddenly appeared.

"'Scuse me, 'scuse me," Keyes said, shouldering his way through the crowd. He was wearing a heavy veneer of pancake makeup and an expensive-looking tuxedo.

"Mmn," Grace purred. "He's wearing a Brioni."

"That's expensive?" Rinicker asked as Keyes hustled past them, looking both officious and a little harried.

"Gracious, yes," Grace said.

Theodosia saw the boom light poke up high above the crowd and then bob dangerously close to the glass case where the Fabergé egg resided. Then it was pulled back just in the nick of time. One disaster averted, anyway.

"I think they're going to interview Timothy Neville," Rinicker said. He smiled at Grace. "Come on, let's go watch. It might be fun."

But Theodosia and Drayton hung back.

"Did you know about this?" Theodosia asked Drayton. "About the TV people coming in?"

Drayton shook his head. "I had no idea. In fact, I rather despise the idea of a media circus."

"But it's probably good publicity," Theodosia told him. "The show opens on Sunday to the general public, right?"

"I suppose."

"Well, there you go." She also figured that the all-seeing eye of a television camera, poised to capture any sudden moves, might serve as a serious deterrent to anyone who had plans to grab the egg.

Drayton nudged Theodosia. "There's Haley." He lifted an arm and waved. "Haley, over here."

Haley, looking radiant and youthful in her borrowed blue dress, scooted over to join them. "Hey, guys," she bubbled. "What's up?" She'd swept her long blond hair into a topknot and, with high color in her cheeks, looked every inch the ingenue.

"Channel 8 just showed up to film the Fabergé egg," Theodosia said.

Haley brightened. "Really? There's TV here? Cool."

"Youth," Drayton mumbled.

"What's that, Drayton?" Haley asked.

Drayton shrugged. "Nothing. Just making idle chatter."

"Hey," Haley said to Theodosia. "Great dress. And I love that sparkly pin you're wearing."

"Thank you." Theodosia grabbed one of Haley's hands. "And I'm so glad you came with us tonight."

Haley grinned. "Well, I didn't exactly come *with* you."

"You know what I mean. It gave Drayton a good excuse to cash in some of his currency as a board member. To add your name to the list with all the Gold Circle patrons."

"Gotcha," Haley said. She glanced around, a smile playing at the corners of her mouth. "I would so love a drink."

"Let me . . ." Drayton said. He waved a hand at one of the waiters, who saw him, nodded, and started their way. "Here we go. This young man has a fresh tray of drinks for us . . ."

"Wonderful," Theodosia said as the waiter slid to a graceful stop in front of her. He was tall with warm brown eyes and long hair that was pulled neatly into a low ponytail. She grabbed a flute of champagne from the tray and smiled her thanks at the young waiter. Then her smile faltered and she said, "Wait a minute . . . Don't I know you?" His face swam into focus a little more clearly and she stammered, "Aren't you . . . ?"

"Billy Grainger," Haley said.

Theodosia literally felt her jaw drop. "You're . . . one of the waiters here tonight?" Her words came out in a sharp rasp.

Grainger put one hand behind his back and nodded smartly. "At your service, ma'am."

27

❧

By the time Theodosia had recovered her composure, Grainger had moved on with his tray of drinks.

"What's this all about?" Theodosia asked Haley. She had a feeling that Haley had somehow played a trick on them.

"I hardly recognized him without his motorcycle," Drayton said.

But Haley was completely wide-eyed and innocent. "Why are you two acting so weird?" she asked. "This is what Billy does. He's a waiter. I thought you knew that. He works at Ellington's Char House over on Market Street."

"That's all very well and good," Theodosia said. "But what's he doing here?"

"It's no big secret," Haley said. "Ellington's is catering this affair. Which means Billy's working here tonight. Which I think is kind of fun. And the reason I came."

"You *knew* he'd be here?" Theodosia asked.

"Sure," Haley said. "Besides, look at the upside. I get to hang out with him and we can have free drinks all night long."

"They're already free," Theodosia said.

"Well . . . then we'll get really good service," Haley responded.

"Youth," Drayton said. And this time he didn't bother to mumble.

"What can I say?" Theodosia said to Drayton. "Is Haley really that much of a blithe spirit?"

"To answer your question, yes. That girl is totally without guile."

"You didn't think she was trying to put one over on us?"

"I certainly don't know what her rationale would have been."

"Hmm."

"What hmm?" Drayton asked.

"My head's spinning and I've only had one sip of champagne," Theodosia said. "Maybe we need to check out the canapés?" She was grateful Drayton had been so distracted by Rinicker, Haley, and Grainger. He seemed to have completely forgotten about hustling her out of sight.

"Some food might be in order, yes." Drayton took Theodosia's arm and led her toward the buffet table. "It's over this way. Far from the maddening crowd and the bright lights of the television cameras."

The canapés from Ellington's looked delicious. Silver chafing dishes overflowed with crab claws, cheese puffs, and grilled oysters. Crackers, a French farmhouse pâté, cheeses, and smoked fish were spread out on a silver tray.

"What is this delicious-looking cheese, please?" Drayton asked one of the caterers who was standing behind the table.

"That's artisanal blue from Wedgewood Farms up near Camden."

"Excellent," Drayton said.

The server smiled. "It really is, sir. I think you'll enjoy it."

"It looks like someone besides me is an oyster lover," a voice at Theodosia's elbow said.

She glanced up to find Agent Zimmer smiling at her. He looked so relaxed and dashing that she almost didn't recognize him. "Hello," she said, caught off guard. "Fancy seeing you here. Are you flying solo tonight or did you drag your trusty sidekick along with you?"

"Hurley's around here somewhere. Probably grabbing a drink."

"I didn't know agents were allowed to drink on duty," Theodosia said.

Zimmer cocked his head. "Who says we're on duty?"

"Oh . . . okay." *Hmm,* Theodosia thought to herself. *He is attractive in a kind of tight-jawed law-enforcement way.*

"Excuse me," Drayton said. He reached between the two of them and grabbed a cracker. "Nice tux," he said to Zimmer.

"Thank you," Zimmer said. "It's rented."

"I thought it might be," Drayton said. "Well, we'll see you around." He gave Theodosia a look that clearly said, *Follow me,* and led her toward a cluster of high, round tables and stools.

Theodosia figured that the Heritage Society had hoped to make the area resemble a convivial wine bar, though it looked more like rented tables with a few potted plants scattered around.

"That was awkward," Drayton said as they pushed through the crowd, balancing their plates and glasses.

"I think he was just trying to be nice," Theodosia said. *And maybe something more? Like ask me for a date?*

"He's working," Drayton said. "And maybe trying to work you over, too."

"Maybe." Theodosia eased herself onto one of the high stools, being mindful of her short dress. "Oh well, at least we haven't run into Professor Shepley."

"I guess he really did decide to drive back to Savannah, like he told us," Drayton said. "So he's out of the picture."

"I hope so. Unless the professor decides to pop in as a surprise guest tonight, not unlike Billy Grainger."

"Grainger's not technically a guest, because he's working."

Theodosia rolled her eyes. "You know what I mean."

They nibbled and talked for a good ten minutes. All the while, Theodosia kept an eye on the crowd, watching for anyone who might look a little strange, a little like an interloper. Maybe somebody who was . . . from Eastern Europe?"

"Have you spotted any international party crashers yet?" Drayton asked.

"How did you know that's what I was doing?" Then, "Am I that obvious?"

Drayton picked delicately at a crab claw. "Yes. And in case you're wondering, my stomach is twisted up in knots, too. Ever since we ran into Agent Zimmer."

"He must be worried," Theodosia said. "Just as we are. I mean . . . I keep waiting for a gang of thieves to crash through one of the walls in a Hummer."

"That's unlikely," Drayton said. "Since the exterior walls are one-hundred-year-old granite."

"Good heavens, look who's here," a familiar voice cried out.

Theodosia gazed across the top of her champagne glass to find Sabrina Andros smiling at her, her grin so expansive it looked as if she'd just won the Powerball. Standing right behind her, looking trim in his tuxedo, was Luke Andros.

"I thought you two were on your way to South America," Theodosia blurted out. What she was really thinking was, *Holy cats, now I have to worry about the two of you?*

"Goodness," Sabrina said, her smile faltering. "How did you happen to know our itinerary?"

"Um . . . Grace Dawson mentioned it to me," Theodosia said. "I guess she ran into you at the spa yesterday?"

"Isn't she the unfiltered little chatterbox," Sabrina said. "And, yes, Luke is making a run to meet with a potential customer. But he's planning to leave first thing tomorrow morning." She glanced around. "We certainly didn't want to miss *this*. It's the first big gala we've ever been to at the Heritage Society." She giggled slightly. "It's thrilling to find so many old Charleston families in attendance."

"I'm glad you're enjoying yourselves," Drayton said.

"We weren't about to miss seeing the Fabergé egg, either," Luke said. "You might say we're raving Fabergé fans. We once made a side trip during a visit to Saint Petersburg just to take in the Fabergé Museum."

"It whet our appetite to come and see this one," Sabrina said.

"We've always secretly lusted after Fabergé eggs," Luke said.

"Who doesn't?" Theodosia said. Her throat was starting to feel dry and she was getting a strange sense of impending doom. Were these people jewel thieves? Had they robbed Heart's Desire and now had plans to abscond with the Fabergé egg? Or were they just clumsy social climbers?

"But, of course, a Fabergé egg is prohibitively expensive," Luke added.

"Pity," Sabrina said, her eyes glittering. She moved closer to Theodosia and said, rather coyly, "That flower pin you're wearing is extraordinarily gorgeous, too. I can't seem to take my eyes off it."

"It certainly is a beauty," Luke echoed.

"I have to ask," Sabrina said. "Is it yours, something you inherited? Or did you borrow it from a jeweler just for this particular occasion? I mean, it looks like it's worth a bloody fortune."

Theodosia didn't know what to say, so she said, "Thank you. And the pin doesn't belong to me. It's definitely on loan." Her eyes sought out Drayton's. "In fact, Drayton was just saying that it's probably time to put it back in the safe downstairs. Weren't you, Drayton?"

"Indeed, yes," Drayton said, picking up his cue nicely. "One can never be too careful. Even in a tony crowd like this."

Luke Andros peered at Theodosia's ruby pin, moving in a little too close for comfort. "Look at those rubies and diamonds. I'd say it's classic Bulgari."

"You rarely see workmanship of that caliber anymore," Sabrina said. "Yes, I'd say it's worth a fortune."

Theodosia watched Sabrina and Luke slink through the crowd, shaking hands and shamelessly introducing themselves along the way. "Those two give me the creeps."

"I hear you," Drayton said. "There's something odd about them."

"And you're right about this pin."

"How's that?"

"I . . . I don't think I should wear it anymore."

"Now you're listening to reason. You feel spooked, huh?"

"I didn't until Sabrina and Luke Andros showed up and started making such a big deal of it." Theodosia fumbled with the clasp and gently unclipped the ruby and diamond pin from her dress. "Here," she said, holding it out to Drayton. "You take it."

Drayton's hands flew up in a defensive posture. "I don't want it."

"We need to do something to keep it safe."

Haley came wafting by their table at that exact moment.

"Haley," Drayton said, crooking a finger at her. "Do me a favor, will you?"

"Sure," she said. "Your wish is my command. What's up?"

"Have you seen Timothy since you've been here?"

"Um . . . sure," Haley said. "Like ten seconds ago. He just finished doing a sound bite for that TV guy with the fake-bake tan."

"Go ask Timothy for the key to his private office, will you?" Drayton asked. "Tell him it's for me. That I want to lock something away for safekeeping."

"Okay," Haley said.

Drayton got up from the table. "We'll meet you over by the door, right next to that display of Etruscan coins."

Haley shot him a salute. "Be right back."

"Thank you," Theodosia said to Drayton as they strolled back toward the main door. "I think we'll both feel better when that pin is under lock and key. You were right, wearing it tonight was kind of reckless."

"It does feel as though something's about to happen, doesn't it?"

The words had barely left Drayton's mouth when a thin, high cry pierced the air.

"What on earth?" Drayton said. His head spun around. "It sounded like a wounded animal."

"But out in the hallway?" Theodosia said.

They both ducked through the doorway only to run smack-dab into Delaine. Her face was pink and puffy and streaked with tears; her shoulders heaved up and down with emotion.

"Delaine," Theodosia cried. "Honey, what's wrong? What happened?"

"Re-re-naldo!" Delaine moaned. "He's so mean and hateful!"

Renaldo Gilles, Delaine's boyfriend du jour, was hovering a few feet away, looking decidedly awkward.

Theodosia advanced on Gilles. "What did you *do* to her?"

Gilles looked panic-stricken. "Nothing. She just suddenly broke into hysterics."

"I can see she's upset. The question is why?"

Gilles spread his arms apart in the manner of a European shrug. "I *told* her I couldn't remain here indefinitely. I made it perfectly clear that I had to return to France, that my company would *fire* me if I didn't come back."

Delaine fanned herself madly as she quavered, "You told me you were going to stay *longer*."

"I did stay longer," Gilles said. "Almost an extra two

weeks. But . . . ah, what's the use." He waved his arms. *"Mon Dieu."*

Drayton glanced at Theodosia and said, in a low voice, "Lovers' quarrel."

Theodosia nodded. It wasn't the first time she'd seen Delaine fall apart over a man. She was clearly in pain now, but she'd get over it. She always did.

But for now, Delaine was quite content to wallow in the throes of her self-induced pity party. "What am I going to do?" she asked, throwing herself into Theodosia's arms.

Theodosia hugged her gently for a few moments, then pried Delaine's fingernails off her shoulders, where she was sure they'd left some serious indentations. "You're going to wipe away those tears and go join the party," she told her. "Take Gilles with you, don't take Gilles, whatever. Go talk to your friends or even another man if you feel like it. But don't let this silly little flirtation define you. You're better than this."

Delaine blinked at Theodosia and sniffled. "I am, aren't I?" Her eyes regained some of their fierce glitter. "I'm a good-looking woman. I'm still in my prime."

"You're a knockout."

"Well, I . . . do you . . . do you have a Kleenex?" Delaine sniffled again. "Goodness, I must look a fright."

Theodosia dug in her beaded clutch and handed Delaine a tissue. Delaine wiped at her eyes and managed an uneven smile. "Is my mascara all smeary?"

"Not too bad." She wasn't about to tell Delaine that she had a serious case of raccoon eyes.

"Help me?" Delaine asked, helplessly.

Theodosia wiped away the smudges from beneath Delaine's eyes as best she could. "There. All fixed. Feel better now?"

"Not really," Delaine said. "But at least I feel a tiny bit more presentable."

"There you go," Drayton said in a false hearty tone. "That's ninety percent of it right there."

Gilles was tapping his foot now. "Well, have you decided? Are we going in or not?"

Delaine lifted her chin. "You may escort me, yes. But only for the time being."

Theodosia let out a sigh of relief as Delaine preceded Gilles into the party.

Drayton watched them go. "That poor Frenchman is like a lamb to the slaughter," he said. "No man has a fighting chance against Delaine."

"She's one of a kind, that's for sure." Theodosia mustered a quick smile as they strolled back into the Great Hall to rejoin the party. "Oh good. Here comes Haley."

Haley came running up and immediately dangled a little brass key in front of Drayton's nose. "I got the key. But Timothy made me promise to bring it back to him immediately. Once you lock up whatever little treasure it is you're locking up."

"Not a problem," Drayton said, reaching for the key.

Haley snatched it back out of his research. "What's so important, anyway?" She gave an impish grin and her eyes danced with curiosity.

Theodosia handed the ruby-and-diamond brooch to Haley. "We're trying to keep this safe."

Haley gazed at it. "This sure is some fancy hunk of jewelry." Now there was reverence in her voice. "Where'd you get it, anyway?" She cradled the pin in the palm of her hand.

"Brooke loaned it to me," Theodosia said. "It was one of the few pieces that wasn't stolen during the robbery."

"Our dear Theodosia had a crazy notion that wearing that fancy pin might lure the jewel thieves out of hiding," Drayton explained.

"And did it?" Haley asked.

"Not as far as we know," Theodosia said.

"So you want me to . . . what? Take this pin and lock it up?" Haley asked.

"That would be great," Theodosia said.

"Just put it in Timothy's desk," Drayton said.

Haley held the pin up to her dress. "It's so gorgeous, maybe I should wear it."

"We'd rather you didn't," Drayton said.

"It's probably more prudent if you just kept it out of sight," Theodosia said, glancing around. Nobody was watching, but she still felt jittery. "Maybe hide it in your pocket or something." She knew the dress Haley was wearing had two deep pockets hidden in the folds of the voluminous skirt.

But Haley was still entranced. She held the bauble up to the light, studying it. "Holy guacamole, this thing looks expensive." She grinned as it twinkled and shimmered, catching the overhead lights.

"Haley . . ." Drayton's voice carried a warning tone.

"Okay, okay," Haley said, closing her hand around the pin. "I hear you. I'll run down to Timothy's office and lock it up nice and tight so it'll be safe from prying eyes and nefarious jewel thieves."

"Thank you," Theodosia said as Haley skipped away.

28

❧

With the ruby–and–diamond pin safely on its way to Timothy's office, Theodosia suddenly felt a million times lighter. Nothing was going to happen tonight, she assured herself. The Fabergé egg was safe and, come Monday morning, she would redouble her efforts to help Brooke. But tonight she was going to relax and enjoy the party. She might even flirt with Agent Zimmer if she felt like it. And, by the way, she wanted to take a careful look at all the splendid objects that the Heritage Society had on view throughout the room.

"Those Etruscan coins," Theodosia said, pointing to a scatter of brass coins that lay on a drift of black velvet. "What do they date back to?"

"I'm glad you asked," Drayton said. "These particular coins hail from the third century BC. You see the gold one with the lion's . . ."

A tiny, shrill scream, almost a blip of a scream, echoed from out in the hallway.

The sound didn't register with Drayton, but Theodosia

picked up on it instantly. Her heart did a rapid flip-flop and then leapt into her throat. "Did you hear that?"

"Excuse me . . . what?" Drayton said. He'd been in the middle of speechifying.

"That little noise?"

Drayton cocked an eye at her. "Is Delaine making another scene? Startling everyone with one of her mouse shrieks?"

Another blip of a scream sounded, and this time it was slightly more distinct.

"Dear Lord," Theodosia said. "That sounded just like Haley!"

"*Our* Haley . . . Where?"

"I think . . . out in the hallway," Theodosia said. Deep in her heart she *knew* something was wrong. Felt it in her bones. So without another word to Drayton, she lunged for the door.

Drayton spun and followed on her heels. "We probably shouldn't . . ." he began.

But Theodosia was already out the door and five steps ahead of him. "There!" she screamed. She flung out an arm and pointed toward the far end of the corridor, where a trio of shadowy figures danced and ducked and tangled in a mighty struggle. "Haley?" she cried out.

"Theo!" Haley's piteous scream came back. "Help me!" Haley was twisting and turning, trying to escape the grip of two men.

"I'll alert security," Drayton said. "Grab those FBI . . ."

Theodosia snagged his sleeve and tried to pull him along. "No time. We have to help Haley *now*."

"But the . . ."

Theodosia took off as though someone had fired a starter's gun, leaving Drayton in her wake. She pounded down the hallway toward Haley. "Hang on, Haley!" Just as her slippery shoes started to gain traction on the thick carpet, a door flew open and she was swatted aside like a bug. Screeching, her right shoulder exploding with a flash of pain, she flailed out and stumbled, then crashed down hard on one knee.

The door whapped shut as Billy Grainger careened out of the small catering kitchen. He cut in front of Theodosia, struggling valiantly to steady his tray of champagne flutes, wobbling and swaying for a few seconds, fighting to keep his tray level and regain his balance. No such luck. He stumbled badly, causing the glasses to topple sideways and crash into one another. Foamy gluts of champagne spewed everywhere.

"You!" Theodosia cried as the spatter of liquid hit her. She batted at Grainger from where she was still half sprawled on the floor. "Help me!"

"Watch where you're going!" Grainger yelled angrily as he tried to pull himself up.

"No!" Theodosia screamed back at him, gesturing and trying to make him understand. "A couple of guys just grabbed Haley. You have to help us!"

Grainger's face drained white. "What?" he hissed.

"Down there," Theodosia flung out an arm. "Two guys grabbed Haley and are trying to drag her . . ."

As Theodosia and Grainger struggled to regain their footing, the lights flicked off and the entire hallway was plunged into darkness.

"Where'd they go?" Grainger cried as he whirled about frantically. They could hear Haley screaming and struggling, but couldn't see her.

Flailing a hand out, Theodosia located a wall and fought to guide herself along. While down at the far end of the hallway, a single figure stepped out of the shadows and said, in the cold, flat tone of an undertaker, "Pick the girl up and bring her along."

"C'mon!" Theodosia called to Drayton and Grainger, trying to rally them in the darkness. "We've got to help Haley."

But as the double doors clanged shut at the far end of the hallway, they were the only ones left fighting their way down the darkened corridor.

"Where'd they disappear to?" Grainger asked.

"Dragged her outside," Theodosia huffed.

"How many guys?" Drayton asked.

"I don't know," Theodosia said. "Maybe . . . three?"

"So, a gang," Drayton panted as he struggled to keep up with them.

When they finally reached the far end of the corridor, a small light shone on the reception desk. Theodosia clattered her way across the marble entry as Drayton and Grainger followed in her wake. She slammed the double doors open wide, almost decapitating the carefully manicured topiaries of Czar Nicholas and Czarina Alexandra in the process.

"I don't see anybody," Grainger said. He was glancing about feverishly, quivering like a Brittany spaniel on point.

Theodosia, Drayton, and Grainger all stood stock-still for a few moments, searching for the men who'd just carted off Haley. Streetlights shone dimly, a sliver of moonlight dappled the sidewalk, but they saw nothing.

"Where is she?" Drayton asked.

Suddenly, there was a telltale blur of movement from far down the row of parked cars. Theodosia caught it out of the corner of her eye and said, "There they are!"

It was dark as pitch, but Theodosia could see that Haley was still putting up a valiant struggle. Heads bobbed, bodies twisted, arms flew wildly, and then someone—probably Haley?—was rudely shoved into the backseat of a long, dark car.

"Let's go!" Theodosia cried.

Three abreast, they thundered down the sidewalk. But they'd covered only half the distance to the dark car when its lights flashed on. Then the car's engine roared to life and, a millisecond later, it squealed away from the curb.

"Dear Lord, she's gone," Theodosia cried. She felt like sinking to her knees in despair. Instead, she spun toward Grainger and snarled, "You better not be in on this."

"I'm not, I'm not," he cried.

"Then, who took her?"

Grainger threw up his hands in frustration. "I don't know."

"Had to be the jewel thieves," Drayton said. "I think our worst fear just came true. They saw that jeweled pin and . . ."

"We're going after them," Theodosia said, making a snap decision and darting across the street. "Come on. Everybody into my Jeep."

They all piled in, and she took off like it was the start of the Indianapolis 500, gunning her engine, breaking a nail as she snapped her seat belt closed.

"Where'd they go? Where'd they go?" Drayton quavered as they rocketed down the street.

"Back down King Street," Grainger said. "And then I think they turned left on Tradd."

"You think or you know?" Theodosia demanded. She was accelerating like crazy, weaving down King Street, throwing caution to the wind, hoping she wouldn't sideswipe a car or kill a hapless pedestrian.

"Turn left," Grainger shouted.

Theodosia squealed into the turn. She could feel the back end of her Jeep ready to let go, swinging ever so slightly with the centrifugal force. At the last moment, her tires dug in and found purchase. She fishtailed like crazy for a hundred yards and then straightened out.

Grainger leaned forward and squinted. "I'm positive that's the car up ahead. Same curved taillights."

Theodosia goosed her car faster.

"Be careful," Drayton cautioned.

"No fear," Theodosia said. She reached down, grabbed her beaded bag, and tossed it over the backseat to Drayton. "Dig out my cell phone and call Tidwell. Be quick."

Drayton panicked. "Call him? How?"

"Speed dial," Theodosia said through gritted teeth.

Grainger was riding shotgun, hanging on for dear life, but doing his best to spot for her. "I think they're turning again. Yeah, that's them. It has to be. Looks like they're headed for the harbor."

"Andros!" Theodosia snarled. "It has to be Luke Andros who grabbed Haley. I'll bet that jackhole is going to put her on his boat and take off." She had a sudden and terrible vision of a boat speeding out into the fog as the Atlantic rushed in, and Haley being dumped overboard into bitter cold water. Could Haley swim? Could she even dog paddle? And if they launched a rescue boat in time, would they even be able to spot her among the choppy waves?

"Theo!" Drayton cried. "I've got Tidwell on the line. What do you want me to tell him?"

She clutched the steering wheel as they flew along at breakneck speed. "Just hold the phone up to my mouth. I'll do the talking."

"Miss Browning?" came Tidwell's steady voice. "What?"

"We need help bad," Theodosia cried. "Haley's been kidnapped by Luke Andros and two of his gang members." She gave him a rapid-fire version of what had gone down. "We're pretty sure they're headed for Charleston Harbor."

"Probably headed for the Charleston Yacht Club!" Grainger yelled.

"The Charleston Yacht Club," Theodosia told Tidwell. "Can you alert the Coast Guard and pull out all the stops? I think Andros is going to try to make a getaway on one of his yachts." She listened to Tidwell for another half minute, nodded even though he couldn't see her, and said, "We'll be there." Then she said, "Okay, Drayton, you can hang up now."

"What?" Drayton asked. "What's going on?"

"Tidwell's going to meet us at the Charleston Yacht Club,"

Theodosia said. "He's says he's going to commandeer a Coast Guard ship if he has to."

"Dear Lord," Drayton said, gripping the back of Theodosia's seat. "It's going to be an international incident."

Theodosia fought to coax more speed from her vehicle. She made a wide, careening turn onto Meeting Street, almost clipping the wrought-iron light standard on the corner. She trounced down on the accelerator and ran hard for two blocks, and then twisted left on Atlantic Street, chasing after the dark car.

They whipped past the Featherbed House B and B and the historic Ramsey-Hay House, never losing sight of the car ahead, but never quite catching up to it, either.

"Turning on East Bay Street now," Grainger called out. "Yup, they're headed for the yacht club."

Theodosia turned, too, whipping past White Point Garden. Past the row of cannons, the rose beds, the bandstand, and the spot where an old pirate gallows had once stood. Fog was starting to roll in now, little puffs that reminded her of dank, dirty clouds, and she was forced to curtail her speed as the moisture condensed on her windshield. Even with her wipers beating, it was getting difficult to see.

"Parking lot up ahead," Grainger said, pointing. "Watch out, don't clip that signpost."

Theodosia cranked the steering wheel hard and shot into what was a practically deserted parking lot. A blue Toyota sat in one corner, a long, black car was hunkered in the opposite corner.

"Is that the car? Is that the car we were chasing?" Drayton asked.

"I think so," Theodosia said.

"Pull in tight behind it so you can block it," Grainger advised.

Theodosia rammed her Jeep up against the back of the

dark car and sat for a split second, trying to collect herself. Then she jerked the key from the ignition and kicked open the door. "Let's go!"

It was a good two hundred yards down to the far pier, the length of two football fields, and they were all tired and winded when they finally arrived.

"You see anything?" Drayton asked as they tentatively stepped out onto the wooden pier. A chill drizzle had started up, obscuring everyone's vision.

"It looks like Andros is still here," Theodosia whispered. Between the bobbling masts and clanking halyards, she could see two large yachts sitting at the end of the pier. Music and lights and laughter had flowed freely from them last night, but tonight they were silent. "I think we're in time. We just need to, you know . . . be careful and stay quiet."

They tiptoed down the pier, boards creaking beneath their feet, rain pattering down, the water splishing and splashing as it swirled around the boats that were moored there. They were hoping against hope that they could somehow steal on board Andros's yacht and rescue Haley.

But when they reached the far end of the dock, they saw . . . nothing. No kidnappers milling about, no crew ready to cast off lines, no sign of struggle, and no Haley. Just two dark yachts bobbing in the water. Apparently deserted.

"They're not here." Drayton exhaled hard in disbelief.

"Did we lose them during the chase?" Theodosia asked. She put a hand to her mouth, puzzled. "How could that have happened?"

"I'm positive that was their car back in the parking lot," Grainger said.

A sudden, low, throaty rumble from a boat two piers over caught their attention. Then lights flashed on and lines were cast off amid a few mumbled shouts.

"Oh no," Theodosia cried as she gazed across a raft of bobbing boats toward the other dock. She couldn't believe what was happening. "There's a different boat. Haley must be on a different boat!"

"It's pulling away," Drayton said, as the prow of a large yacht suddenly sliced into view.

"Let's go," Grainger said. "Maybe we can catch it."

They rushed back down the long pier, ran through a small picnic area and past the Charleston Yacht Club's clubhouse. Then they pounded out onto the dock where the ship had just pulled away.

And it really had pulled away. A yacht at least fifty feet in length churned up a froth of water in its wake, the glow of its running lights slowly disappearing in the dark.

"We're too late," Theodosia gasped as rain started to pour down harder. "She's gone."

"If Haley really was on that boat," Drayton said.

"She's on it," Theodosia said. "I know she is. I can feel it." She ground her teeth together and called out, "Haley!" It was a long, agonizing cry that barely hung in the air before it was muffled by the fog.

"Now what?" Drayton asked.

Theodosia's shoulders slumped. "Now we try to call Tidwell again." She reached a hand out. "Gimme the phone."

Drayton blanched. "I think it's . . . still in your car."

"I'll run back and grab it," Grainger said.

But before he could make a move, the loud, high-pitched blare of a horn pierced the air. The horn blatted again and then a brilliant bright light flashed on.

"What on earth?" Drayton murmured as the light swooped sideways and suddenly shone directly on them, bathing them in a white glow and practically blinding them with its glare.

Like a ghost ship emerging from a bank of fog, a Coast Guard ship suddenly and miraculously glided into sight. It was an RB-M, one of the new, sleek, forty-five-foot response boats used for search and rescue.

Up on deck, a man's voice, clearly enhanced by the aid of

a loudspeaker, shouted down to them. "Stay where you are. Do not try to board us. We're going to swing in close and attempt to pick you up."

Theodosia was awestruck. She didn't know whether to dance or cry. "Oh my gosh, Tidwell really did it! The man actually commandeered a Coast Guard vessel!"

The words were barely out of Theodosia's mouth when Tidwell leaned out over the railing and hailed her. "Ahoy," he called. Wind slicking back his hair, a yellow rain jacket billowing out around him, he gazed solemnly down at them. "How many?" he called out.

"Three of us," Theodosia called back. "Please hurry!"

29

With a loud *clang*, a metal ladder was slung over the side of the ship and Theodosia, Drayton, and Billy Grainger scrambled aboard.

"I can't believe you commandeered a ship," Theodosia said to Tidwell. Her voice caught in her throat, tears of gratitude welled in her eyes.

But Tidwell was completely focused on the task at hand. "Hang on," he told them, "we're going to heave about."

Grainger stepped up to Tidwell. "Is the boat that took off with Haley still in sight?"

Nonplussed, Tidwell stared at Grainger. "Who might you be?"

"Boyfriend," Drayton said, as if that explained everything. And it probably did.

"Kindly stay out of my way," Tidwell said.

Two Coast Guardsmen scrambled to put life jackets on Theodosia, Drayton, and Grainger. Then the ship's motors revved to an ear-splitting pitch and they roared out into the deep waters of Charleston Harbor.

Out on fairly open water, the wind and rain cut like a knife. They all huddled together next to the small wheelhouse. They were shivering like crazy and hanging on for dear life.

Wind and rain stinging her eyes, Theodosia leaned sideways and caught sight of the boat they were chasing. It was dead ahead, but a long way ahead. She steadied herself and lurched over to a side railing where one of the Coast Guardsmen was positioned.

The Coast Guardsman saw her fear and frustration and said, "Fast boat." His name tag said BEATTY and he looked grim.

"You think we can catch them?" Theodosia asked.

"Lieutenant Commander's pouring it on hard as he can," Beatty said.

"But is this boat faster?"

He gave a quick nod. "I think so. If he punches it all the way up to forty-five knots."

As minutes passed, and Theodosia hunched and held her breath, she saw that they were slowly but surely gaining on the boat directly ahead of them.

Tidwell duckwalked his way over to her. "Who is it?" he asked her. "Who took the girl?" He was standing with his legs splayed apart like an old sea captain. His orange life jacket billowed out around him like a spinnaker.

"I'm positive it was Luke Andros," Theodosia said. "Here I thought he was going to go after the Fabergé egg, but he grabbed Haley and the ruby-and-diamond brooch instead."

"Ruby brooch?"

Theodosia waved a hand. "It's a long story. But at least the Fabergé egg is safe."

"Who says there isn't another crew going after the egg?" Tidwell asked.

His words sent Theodosia into a stunned silence. She'd never imagined that type of scenario. Was kidnapping Haley simply a plot to lure them all away from the Heritage Society? Was there a second crew waiting in the wings? A crew all set to go storming in and grab the Fabergé egg? If kidnapping Haley was just a distraction for the real smash-and-grab, then she had screwed up royally!

Theodosia grabbed Tidwell by the front of his shirt. "You've got to get in touch with the Heritage Society!" she screamed. "Make sure everything is okay."

Tidwell frowned at her. "I just spoke to one of my men ten minutes ago."

"Call him again. Please."

"If it would make you happy . . ."

"It really would," Theodosia said.

Tidwell disappeared into the wheelhouse while Theodosia kept watch on deck. Up ahead, to their right, were the lights of Fort Sumter. Once they passed that, there was nothing ahead of them but a dark expanse of Atlantic Ocean.

And still they gave chase. Giant waves beat against the sides of the boat, thundering in her ears, keeping time with her heartbeat.

Theodosia felt like they were going to chase them all the way to the Azores. Or the west coast of Africa. But no, that couldn't happen. So where was Andros really headed? Up the inland waterway? Down to the Florida Keys or the Caribbean, where he could elude them among thousands of tiny islands? No, the Coast Guard wouldn't let that happen. She had faith in them.

Tidwell came back out on deck.

"What's happening at the Heritage Society?" she asked.

"Nothing," Tidwell said.

"Thank goodness."

Little by little, they were catching up. Even Drayton clutched at the railing to watch.

"They're doing it, by george," he said. "We're catching up."

"Pulling closer," Theodosia said.

When they were little more than fifty yards back, Lieutenant Commander Barley gave a hand signal and a Coast Guardsman standing in the prow of the ship shone a bright spotlight on the boat ahead of them. Then Barley got on the horn and ordered it to pull over, by order of the United States Coast Guard.

The boat carrying Haley kept churning away.

"Try to pull up to their starboard side," Tidwell yelled above the roar of the engines and the pounding of the rain. "Try to force them over toward shore."

"We have to be careful," one of the Coast Guardsmen warned. "There are dangerous shoals over there."

"Do it anyway," Tidwell snarled.

The Coast Guard ship cut just right of the boat and then jigged a hard left, almost pulling up alongside.

"Throw some more spots on that ship," Barley ordered.

Two bright spotlights split the air and then suddenly converged on the back of the boat.

Like a key light bursting on in a stage play, Haley was suddenly silhouetted in the back of the boat. She was waving her arms wildly at them.

"There she is!" Theodosia called out. "We've got to get her."

Suddenly, someone grabbed Haley from behind and tried to pull her down.

"Oh no," Theodosia said as she watched Haley struggling with a dark figure.

The Coast Guard boat jigged left and smashed up against the yacht.

"Push in a little closer if you can," Theodosia cried out. She was hoping they could toss a line onto the runaway yacht, try to hook it like an ornery steer.

The spotlights from high atop the Coast Guard ship scoured the darkness and then converged again on the two figures.

"Look at Haley!" Drayton yelled out. "She's fighting like crazy."

"Dear Lord," Theodosia cried, swelling with pride as she watched. "She's managed to break free."

Then, suddenly, they saw Haley spin around and run toward the figure she'd just been struggling with. The two figures morphed into one as they grappled with each other at the very back of the boat. Then, slowly, horrifically, they both toppled over the railing and into the ocean!

"Man overboard," cried one of the Coast Guardsmen.

"There are two people overboard!" Theodosia cried. "We don't care about the kidnapper, but we've got to rescue Haley as fast as possible."

Now the lights were aimed at the frothing sea where two heads bobbed in the choppy waters.

"There she is," Theodosia cried as a Coast Guardsman tossed two life preservers directly at the struggling figures.

Haley immediately grabbed one of the rings and wrapped an arm around it. The Coast Guardsman quickly pulled up the slack and began to reel her in.

"I think he's got her," Theodosia said.

"Of course he has," Tidwell said. But he was grinning happily.

"They've got her, really?" Drayton asked.

"Here she comes," Theodosia said. She could see Haley at the side of the boat, reaching a hand up as one of the Coast Guardsmen bent down to grab her.

"Now for Andros," Tidwell said, as one of the Coast Guardsmen struggled to reel in the second person.

"Andros," Theodosia spat out. "They ought to just let him flounder out there. Wait for him to swim ashore like a drowned rat and then put the cuffs on him."

Drayton scurried to the fore of the boat and huddled right

behind one of the Coast Guardsmen who was manning the lines. He stared into the choppy waters, did a kind of double take, wiped at his eyes, and then gestured wildly for Theodosia to come up and join him.

Haley was just being hauled up the side and into the boat.

"Is she okay?" Theodosia called out.

"I'm okay," Haley said as soon as she caught sight of them. She was soaked to the bone and her teeth chattered like castanets. "I'm wet and freezing to death, but I'm okay." She seemed fairly calm, in spite of the fact that she'd just been hauled out of the water like a wounded sea turtle.

"Can somebody please wrap a towel around her?" Theodosia asked. "For goodness' sakes, we don't want her to get hypothermia."

One of the Coast Guardsmen quickly shook open a Mylar thermal blanket and wrapped it tightly around Haley's shoulders. "This is better," he said. "It's reflective so it'll trap her body heat."

"Look at this," Drayton cried out. He was pointing at the other figure who was being hauled in roughly. "Look what got dragged up in the nets."

Theodosia leaned over the railing and strained to make out the struggling figure. In the dark mist, it was hard to see just who it was. But whoever they were, they were angry as hell. She could see legs churning and arms waving. Was it Luke Andros? Was he the one who'd tried to spirit Haley away and then planned to drop her overboard without a second thought? Probably. Well, she'd have a few choice words for him. And if they made anyone's ears turn red, then too bad.

"Here they come!" Drayton yelled.

Theodosia pushed her way closer to where two Coast Guardsmen struggled to pull a body over the railing.

"That's it," one of them yelled. "Get under his arms."

Theodosia waited, teeth practically bared, ready to unleash

her anger on Luke Andros. She'd take care of Sabrina, too, once they'd finally corralled that runaway boat.

"Here we go!" the second Coast Guardsman called out.

"Like a lunker on a hook!" Drayton cried. He flung his arms up in the air, like a referee signaling a touchdown.

A body tumbled over the side of the boat and fell, *kersplat*, onto the heaving, wet deck of the Coast Guard ship.

Theodosia lurched forward angrily. This was the jerk who'd kidnapped Haley in order to steal the ruby-and-diamond brooch. Probably the same mastermind who'd engineered the robbery at Heart's Desire, and then run like a weasel in the night as Kaitlin lay dying.

"Let me through!" Theodosia cried. Three Coast Guardsmen stepped back as she kicked the pointy toe of her high heel at the person who lay heaving on the deck.

"Uhh," moaned the figure. An arm raised up and Theodosia could see a faint tattoo mark on the wrist.

"How dare you," Theodosia began. "How dare you . . ." Before she could say one more word, the pathetic figure spit out a glut of water and turned its weary head to stare at her.

Theodosia rocked back on her heels, her mind reeling in disbelief. All she managed to blurt out was, "Grace? Is that you?"

30

⚜

They all huddled on the deck of the Coast Guard ship. Theodosia with an arm around Haley, Drayton on her other side, Billy Grainger standing right behind Haley, gently kneading her shoulders.

Grace Dawson had been tied up and was being guarded belowdecks. Two of her minions had also been captured and a Coast Guardsman had taken the wheel of Grace's yacht and was guiding it back to the harbor.

"It was Grace all along," Theodosia said. "She was the one who had the gang. Pity we only caught two of them when we stopped their ship."

"I suppose the others got away," Drayton said.

Tidwell stepped out of the wheelhouse. "Not to worry. I already sent a SWAT team to Grace Dawson's house. And I'm pleased to say three others have been apprehended."

"Wait a minute." Drayton looked totally befuddled. "Grace had a gang?"

"I told you one of the robbers might have been a woman," Theodosia said. "It looks as though Grace was the leader."

"She was their leader," Tidwell said.

"So who are the other guys?" Drayton asked.

"Paid thugs," Tidwell said. "Recruited to help her carry out the Heart's Desire robbery."

"And then they were going to go after the Fabergé egg," Theodosia said. "But they chickened out."

"Probably scared off by too much security," Tidwell said. "Which is why their fallback was to steal your ruby-and-diamond pin." He opened his hand and there it was, glimmering and elegant, looking none the worse for wear.

"Thank you," Theodosia said as she accepted the pin. "I can't wait to return this to Brooke."

"And tell her that the mystery's been solved," Haley said.

"That Kaitlin's murder has been solved," Theodosia said in a quiet tone.

Drayton still looked puzzled. "I was under the impression that Grace Dawson was an extremely wealthy woman. That her late husband owned a Mercedes dealership."

"Doubtful," Tidwell said. "I'd be willing to bet that her life is a complete fabrication. I've got investigators going through her house right now." His cell phone shrilled and he stepped out of the circle to answer it. "Yes?" he said. "Go ahead."

"Your investigators?" Theodosia asked him as he listened on his phone.

Tidwell frowned at her but nodded his head.

"Did they find anything?"

Tidwell held up a paw. "Wait a minute . . . I'm having trouble hearing you. Speak up." Then the connection seemed to improve because he suddenly seemed on full alert. "Is that so? Really. Well, get a crime scene team in there immediately. That's right, photograph everything. No, better yet, videotape it. We'll want to take everything into court for show-and-tell." He listened for another ten seconds and said, "That's exactly right—it's a murder charge now."

"What?" Theodosia demanded once he'd hung up.

Tidwell's eyes had taken on an odd light. Probably the light of victory. "Would you believe the woman's bedroom looks like Ali Baba's treasure cave?"

"No!" Drayton exclaimed.

"Grace must have been a modern-day pirate," Theodosia said. "Dip over to Hilton Head for a quick heist, then scoot down to Miami for another raid."

"And Lionel Rinicker wasn't in on it?" Drayton asked.

Tidwell shook his head. "He doesn't appear to have been."

"Grace was using him as cover," Theodosia said. "Getting introductions to all the right people, going to the opera, the chamber music society, all the charity events. Meeting all the right people."

"Rinicker's going to be awfully stunned when he finds out that his girlfriend is an international jewel thief," Haley said.

"Ex-girlfriend," Drayton said.

Theodosia touched a hand to Haley again, reassuring herself that the girl was okay. "What a night. And to think that the FBI missed out on this."

"I have a feeling you'll be seeing Special Agent Zimmer again," Drayton said with a mousy grin. "And when you do, just think of the conversation starter you'll have for your first date."

Haley perked up. "You're going to date that guy? Cool."

"Maybe," Theodosia said.

"Hey there," Lieutenant Commander Barley called as he leaned out of the wheelhouse. "Why don't you folks try to crowd in here and get warm? Grab a hot drink if you want."

They all moved stiffly inside, grateful to be out of the wind and pouring rain.

"What have we got in the thermos?" Barley asked one of his Coast Guardsmen.

The young ensign, the same one who'd helped haul Haley in, shrugged and said, "I don't know. I think just some hot tea."

Drayton caught Theodosia's eye and gave a slow wink.

"Is that okay?" the young man asked.

Theodosia smiled. "I'd say it's just about perfect."

FAVORITE RECIPES FROM
The Indigo Tea Shop

Drayton's Devonshire Cream

4 oz. mascarpone sweet cheese
1 cup heavy whipping cream
1 tsp. vanilla
2 Tbsp. sugar

PLACE ingredients in a large bowl and beat on high until the mixture holds its shape and resembles softly whipped cream. Cover and refrigerate until serving time. Yields 1½ cups.

Strawberry Cream Cheese Tea Sandwiches

6 oz. cream cheese, softened
2 Tbsp. strawberry preserves
10 slices thin white bread

COMBINE cream cheese and strawberry preserves. Using a small, round cutter, cut 3 rounds out of each slice of bread, discarding the crusts. Spread half the rounds with the cream cheese mixture, then top with the remaining bread rounds. Yields 15 tea sandwiches.

Cheesy Corn Chowder

½ cup water
2 cups potatoes, diced
1 cup carrots, sliced
1 cup celery, chopped
1 tsp. salt
¼ tsp. pepper
2 cups cream-style corn
1½ cups milk
⅔ cup Cheddar cheese, grated

IN saucepan, combine water, potatoes, carrots, celery, salt, and pepper. Cover and simmer for 10 minutes. Add cream-style corn and simmer for an additional 5 minutes. Add milk and grated cheese and stir until heated through (do not boil). Yields 4 servings.

Zucchini Quiche

1 cup onions, chopped
1 cup Bisquick
4 eggs

½ cup oil
½ cup Parmesan cheese, grated
¼ tsp. salt
3 to 3½ cups grated zucchini

PREHEAT oven to 350 degrees. Mix all ingredients except
zucchini in a bowl. Add zucchini last and stir gently. Pour
into a buttered 9-inch pie plate. Bake about 30 to 40 minutes until golden brown. Yields 4 servings.

Charleston Chocolate Brownie Tortes

3 egg whites
½ tsp. vanilla
Dash of salt
¾ cup sugar
¾ cup chocolate wafers, crumbled
½ cup chopped walnuts
Whipped cream or Cool Whip for topping

PREHEAT oven to 325 degrees. Beat egg whites, vanilla,
and dash of salt until mixture yields soft peaks. Gradually
add in ¾ cup of sugar, then beat to stiff peaks. Fold in ¾
cups of crumbled chocolate wafers and ½ cup chopped
walnuts. Spread mixture in a buttered 9-inch pie plate.
Bake for 35 minutes. Cool torte well, then top with
whipped cream. Chill for at least 3 hours before serving.
Yields 6 servings.

Prosciutto and Fig Butter Tea Sandwiches

1 French baguette
Butter as needed
1 jar fig jam
8 oz. prosciutto ham
1 pear, sliced into very thin slices
Bibb lettuce
Salt and pepper to taste

SLICE a French baguette lengthwise. Spread the bottom half with butter and the top half with fig jam. On bottom half, layer on prosciutto ham, sliced pears, and Bibb lettuce. Season with salt and pepper. Add top to sandwich and cut into pieces. Yields approximately 9 to 10 pieces.

Cranberry Cream Scones

2¼ cup all-purpose flour
½ cup sugar
1 Tbsp. baking powder
½ tsp. salt
¼ cup butter
2 eggs
¾ cup heavy cream
1 tsp. grated orange peel
¾ cup cranberries, fresh or frozen

PREHEAT oven to 425 degrees. Combine flour, sugar, baking powder, and salt. Cut in butter until mixture is coarse and crumbly. Mix eggs, cream, and orange peel in a separate bowl. Add egg mixture to flour mixture. Add cranberries and combine gently. Turn dough out onto a floured work surface and pat into a circle, kneading as little as possible. Cut into 12 rounds or wedges and place on a greased baking sheet. Bake for 14 to 16 minutes or until golden brown. Yields 12 scones.

Drayton's Shortbread Squares

> 2 cups flour, sifted
> 2 Tbsp. sugar
> 3 tsp. baking powder
> ½ tsp. salt
> ½ cup butter
> 1 egg, beaten
> ⅔ cup milk
> Strawberries or blueberries

PREHEAT oven to 450 degrees. Mix together flour, sugar, baking powder, and salt. Cut in butter until mixture becomes coarse. Combine egg and milk, and add to dry ingredients, stirring only to moisten. Spread mixture in greased 8-inch-by-8-inch baking pan. Bake for 16 to 18 minutes. Cool for 5 minutes, then cut into squares and remove from pan. Serve warm, topped with strawberries or blueberries. Yields 9 squares.

Waldorf Tea Sandwiches

1 cup grated apples
¼ cup minced celery
½ cup finely chopped walnuts
¼ cup mayonnaise, or as needed
12 slices cinnamon-raisin bread

MIX together apples, celery, walnuts, and mayonnaise. Cut crusts off 12 slices of bread and butter the bread. Spread apple-walnut mixture on 6 of the slices. Top with the other 6 slices and cut in half diagonally. Yields 12 tea sandwiches.

Haley's Beef Stroganoff

4 Tbsp. oil
1 medium onion, chopped
6 oz. beef strips
2 Tbsp. flour
Salt and pepper to taste
1 lb. mushrooms, sliced
¼ cup sour cream

HEAT 2 Tbsp. oil in a large skillet. Add onions and cook until soft. Set aside. Coat beef strips with flour, salt, and pepper. Add another 2 Tbsp. oil to skillet and cook beef strips over medium-high heat for about 4 minutes. Set aside strips. Add mushrooms to skillet and cook. Add cooked onions and cooked beef strips to mushrooms, stir-

ring gently. Add sour cream and warm it—do not over-
cook as it will separate! Serve beef Stroganoff over buttered
noodles or rice. Yields 2 to 3 servings.

Chocolate Chip Scones

2½ cups all-purpose flour
½ cup sugar
2 tsp. baking powder
½ tsp. salt
½ cup butter, softened
¾ cup sour cream
1 egg
½ tsp. vanilla
1 cup chocolate chips

PREHEAT oven to 375 degrees. Combine flour, sugar, baking powder, and salt. Cut in butter until mixture is crumbly and coarse. In another bowl, combine sour cream, egg,
and vanilla. Add sour cream mixture to flour mixture and
stir until moistened. Stir in chocolate chips. (If mixture
seems dry, add a little cream.) Place dough on lightly
floured surface and gently knead 8 or 10 times. Divide
dough into halves and pat each half into a 7-inch circle.
Place each circle on a large, greased baking sheet. Score
each circle into 6 wedges, but do not separate. Bake 25 to
30 minutes or until scones are lightly browned. Cool 10
minutes, and then gently separate scones. Yields 12 scones.

TEA TIME TIPS FROM
Laura Childs

Tropical Tea

Celebrate the summer months with a salute to the tropics. Go wild with as many floral bouquets as you can fit on your table, then add a roost of pretty feathered birds from the craft store. If you have a floral tablecloth, napkins, and dishes, so much the better. Serve curried chicken salad in pineapple halves, banana nut scones, and small slivers of mushroom and cheese quiche. An oolong tea is perfect and so is an iced tea infusion of raspberry and hibiscus if the weather is hot.

Duchess of Devonshire Tea

Pull out your crisp white tablecloth and decorate it with anything that's British themed. We're talking Shelley china, statues of Big Ben, even plates that bear the Queen's likeness. English tea roses would make an elegant centerpiece. Your first course will naturally be buttermilk scones with froths of Devonshire cream. Move on to a mandarin orange salad topped with sliced almonds, smoked chicken and fig butter tea sandwiches on white bread, and smoked salmon and cream cheese tea sandwiches on dark bread. Consider an English trifle for dessert and serve rich Ceylon tea.

Edgar Allan Poe Tea

Who doesn't love an autumn tea? And dear Mr. Poe can certainly set the mood for Halloween. Think cinnamon-apple scones, chicken salad with cranberries on nut bread, corn chowder, and gingerbread bars. Liven up your table with crocks filled with colorful leaves, black crows from the craft store, and candles dripping rivulets of wax. Make color copies of Poe's book covers to use as place mats. Mix it up with two different teas, perhaps a smoky Lapsang souchong and a spiced plum tea.

Shabby Chic Tea

This is a fabulous excuse to pull out everything that's lacy and floral. Start with a floral tablecloth, and then layer it with a lace tablecloth. Keep the theme going with floral napkins and teacups—if everything's mismatched, so much the better! For a centerpiece, pop pink peonies into a glass jar or cream-colored crockery and cluster some framed photos and pretty tins around it. If you're doing a buffet, you could even add painted birdhouses and vintage purses as a backdrop. Serve Cheddar cheese quiche, shrimp salad tea sandwiches, cream scones, and biscotti. A Keemun tea would be delicious, but so would peaches and ginger iced tea served in a large glass container with a spigot!

Lavender Dreams Tea

The mood is laid-back and elegant for this luncheon or after-noon tea. Decorate your table with a lavender tablecloth and your favorite purple flowers displayed in a crystal vase. Lay dried lavender around for an elegant, aromatic effect. Serve lavender scones, chicken salad on nut bread, and lavender shortbread cookies or tea bread. An Assam or Earl Grey tea would be perfect. Packets of lavender seeds make memorable party favors. Classical music is a must.

Maharaja's Tea Party

This is your chance to channel the richness of India and the exuberance of Bollywood. Decorate your table with an Indian-print tablecloth or napkins. For your centerpiece, fill a large colorful bowl with floating candles and flowers. Add an elephant statuette and sprinkle some colorful "jewels" from the party store on your table. Go wild with table-ware, too—colors of orange, hot pink, and red are perfect. Serve raspberry and rosewater scones, fresh papaya, cream cheese and cucumber tea sandwiches, and Indian tea bis-cuits. Darjeeling tea makes the perfect complement, and don't forget to pass out washable henna tattoos to all your guests!

TEA RESOURCES

TEA MAGAZINES AND PUBLICATIONS

Tea Time—A luscious magazine profiling tea and tea lore. Filled with glossy photos and wonderful recipes. (teatimemagazine.com)

Southern Lady—From the publishers of *Tea Time* with a focus on people and places in the South as well as wonderful teatime recipes. (southernladymagazine.com)

The Tea House Times—Go to theteahousetimes.com for subscription information and dozens of links to tea shops, purveyors of tea, gift shops, and tea events.

Victoria—Articles and pictorials on homes, home design, gardens, and tea. (victoriamag.com)

Texas Tea & Travel—Highlighting Texas and other Southern tea rooms, tea events, and fun travel. (teaintexas.com)

Fresh Cup Magazine—For tea and coffee professionals. (freshcup.com)

Tea & Coffee—Trade journal for the tea and coffee industry. (teaandcoffee.net)

Bruce Richardson—This author has written several definitive books on tea. (elmwoodinn.com/books)

Jane Pettigrew—This author has written thirteen books on the varied aspects of tea and its history and culture. (janepettigrew.com/books)

A Tea Reader—by Katrina Ávila Munichiello, an anthology of tea stories and reflections.

AMERICAN TEA PLANTATIONS

Charleston Tea Plantation—The oldest and largest tea plantation in the United States. Order their fine black tea or schedule a visit at bigelowtea.com.

Fairhope Tea Plantation—Tea plantation in Fairhope, Alabama.

The Great Mississippi Tea Company—Up-and-coming Mississippi tea farm about ready to go into production. (greatmsteacompany .com)

Sakuma Brothers Farm—This tea garden just outside Burlington, WA, has been growing white and green tea for more than a dozen years. (sakumamarket.com)

Big Island Tea—Organic artisan tea from Hawaii. (bigislandtea.com)

Mauna Kea Tea—Organic green and oolong tea from Hawaii's Big Island. (maunakeatea.com)

Onomea Tea—Nine-acre tea estate near Hilo, Hawaii. (onomeatea .com)

Moonrise Tea—Organic teas grown on Hawaii's Big Island and packed in rice paper pouches. (moonrisetea.com)

TEA WEBSITES AND INTERESTING BLOGS

Teamap.com—Directory of hundreds of tea shops in the U.S. and Canada.

Afternoontea.co.uk—Guide to tea rooms in the UK.

Cookingwithideas.typepad.com—Recipes and book reviews for the bibliochef.

Cuppatea4sheri.blogspot.com—Amazing recipes.

Seedrack.com—Order *Camellia sinensis* seeds and grow your own tea!

Friendshiptea.net—Tea shop reviews, recipes, and more.

RTbookreviews.com—Wonderful romance and mystery book review site.

Adelightsomelife.com—Tea, gardening, and cottage crafts.

Theladiestea.com—Networking platform for women.

Jennybakes.com—Fabulous recipes from a real make-it-from-scratch baker.

Southernwritersmagazine.com—Inspiration, writing advice, and author interviews of Southern writers.

Thedailytea.com—Formerly *Tea Magazine*, this online publication is filled with tea news, recipes, inspiration, and tea travel.

Allteapots.com—Teapots from around the world.

Fireflyvodka.com—South Carolina purveyors of Sweet Tea Vodka, Raspberry Tea Vodka, Peach Tea Vodka, and more. Just visiting this website is a trip in itself!

Teasquared.blogspot.com—Fun, well-written blog about tea, tea shops, and tea musings.

Blog.bernideens.com—Bernideen's teatime blog about tea, baking, decorating, and gardening.

Teapages.net—All things tea.

Possibili-teas.net—Tea consultants with a terrific monthly newsletter.

Relevanttealeaf.blogspot.com—All about tea.

Baking.about.com—Carroll Pellegrinelli writes a terrific baking blog complete with recipes and photo instructions.

Stephcupoftea.blogspot.com—Blog on tea, food, and inspiration.

Teawithfriends.blogspot.com—Lovely blog on tea, friendship, and tea accoutrements.

Teaescapade.wordpress.com—Enjoyable tea blog.

Bellaonline.com/site/tea—Features and forums on tea.

Lattesandlife.com—Witty musings on life.

Napkinfoldingguide.com—Photo illustrations of twenty-seven different (and sometimes elaborate) napkin folds.

Worldteaexpo.com—This premier business-to-business trade show features more than three hundred tea suppliers, vendors, and tea innovators.

Sweetgrassbaskets.net—One of several websites where you can buy sweetgrass baskets direct from the artists.

Goldendelighthoney.com—Carolina honey to sweeten your tea.

Fatcatscones.com—Frozen ready-to-bake scones.

Kingarthurflour.com—One of the best flours for baking. This is what many professional pastry chefs use.

Teagw.com—Visit this website and click on Products to find dreamy tea pillows filled with jasmine, rose, lavender, and green tea.

Californiateahouse.com—Order Machu's Blend, a special herbal tea for dogs that promotes healthy skin, lowers stress, and aids digestion.

Vintageteaworks.com—This company offers six unique wine-flavored tea blends that celebrate wine and respect the tea.

Downtonabbeycooks.com—A *Downton Abbey* blog with news and recipes. You can also order their book *Abbey Cooks Entertain*.

Auntannie.com—Crafting site that will teach you how to make your own petal envelopes, pillow boxes, gift bags, etc.

Victorianhousescones.com—Scone, biscuit, and cookie mixes for both retail and wholesale orders. Plus baking and scone-making tips.

Harney.com—Contact Harney & Sons to order their *Titanic* Blend loose leaf tea or their RMS *Titanic* tea sachets.

Englishteastore.com—Buy a jar of English Double Devon Cream here as well as British foods and candies.

Stickyfingersbakeries.com—Scone Mixes and English Curds.

PURVEYORS OF FINE TEA

Adagio.com

Harney.com

Stashtea.com

Republicoftea.com

Teazaanti.com

Bigelowtea.com

Celestialseasonings.com

Goldenmoontea.com

Uptontea.com

VISITING CHARLESTON

Charleston.com—Travel and hotel guide.

Charlestoncvb.com—The official Charleston convention and visitor bureau.

Charlestontour.wordpress.com—Private tours of homes and gardens, some including lunch or tea.

Culinarytoursofcharleston.com—Sample specialties from Charleston's local eateries, markets, and bakeries.

Poogansporch.com—This restored Victorian house serves traditional low-country cuisine. Be sure to ask about Poogan!

Preservationsociety.org—Hosts Charleston's annual Fall Candlelight Tour.

Palmettocarriage.com—Horse-drawn carriage rides.

Charlestonharbortours.com—Boat tours and harbor cruises.

Ghostwalk.net—Stroll into Charleston's haunted history. Ask them about the "original" Theodosia!

CharlestonTours.net—Ghost tours plus tours of plantations and historic homes.

Follybeach.com—Official guide to Folly Beach activities, hotels, rentals, restaurants, and events.

Turn the page for a preview of
the next Tea Shop mystery from Laura Childs

PEKOE MOST POISON

*Available in hardcover March 2017
from Berkley Prime Crime*

Palmettos swayed lazily in the soft breeze, daffodils bobbed their shaggy heads as Theodosia Browning stepped quickly along the brick pathway that wound through a bountiful front yard garden and up to the polished double doors of the Calhoun Mansion. Pausing, she pulled back the enormous brass boar's head door knocker . . . nothing wimpy about this place . . . and let it crash against the metal plate.

Claaaang. The sound echoed deep within the house as the boar's eyes glittered and glared at her.

Turning to face Drayton, her friend and tea sommelier, Theodosia said, "This should be fun. I've never visited Doreen's home before."

"You'll like it," Drayton said. "It's a grand old place. Built back in the early eighteen hundreds by Emerson Calhoun, one of Charleston's early indigo barons."

"I guess we're lucky to be invited then," she said. Their hostess, Doreen Briggs, also known to her close friends as "Dolly," was president of the Ladies Opera Auxiliary and one of the leading social powerhouses in Charleston, South Carolina. Theodosia had always thought of Doreen as being slightly bubbleheaded, but that could be a carefully cultivated act, aimed to deflect from all the philanthropic work that she and her husband were involved in.

A few seconds later, the front door creaked open and Theodosia and Drayton were greeted by a vision so strange it could have been a drug-induced hookah dream straight out of *Alice in Wonderland*. The man who answered the door was dressed in a powder blue velvet waistcoat, cream-colored slacks, and spit-polished black buckle boots. But it wasn't his formal, quasi-Edwardian attire that made him so bizarre. It was the giant white velvet rat head perched atop his head and shoulders. Yes, white velvet, just like the fur of a properly groomed, semi-dandy white rat. Complete with round ears, long snout bristling with whiskers, and bright pink eyes.

"Welcome," the rat said to them as he placed one white-gloved hand (paw?) behind his back and bowed deeply.

At which point Theodosia arched her carefully waxed brows and said, as a not-so-subtle aside to Drayton, "When the invitation specified a 'Charleston rat tea,' they weren't just whistling Dixie."

It was a rat tea. Of sorts. Drayton had filled her in on the history of the quaint rat tea custom on their stroll over from the Indigo Tea Shop, where they brewed all manner of tea, fed and charmed customers, and made a fairly comfortable living.

"Seventy-five years ago," Drayton said, "rat teas were all the rage in Charleston. You see, at the advent of World War Two, our fair city underwent a tremendous population explosion as war workers arrived at the navy shipyard in droves."

"I get that," Theodosia had said. "But what's with the rats specifically?"

"Ah," Drayton said. "With the increased populace, downtown merchants were thriving. Because they were so frantically busy, they began tossing their garbage out onto the sidewalks, which immediately attracted a huge influx of rats. The local public health officials, fearing some kind of ghastly epidemic, quickly spearheaded a 'rat torpedo' campaign. Volunteers were tasked with wrapping poisoned bait in small folded bits of newspaper and sticking them in alleys and crawl spaces."

Theodosia listened, fascinated, as Drayton continued his story.

"These rat torpedoes were so effective," Drayton said, "that prominent society ladies even held fancy 'rat teas' to help promote the campaign."

"And the rats were eventually eradicated?" Theodosia had asked.

"Charleston became a public health model," Drayton said. "Several major cities even sent representatives to study our method."

The blue rat at the door was still nodding to them as Theodosia and Drayton stepped inside the foyer. Here, they were greeted by a second rat wearing a pastel pink coat. This rat was equally polite.

"Good afternoon," pink rat said.

"I feel like I've been drinking to excess," Theodosia said. "Seeing pink rats instead of pink elephants."

"This way, please," pink rat said to them in carefully modulated tones.

They followed him down a long, red-tiled hallway where oil paintings dark with crackle glaze hung on the walls and the hum of conversation grew louder with each step they took. Then pink rat turned suddenly and ushered them into an enormous sunlit parlor where fifty or so guests milled about and a half-dozen elegant tea tables were carefully arranged.

Pink rat consulted his clipboard. "Miss Browning, Mr. Conneley, you're both to be seated at table six."

"Thank you," Drayton said.

"Do I know you?" Theodosia asked pink rat. Her blue eyes sparkled with curiosity and her voice was slightly teasing. She was a woman of rare and fair beauty even though she'd be the first to pooh-pooh anyone who told her so. But with her masses of auburn hair, English rose complexion, and captivating smile, she certainly stood out in a crowd.

"I don't think so, ma'am," pink rat said as he spun on the heels of his buckle boots and hastened off to escort another group of guests to their table.

"Who *was* that?" Theodosia asked as her eyes skittered around the rather grand room, taking in the crystal chandelier, enormous marble fireplace, gaggle of upscale-looking guests, as well as tea tables set with Wedgwood china and Reed & Barton silver. "He sounded so familiar. The rat guy, I mean."

"No idea," Drayton said as he regarded the table settings. "But isn't this lovely? And what fun to stage a madcap homage to the rat teas of yesteryear." Drayton was beginning to rhapsodize, one of the most endearing qualities of this debonair, sixty-something tea sommelier, while Theodosia was suddenly fizzing with curiosity. Why had she been invited when she had just a nodding acquaintance with Doreen Briggs? And who were these white rat butlers, anyway? Professional servers shanghaied from a local catering company? Or actors who'd been hired to wear costumes and playact a rather bizarre role?

These were the kind of things Theodosia wondered about. These were the things that kept her brain whirring at night when she should have been fast asleep.

* * *

"Drayton!" an excited voice shrilled. Theodosia and Drayton turned to find Doreen Briggs closing on them like a five-foot-two-inch heat-seeking missile. She charged up to Drayton, rose on tiptoes to administer a profusion of air kisses, and then flashed an enormous smile at Theodosia. "Theodosia," she said. "So good of you to come." Doreen gripped her hand firmly, pumped her arm. "Welcome to my home."

"Thank you for inviting me," Theodosia said. "And I must say, you have a very lovely home."

"It is cozy, isn't it?" Doreen said. Her green eyes glinted almost coquettishly, her reddish-blond hair cascaded around her face in a forest of curls that didn't seem quite natural for a woman in her late fifties.

"We're thrilled to be here," Drayton added.

Doreen, who was stuffed into a pastel pink shantung silk dress with a rope of pearls around her neck, waved a hand that was festooned with sparkling diamond rings, and said, "Don't you think this is jolly fun? The rat tea theme, I mean? Aren't my liveried rats just adorable?"

"Charming," Theodosia responded. Truthfully, she thought the rats—she'd seen at least four of them moving officiously around the room—were a little strange. But this was a woman who supported the arts, gave money to service dog organizations, and was on the verge of bequeathing a sizable grant to Drayton's beloved Heritage Society, so she was willing to cut her a good deal of slack.

"Where's Beau?" Drayton asked. "He's certainly here today, isn't he?" Beau Briggs was Doreen's husband, a self-professed entrepreneur who owned apartment buildings in North Charleston and was a partner in the newly opened Gilded Magnolia Spa on King Street.

Doreen pushed back a strand of frizzled hair. "He's around here somewhere. Probably bending the ear of one of our guests, talking about one of his pet business projects." She put a hand on Theodosia's arm and said, "Isn't it cute when men work themselves into a tizzy over business? I love how they think they're masters of the universe when it's really we women who run things."

"And a fine job you ladies do," Drayton said.

"Aren't you the most politically correct gentleman yet," Doreen fawned. "You'll have to indoctrinate Beau with some of your fine, liberal ideas." She managed a quick sip of air and said, "We're sitting right here." Then she waved a chubby hand. "Your table is right next to us."

"I'm looking forward to meeting your husband," Theodosia said. She'd heard so much about the man who'd helped create Gilded Magnolia Spa. Magazines had run full-color spreads, health and beauty editors had rhapsodized about it in articles, and the ladies-who-lunch types, who shopped at Bob Ellis Shoes and Hampden Clothing, had been exchanging whispers about the spa's gold foil facials and amazing electrostim lifts.

"I imagine Beau will pop up any moment," Doreen said as she glanced around the room. Then her face lit up and she cried, "There he is." She waved a hand as bracelets clanked. "Beau!" Her voice rose higher. "Yes, I'm talking to you, hunky monkey . . . who do you *think* I'm waving at like a crazy lady? Get over here and say hello to Theodosia and Drayton."

Beau Briggs, who was forty pounds overweight, with slicked-back red hair, the jowls of a shar-pei, and perfectly steam-cleaned pores, came huffing over to join them.

"Dolly," he said. "What?" His pink sport coat was stretched around his midsection, the gold buttons looking about ready to burst and go airborne. Theodosia decided Beau might partake of his own spa's skin care regimen, but not their low-cal smoothies and fruit salads.

"These are the people I was telling you about," Doreen

said. "Theodosia and Drayton. They run that lovely Indigo Tea Shop over on Church Street. You remember, they bake those chocolate chip scones that you adore so much?"

Beau turned an expectant smile on them. "I hope you brought some along?"

Doreen gave him a playful slap. "Silly boy. You know our caterers are handling the scones and tea sandwiches today. Theodosia and Drayton are our guests. They're here to partake of tea, not serve it."

"A respite," Drayton said, trying to be jocular.

"Then sit down, sit down," Doreen said as all around them guests began taking their seats. "Oh!" She spun around to position herself at the head table, all the while looking a little scattered. "I suppose it's high time I get this fancy tea started." She glanced down, looking slightly perturbed. "Now, where did I put my silver bell?"

The tea turned out to be a lovely affair, albeit a trifle strange. The rat theme continued as everyone took their places and more liveried rats came scurrying out of the kitchen. They carried steaming teapots in white-gloved hands, pouring out servings of Darjeeling and Assam tea. By the time silver trays overflowing with cinnamon and lemon poppy seed scones arrived, Theodosia was well past her initial surprise. In fact, she was able to sit back and enjoy herself as Drayton did the heavy lifting, chatting merrily with all the guests as their table, most of whom she had only a nodding acquaintance with. Then again, Drayton was a stickler for politeness and decorum. And tended to be a lot more social than she was.

Let's see now, Theodosia thought after they'd gone around the table and made hasty introductions. The two blondes, Dree and Diana, were on the board of directors for the Charleston Symphony. The woman in the fire-engine red suit . . . Twilby . . . Eleanor Twilby? . . . was the executive director of . . . something. And then . . . well, she just wasn't sure. But the crab and Gruyère cheese quiche she was digging into was incredibly creamy and delicious.

Doreen turned in her chair and tapped Theodosia on the shoulder. "Having fun?" she asked.

Theodosia, caught with a bite of food in her mouth, chewed quickly and swallowed. "This quiche is incredible!" She really meant it. "I'll have to get the recipe. Haley would love it." Haley was her chef and chief baker back at the Indigo Tea Shop.

"Carolina blue crab," Doreen said in a conspiratorial whisper. "Baked by Crispin's Catering. They're brand-new here in Charleston and making quite a splash. We even tapped them to cater all the appetizers for our grand opening party at Gilded Magnolia Spa next Saturday."

"You have quite a large group here today," Theodosia said. "Are most of them spa customers?"

"It's a sprinkling of all sorts of people," Doreen said. "Spa members, media people, a few friends and neighbors, some business associates." She raised a hand to one of the rat waiters and said, "We're going to need a fresh pot of this orange pekoe tea for Beau." And to Theodosia: "It's his favorite."

"One of Drayton's recommendations?" Theodosia asked.

"Oh, absolutely," Doreen said. "I consulted with Drayton on all the teas we're serving here today. As usual, he was spot-on."

"He's the best tea sommelier I've ever encountered. We're fortunate to have him at the Indigo Tea Shop."

"Watch out someone doesn't try to steal him away," Doreen said. She turned, held up Beau's teacup for the waiter to pour him a fresh cup of tea, and said, "Just set the teapot on the warmer, please."

The pink rat leaned forward, set down the teapot, and, in the process, the edge of his sleeve brushed against one of the tall white tapers.

"Watch the! . . ." Doreen cried out as the candle wobbled dangerously in its silver holder.

But it was too late.

The burning candle bobbled and swayed for a couple more seconds and then tipped onto the table. It landed, flame burning bright, right in the middle of an enormous, frothy centerpiece. As if someone had doused it with gasoline, a ring of dancing fire burst forth. A split second later, the decorator-done arrangement of silk flowers, pinecones, twisted vines, and dried moss was a boiling, seething inferno.

As the guests at Doreen's table began to scream, two people leapt to their feet and began beating at the crackling flames with linen napkins. Their efforts just served to fan the flames and set one of the napkins on fire. It twisted and blazed like an impromptu torch until the person waving it suddenly dropped it onto the table.

Beau Briggs, as if just realizing they might all be in mortal danger, suddenly jumped to his feet, knocking his chair over backward. "Somebody get a fire extinguisher!" he yelped as flames continued to dance and scorch the tabletop. Now everyone from his table was jigging around in a fearful, nervous rugbylike scrum, while people from other tables were rushing over to shout suggestions. Doreen, no help at all, put her hands on her head and let loose a series of high-pitched yips.

"Somebody do something!" a woman in a black leather dress screamed.

At which point Theodosia grabbed the teapot from her table, elbowed her way through the gaggle of guests, and poured the tea directly onto the flames.

There was a loud hiss as an enormous billow of black smoke swirled upward. But the tea had done the trick. The fire had fizzled out, leaving only the remnants of a singed and seared centerpiece swimming in a brown puddle of Darjeeling tea.

"Thank you," Beau cried out. "Thank you!"

"Good work," Drayton said to Theodosia, just as blue rat arrived, fumbling with a bright-red fire extinguisher. He aimed the nozzle at the table and proceeded to spray white, foamy gunk all over the remaining plates of food.

"Stop, stop," Beau yelled at the rat. He lifted his hands to indicate they were all fine, that the danger was over, even as a few tendrils of smoke continued to spiral up from the charred centerpiece.

"Goodness," Doreen squealed, nervously patting her heart with one hand. "That was absolutely terrifying. We could have . . . all been . . ." She spun around toward Theodosia, a look of gratitude washing across her face. "Thank you, my dear, for such quick, decisive thinking."

"But your tea party's been ruined," Theodosia said with a rueful smile. "I'm so sorry." The head table, which had looked so elegant and refined a few minutes earlier, was now a burned and blistered wreck. The ceiling above was horribly smudged.

"We'll salvage this party yet," Beau said. Undeterred, he pulled himself to his full height and raised his hands like a fiery evangelist, ready to address the upturned, still-stunned faces of all his guests.

"I don't know how," Doreen muttered.

"My dear friends," Beau said. "Please pardon the inconvenience." He pulled a hankie from his jacket pocket and mopped at his florid face as a spatter of applause broke out. He acknowledged the applause with a slightly uneven smile and continued. "Even though everything is firmly under control, I think it's best that we finish our . . . ahem, that we adjourn to . . ." Stumbling over his words, he halted midsentence as a tremendous shudder ran through his entire body. It shook his shoulders, jiggled his belly, and made his knees knock together. Then his eyes popped open to twice their normal size and he let out a cough, razor sharp and harsh. That cough quickly became a series of coughs that racked his body and morphed into a high-pitched, thready-sounding wheeze.

Doreen, looking properly concerned, held out a glass of water for her husband. "Please drink this, dear."

As Beau struggled to grab the water, his hands began to shake violently. He managed to just barely grasp the glass and lift it shakily to his lips.

"I just need . . ." Beau managed to croak out.

But just as he was about to take a much-needed sip of water, his head suddenly flew backward and he let loose a loud choke that sounded like the bark of an angry seal. The water glass slipped from his hand.

Crash! Shards of glass flew everywhere.

"Beau?" Doreen said in a small, scared voice, as if she sensed something was catastrophically wrong.

Beau was waving both hands in front of his face now, gasping for breath and hacking loudly. "Wha . . . bwa . . ." He fought to get his words out, but simply couldn't manage it.

At least five sets of hands stretched out to help him, all holding water glasses. Instead of grabbing one of the glasses, Beau struggled to pick up his cup of tea. He managed to get his teacup halfway to his lips before his right hand convulsed into a rigid claw and the cup slipped from his grasp. As it clattered to the table, he clutched frantically at his throat. Eyes fluttering like crazy as they rolled back in his head, he managed a hoarse groan. Then, as if made of rubber, his legs gave way completely.

Bam! Beau dropped to the floor like a sack of potatoes, smacking his forehead on the sharp edge of the table on his way down.

In a frenzy now, screeching for help, Doreen bent over and tried to grab him. But Beau was so heavy and unwieldy that all she managed to do was bunch his shirt above his jacket collar. "He's not breathing!" she screamed. "Does anyone know the Heimlich maneuver?"

One man from a nearby table immediately sprang to his feet and came flying around to help. He knelt down directly behind Beau, wrapped his arms around his chest, and pulled him halfway upright. Then, locking his hands under Beau's sternum, the man pulled his arms tight, making quick upward thrusts.

Beau's eyes flickered open, then turned glassy as white foam dribbled from his mouth.

"It's working, it's working!" Doreen cried. "He blinked his eyes."

"Thank goodness," Drayton said. He sank into his chair as the Good Samaritan continued to thump and bump poor Beau Briggs.

"Is he coming around?" Doreen asked in a tremulous voice as Beau's head jerked back and forth spasmodically and then lolled to one side as if his neck were made of Silly Putty.

"His color's looking better," the skinny woman in black leather cried out. "His face isn't purple anymore."

"That's good?" Doreen asked. Then, as if to reassure herself, said, "That's good."

Meanwhile, the man who was still administering the Heimlich maneuver was struggling mightily and beginning to lose steam. "If I could just . . ." he grunted out, trying to catch his breath. ". . . Dislodge whatever he's got caught in his throat. Try to get him breathing on his own." He pulled and thrust harder and harder, his own face turning a violent shade of red. "Where's the ambulance?" the man gasped. "Where are the EMTs?"

"On their way!" the pink rat cried. "I can hear sirens now."

"Can somebody take over here?" the Good Samaritan gasped.

A man in a white dinner jacket sprang into action. He employed a different technique. He bent Beau forward and thumped him hard on the back. But nothing seemed to be working. Beau's eyes, open wide but unseeing, looked like two boiled eggs. His bulbous body was as limp and unresponsive as a noodle.

"I don't think that technique is going to work," Theodosia said in a quiet voice.

Drayton heard her and frowned, his eyes going wide with alarm. "Why would you say that? What do you think is wrong with him?"

"You see that white foam dribbling from his mouth?" Theodosia said. "You see his pale, almost waxy complexion? I think he's ingested some sort of poison."

"Poison!" Doreen suddenly screamed at the top of her lungs. "Don't drink the tea! The tea is poisoned!"

The Tea Shop Mysteries by
New York Times Bestselling Author

Laura Childs

DEATH BY DARJEELING
GUNPOWDER GREEN
SHADES OF EARL GREY
THE ENGLISH BREAKFAST MURDER
THE JASMINE MOON MURDER
CHAMOMILE MOURNING
BLOOD ORANGE BREWING
DRAGONWELL DEAD
THE SILVER NEEDLE MURDER
OOLONG DEAD
THE TEABERRY STRANGLER
SCONES & BONES
AGONY OF THE LEAVES
SWEET TEA REVENGE
STEEPED IN EVIL
MING TEA MURDER
DEVONSHIRE SCREAM
PEKOE MOST POISON

"A delightful series."
—The Mystery Reader

"Murder suits [Laura Childs] to a Tea."
—*St. Paul Pioneer Press*

laurachilds.com
penguin.com

M314AS1115